# THE FALL

A Love in O'Leary Novel

MAY ARCHER

Copyright © 2018 by May Archer
All rights reserved.

No part of this book may be reproduced in any form or by any electronic or mechanical means, including information storage and retrieval systems, without written permission from the author, except for the use of brief quotations in a book review.

This book was not written with AI. This author does not give permission for any portion of this book to be used to train AI.

**Cover Art:** Shanoff Designs
**Editing:** Sandra, One Love Editing
**Professional Beta Read:** Leslie Copeland

*All the good bits are theirs, and any mistakes are my own!*

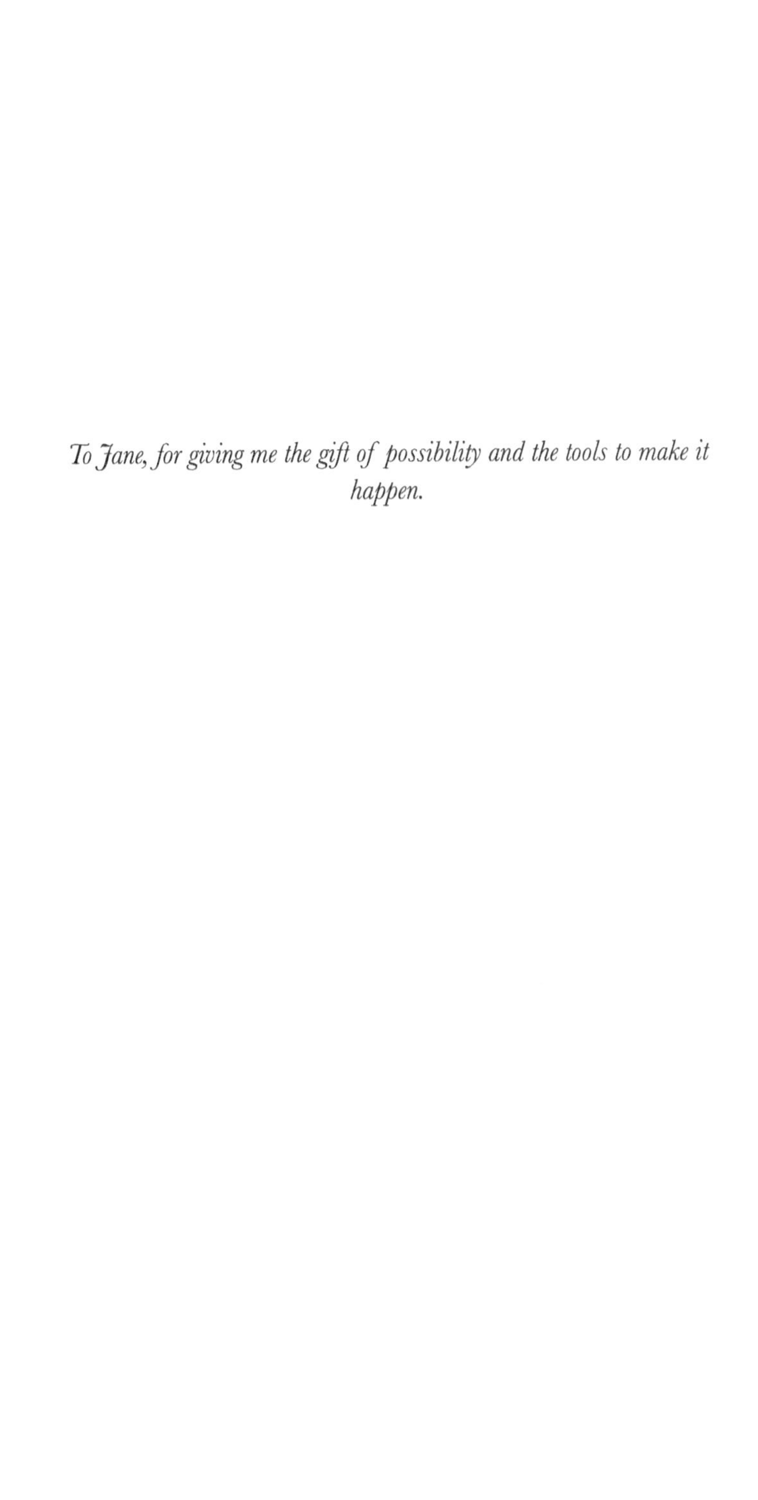

*To Jane, for giving me the gift of possibility and the tools to make it happen.*

## The Fall

"I was in free fall the moment we met, and I just keep falling."

Small town police officer Silas Sloane knows every resident of O'Leary, New York. He's earned the love and respect of its citizens, though living under the small-town microscope grates on him. But though he's good at his job, there's one thing he's not good at: commitments… Until Everett.

Widower Everett Maior, O'Leary's newest citizen, came to the small town kicking and screaming. He never wanted to become primary caretaker for his grandfather and has no interest in living the provincial life. Snarky and superstitious, he's proficient at keeping people at a distance... Until he lays eyes on Silas.

Strange disappearances are plaguing O'Leary, though, even as Silas and Everett find their growing attraction undeniable. Can they find their way to a future together, even as ghosts from the past threaten to tear them apart?

What we call the beginning is often the end. And to make
an end is to make a beginning. The end is where we start
from.

T. S. Eliot

# Chapter One

EVERETT

O'Leary, New York was fucking impossible to get to.

I mean, on the one hand it was as easy as answering the phone to hear my mother crying like the end-times were upon us. It had been a hard year, and in that terror-struck half minute where my body was locked down and my mind was already flailing in anticipatory grief for what-ever new tragedy she was about to share, I'd been easy pickings.

"Grandpa Hen needs your help, Ev," she'd sobbed, and without sparing a single second to think why he might need help or exactly what that help would require, without remembering that Grandpa Hen and I had a relationship that was approximately as cordial as an armed nuclear standoff, I'd agreed.

"Of course," I'd vowed, like a fucking idiot. "Any-thing!" Anything to avert another tragedy, anything to avoid another loss.

As it turned out, *anything* meant me packing up my shit and moving my ass to the backend of nowheresville for an entire academic *year*. It meant me fast-tracking a transitional certificate to teach art to kids who might not be aware that the earth wasn't flat. It meant living with my homophobic throwback of a grandfather, who'd managed to break his leg in three places like the overachiever he was, in The Town That Time Forgot.

*That* was a tragedy and a loss right there.

But despite the hassles of packing and saying temporary goodbyes, of putting our… I mean, *my*… condo up for rent, the preparations for my departure were still easier than the fucking drive itself.

Route 222 between Camden and O'Leary was a serpentine hosebeast, and I was pretty sure it was trying to kill me.

"Fuck!" I breathed, trying to ease my Yaris around yet another hairpin turn that had popped up out of nowhere.

I imagined the road had started out as a footpath through the forest, snaking around rivers and ponds, trees and property lines. No doubt it had been perfectly adequate for taking your cow to market, and I'd bet the endless waves of trees were just *lovely* in the daytime. But trying to drive a tiny Toyota, *in the dark*, around turns so tight it felt like the road was doubling back on itself, I started to feel like the stupid trees were watching and giggling. Like O'Leary didn't want me to come any more than I wanted to go. Too bad it was too late to turn back.

"Leave early," my mom had told me yesterday at my goodbye party. She'd been on the verge of tears, per usual, and giving me the helpless, anxious look that was pretty much her standard these days — the one that made it seem like she was visibly restraining herself from trying to pick me up like a toddler, even though I was nearly thirty and outweighed her by at least twenty-five pounds. "Don't take chances, Ev," she'd begged.

*Pfft. As if*, I'd assured her. The Ev who took chances had died along with my husband Adrian last year. These days, I was self-reliant and responsible. I took care of my own shit, always. You could find my picture in the dictionary next to *competent*. See also: *risk-averse*.

But then, after everyone else had gone home — after my friends and relatives had gone back to their own houses, and families, and lives — I'd looked at the empty walls and the packed suitcases waiting in the spare bedroom, and... well, I'd lost my shit.

Everyone had said, "Wait a year, Ev." and, "Don't make any life-changing decisions in those first grueling months, when grief is fresh and your mind is clouded." And since I was Everett Maior, Rule Follower these days, that's exactly what I'd done.

I'd lived in our condo, which Adrian had decorated in the rustic, urban style he'd loved — a style I'd teasingly called Pottery Barn Puked, just to piss him off so I could make it up to him later. I made the bed every morning, because Adrian used to be fastidious about it, putting every fussy throw pillow into place in a way that would have made him proud.

I'd carved my own pumpkins into works of jack-o'-lantern art, remembering how impressed Adrian used to be by my skill. Then I'd gone out and bought the giant Costco bags of candy we used to pretend were for trick-or-treaters even though there were no kids in our complex, and systematically eaten every piece of it. I'd made myself so sick, I hadn't been able to touch sweets since.

I'd hung Adrian's stocking next to mine last Christmas, on the fussy ceramic hangers he loved, though I was still convinced that Daphne, our resident feline shithead, was going to pull them down and shatter them like ceramic shrapnel bombs. I waited for the Christmas spirit to overtake me. (I was still waiting.)

I'd planted pansies in the window boxes in April, for God's sake, even though I thought they were the most disgustingly simple, chipper flowers in existence, because they were hardy enough to survive a cold snap, and Adrian had always insisted on having the first flowers in the neighborhood. I was determined to keep things up to standard.

I'd been as patient as I possibly could be, and I'd waited for time to work its healing magic. But seeing the essential parts of my life — *our* life — packed into a couple of suitcases, three boxes, and a cat carrier, while I prepared to move to New York without him, had called bullshit on this whole experiment. I didn't feel any closer to okay now than I had at his funeral. My grief wasn't a work in progress but a permanent topographical change.

So I'd dealt with this realization the way any responsible, risk-averse adult would. I'd drunk myself blind on Adrian's aguardiente.

By the time I'd pulled my sorry ass out of bed this morning, showered, and located Daphne at the top of the bedroom closet — seriously, she was *such* a shithead — it had been afternoon; hardly *early*, but the couple renting the place from me were moving in tonight, so there was no way to delay. Besides, I'd been pretty sure I'd rather die than greet Grandpa Hen for the first time in decades with an apology for not arriving Sunday night, as expected.

I hadn't meant it literally, though. And driving down the road through the darkening, late-August twilight, I realized I'd rather have faced off with a disappointed Henry Lattimer, because this road was *spooky*-deserted.

There was no traffic in either direction — not a headlight to be seen. Plus, those crazy technological advances

I'd been used to back in Massachusetts, like *streetlights*, seemed not to have made it to Backwards-land, New York. There had been nothing on either side of the car for miles but relentless trees and unmarked dirt paths.

"The upside here, Daph, is that we can't get lost," I remarked to the cat, who'd finally stopped protesting her imprisonment in the carrier about half an hour before. She ignored me, which was par for the course.

I rubbed my damp palms on the legs of my khaki shorts one at a time and stared at the miniscule amount of road illuminated by my headlights. I fucking hated driving in the dark. There was a reason I'd been the navigator any time Adrian and I had gone on a road trip.

"The bad news, though, is that a tree branch could fall on us at any time. Or we could crash through the brush and our remains won't be found for a decade or longer."

Daphne didn't dignify this with a response, which was probably what I deserved.

Realistically, I couldn't be more than a mile out of town. I remembered that much from my weeks of summer imprisonment in O'Leary as a kid. Soon, the road would open into a wide field, and not long after that came the fork where Route 222 continued on toward Rushton, and Weaver Street headed right toward O'Leary. It wouldn't take more than two minutes.

But a lot could change in two minutes.

Like suddenly deciding you were moving to New York. Or realizing you were in love. Or finding out your husband's pesky acid reflux was actually liver cancer.

The walls of the car started closing in, and I could feel my cheeks flush despite the air conditioning. My heart started beating double-time and there was a familiar cramping in my stomach. *Oh, lovely.* A panic attack was just what I needed. The cherry on the shit-sundae of this whole trip.

I took a deep breath and blew it out, then repeated the process, visualizing a calm and protective shield around the car with every exhale. Doctor Trainor would be so proud. You'd never guess I hadn't suffered from panic attacks until last year, I was such a fucking professional at handling them now.

But tonight, my calm and protective shield was doing jack shit to hold back the tide. My hands started shaking and tingling, and my vision wavered. I tried to guide the car to a gentle stop on the side of the road and…

I swear to God, I saw a man running out of the woods, right at me.

He launched himself out of the tree line at my right, straight out of the brush and into the road. His pale chest glowed in my headlights, like he was some kind of other-worldly creature, and his hair was chin-length and dark, exactly like… exactly like…

At the last possible moment, I yanked the wheel left, sending the car careening through the opposite lane, just as the road curved right. The brakes squealed as I slammed down on the pedal, but there wasn't enough pavement for me to stop. The car sailed over the embankment, weightless for a heartbeat, and in that time when gravity wasn't holding me, I thought that if death was this peaceful, it might be okay.

Then the car slammed into something with a deafening crash, the airbag exploded, catching me in the face, and I was overwhelmed by the tang of metal. I sat there, stunned, even after the airbag deflated, doing a mental assessment. My knee had taken the brunt of the impact, cracking into the center console with bruising force, but I could feel all my fingers. I could feel all my toes.

*Alive, then*, I decided. And apparently, car accidents were an antidote to panic attacks. I'd keep that info in my back pocket.

The headlights were on, but illuminated only a green curtain, since the windshield was so shattered it was impossible to see through. The engine was making an ominous hissing noise, so I turned the key and shut off the car. The headlights cut off with it.

When I heard a shuffling noise from the back seat, I remembered I wasn't alone.

Shit. *Daphne.*

I pushed my door open and then yanked at the door to the back seat, peering inside the cat carrier I'd belted into the car. I swear to God, I'd never been happier to see those accusing blue eyes blinking up at me from her smushed white face.

"You're okay," I told her, unbuckling the carrier and lifting it up so I could see her better. "I've got you, and you're gonna be fine."

She let out a plaintive, guilt-inducing *meow* that rejected any comfort. I rolled my eyes. She'd always been more Adrian's cat than…

*Fuck.* Thinking of Adrian made me remember the guy in the road, and I set the carrier on the ground in the small circle of light spilling from the interior of the car. The guy had been lean and pale, like Adrian, with hair that looked *exactly* as Adrian's had when I'd first met him. And he'd been so damn close to the car.

My stomach churned. Had I hit him? It had all happened so fast.

"Hello!" I yelled into the darkness. "Can you hear me?"

The only response was the chirping of crickets and the tiny, terrifying sounds of the woods.

I scrambled through the thick undergrowth to the passenger's side of the car and pried open the front door digging for my cell. The glass had cracked, but it lit up obediently when I touched the screen… and displayed exactly zero bars of service. Because *of course*.

I had a first aid kit in the glovebox, though, and a vague idea how to use it, so I turned my flashlight on and scanned the road where I'd seen the Adrian-lookalike. I steeled myself to see blood and broken bones. What I found was even scarier.

There was no one in the road. And no sign there'd ever been anyone, either.

Had I… imagined the man somehow? Did panic attacks cause hallucinations? Had I somehow conjured a ghost?

The last time I'd felt so completely alone had been the day of Adrian's funeral, when his mother had turned to cry in his father's arms, and his sister had turned to her boyfriend, and I'd realized the days of sharing my troubles with someone I loved were over. I could take care of myself; of course I could. But Jesus Christ, it was tiring.

I thumped my fist against the trunk.

"This isn't how it was supposed to go, Adrian!" I screamed. "You were supposed to be here with me! We were supposed to do shit *together*." I pushed my fingers against my eyes and found them wet. "If you loved me—"

I broke off before saying something incredibly dumb and stood up straight, pissed at myself.

*If he'd loved me, he'd still be alive?*

I knew better.

Adrian *had* loved me, he'd fought hard, but now he was gone. If there was a heaven or a beyond, if there was any justice in the universe, he would be floating on a cloud somewhere. He was most certainly not materializing just to jump-scare me in the woods of Upstate New York. I had my own broken mind to thank for that.

I limped over to collect my cat and started walking toward O'Leary because there was really nothing else to do. The only way out of the woods, literally and metaphorically, was through them.

# Chapter Two

## SILAS

It was Sunday night, and I was horny as fuck.

I nursed the last quarter of my Allagash Black and glanced across the high-top bar table at my date, a high school physics teacher from Camden named Reggie-Something. I had a victorious little buzz in my blood that had nothing to do with the beer and everything to do with the boldly flirtatious look the blond, blue-eyed man was aiming my way.

Target acquired, thank the hookup gods. If my dick had to make do with my right hand much longer, it was going to mutiny and walk off in protest.

"I really appreciate you meeting me out here," Reggie said, running a finger around the rim of the glass holding the icy remains of his Jack and Coke. "Must be hard for O'Leary's favorite police officer to get away from town."

I shrugged. "Nah, no big deal. Camden's only a couple miles down the road, and I like it here." I grinned. "The Dark Horse has great wings."

If I were being totally honest, I'd rather be at Hoff's, the new bar back in O'Leary, but I *really* preferred not conducting my business in front of my entire town, which was exactly what would've happened if I'd asked Reggie to meet me there. One resident would've called another, a giant game of telephone would've ensued, and Marci at the police station would've been fielding congratulations on my impending wedding by Wednesday. No, thank you.

O'Leary didn't give a shit that I was gay, but they sure as hell cared that I was single.

My parents, on the other hand, were probably just as glad that I'd never felt the desire to present them with a partner they'd have to accept publicly.

"Is that the *only* thing you like around here?" Reggie asked. Another time, his canned responses, exaggerated head-tilt, and batting eyelashes would've made me wince. At this moment, I was too wound up to do anything but play along.

"Definitely not. There's a lot to like." Specifically, I'd like to fuck him. Hard. Maybe in the parking lot first, just to take the edge off, if he was into that.

"O'Leary's a few miles down the road, and it's dangerous in the dark." Reggie smiled, his voice so filled with sultry invitation that my dick throbbed. "You could maybe…"

But what I could maybe do would forever remain a mystery, because my phone chose that precise moment to vibrate across the tabletop so loudly the silverware rattled.

Marci, calling from the station. Shit. Damn. Fuck.

I declined it, knowing she'd call back if it was a true emergency.

When the waitress came by with the bill, I grabbed my wallet before Reggie could move to get his and handed her enough cash to cover dinner and a healthy tip. Virtue-signaling, in case the hookup gods were watching.

"You were saying?" I prompted.

Reggie smiled and opened his mouth.

My phone vibrated again.

*Mother. Fucker.*

I gave Reggie an apologetic smile. "I have to take this."

"Sure," he said. "I'm going to run to the restroom. I'll be *right back*." He hopped down from the stool and turned, then looked back over his shoulder like he wanted to make sure my eyes were trained on his ass.

They were.

"What?" I barked into the phone.

"Hey there, Si! You busy with anything important?"

Marci's voice in my ear was chipper — *too* chipper. The kind of chipper that made my dick instantly deflate because I knew whatever came next was going to wreak havoc on the sexcapades I had planned for the night.

I wondered if Marci had any idea of the effect she had on me.

"I told you, I'm staying with a friend in Camden," I said, which was not a total lie. If things with Reggie had gone south, I would have crashed at my buddy Dare's place for the night. Though they hadn't, so please God, I wouldn't.

"Right, about that. We got a call," she began.

I sighed. I loved being a police officer. Truly. It was the job I'd wanted since I was ten years old, and losing my brother in a car accident years later had only cemented the path I was on.

And I loved O'Leary, too. The residents were some of the best people on earth — kind, salt-of-the-earth, and amazingly open-minded for a town that still celebrated Shoemaker Day every winter in memory of a time when traveling shoemakers were still a thing.

But for a town tiny enough to only employ three full-time and two part-time auxiliary officers, the residents sure managed to manufacture a fuck-ton of drama to get upset over. If anything truly terrible ever happened, they wouldn't know what to do with themselves.

"Let me guess," I said. "Someone else is up in arms over the artwork over at the Cobb place?"

"Artwork," Marci scoffed. "That's not *art*, Si. It's three gigantic metal… *you know what* in various stages of… *you know what.*"

"Phalluses?" I offered, amused despite myself. "Erection?"

"Exactly! Rena Cobb just likes attention," Marci said, with all the bitterness that a woman who'd never broken a rule in her life could harbor for a woman who'd broken every rule in the book and gotten away with it. "Angela Ross says it's going to cause a car accident if it's not taken down. And Karen Mitchener-Martin says it's going to make her give birth!"

I scratched my chin, where my five o'clock shadow was already growing in. "I don't think metal penises work that way, Marci. Not even giant ones."

Marci sighed impatiently. "She's already pregnant, *Si.* She means she's so horrified, it's going to send her into early labor."

I was pretty sure early labor didn't work that way, either, but what did I know?

"But anyway, Mitch just said to remind anyone who called that they can bring it up at the September council meeting and that outrage isn't a public emergency."

I could totally picture our boss saying those exact words. "Good," I told her. "Is that all?"

"No! Thing is, Carmen's on duty tonight, but she got called out on a drunk and disorderly over at Hoff's."

*Christ.* "Jamie Burke again?"

"Yep."

"That's his second one this month."

"Third," Marci corrected.

I pulled at my bottom lip, fingering the scar that ran along it. "Someone needs to talk to him. Remind him to keep his personal grudges from making the police blotter. And maybe talk to Parker over at Hoff's. He's gotta monitor Jamie's intake a little more closely or stop serving him at all."

"Love it. You volunteering to have *that* talk?" she asked pointedly, and I sighed again. I supposed I was.

"But Jamie's not why I called, either," she continued. "There was a disturbance out at the campground."

I frowned. Pickett Campground, which had been owned by Frank and Myrna Lucano for longer than I'd been alive, was on the south end of town, right on the border of Herriman-Sizemore State Park. It catered to the summer tourists who came to hike the trails or go kayaking on Lake Loughton. "What kind of disturbance? I thought the place was mostly closed down for the season, except to locals."

"It is," she agreed. "Frank's got two sites rented through Tuesday, then he's closing down until snowmobile season. But Myrna swears she heard gunshots, and they say one of the campers is missing."

"Myrna thought she was being attacked by a bear last week, and it was only Frank clearing the property with a chainsaw."

Marci laughed. "Most likely someone hunting out of season or a figment of Myrna's imagination," she agreed. "But Frank says the camper paid for four nights and his site's empty."

"His car around?"

"Nothing that easy, I'm afraid. He hiked in through the park."

"You could call Darius Turner," I suggested, happily throwing my friend under the bus. Dare was a State Conservation Officer — a park ranger with a badge and a gun. "If something happened inside the park, it's his jurisdiction."

"Sure, sure," she agreed. "Except there's no proof that anything *did* happen inside the park or that anything happened at all. Si, you know how this works better than I do. The complaint gets reported, we take a statement and check it out, then escalate if necessary. Besides, you can't honestly think that Frank will talk to Dare or any state employee. Not anymore."

Not after the eminent domain case that was going to cost him part of his beloved campground. *Fuck.*

Reggie came out of the restroom, and his eyes immediately locked on mine. I nearly whimpered at the heat there as he sashayed across the room.

"Can't you call Mitch?" I pleaded. "Tell him I'll owe him. Tell him he can borrow my truck whenever he wants for the rest of the year."

"Honey, I tried. I did!" She sounded honestly regretful. "But he's not picking up. And since I knew you were heading out Camden way, I figured maybe you could do a quick drive by and then get back to… you know, whatever you were doing."

Her dropped voice said she knew pretty much *exactly* what I'd been doing. Or hoping to do.

"You're killing me, Marci. Dead."

"Hey! Don't shoot the messenger. I'll keep trying Mitch, too, okay? If I can get him, I'll let you know."

I hung up and scrubbed a hand through my hair in frustration, probably making myself look like a porcupine, but who cared at this point? My evening was shot.

I was ninety-eight percent sure Myrna Lucano had

heard a car backfiring, or a tree branch creaking, or her own arthritic knee cracking; I would've bet my grandfather's Porsche on it. And no doubt the camper had decided to simply hike on to the next location. But as long as there was that two-percent chance something else had happened, I had to check it out, just in case.

The hookup gods were cruel, and they were flighty.

Reggie didn't pause at his own stool, but came around the table directly to mine, resting his forearms on my chest in a proprietary way. "You ready to get out of here, hot stuff?"

I blinked. My dick was so on board with that, I could have cried. But at the same time, I wasn't digging the whole PDA thing. I wasn't closeted, but I had zero desire to parade my hookups around. Either this guy was new to small-town life, or he had no concept of keeping private shit private.

I grabbed his wrists and pulled him away from me a little more deliberately than I might have if I didn't know sex was firmly off the table for tonight.

"Reggie, I just got a call from my dispatcher. There's a situation back in O'Leary."

Reggie frowned. "But it's your night off."

"Yeah," I sighed. "But small-town police officers are never fully *off*. Dates take a back seat to the job."

He took a step away and looked at me cautiously. "Is this, like, a blow-off?" he demanded.

"No! No. *Christ*, no," I assured him. "Literally, any night but tonight. I'm off tomorrow." *If my dick can hold out that long.*

"You promise?"

"Yeah, totally. I'll call you."

I put a hand on his back and ushered him to the front

door. Outside, it was fully dark, and only the ancient red and white Dark Horse sign lit the parking lot.

He pointed his key fob at a little red Nissan parked on the side of the building, and I walked him toward it.

"I could be free Saturday," he announced, turning around to rest his ass against his car. He darted a glance at the front of my jeans and licked his lips in a way that was no doubt designed to make me regret leaving him.

It worked.

"Alright." I nodded. "I'll call you then."

I took another step closer and ducked my head to kiss him. His lips were warm as they met mine, and he gave an appreciative little moan. This guy was easy and uncomplicated, exactly what I wanted.

———

TEN MINUTES LATER, I was driving down Route 222 toward home, my high-beams on and my windows wide open to the cool night breeze. I was trying to clear my head, but driving this road tonight did nothing to improve my mood.

O'Learians called this stretch 'the Camden road,' for obvious reasons, and we all learned to drive by negotiating its many switchbacks and tight turns. Tourists called it a scenic highway and stopped — illegally, I might add — to take pictures, especially when the trees were decked out in scarlet and orange foliage. But for me, this was the road where my brother Matty had been taken from me while he and Molly, his best friend since preschool, had been driving back east to school after a weekend at home.

Matty had lost control of the car. That was the official cause of the accident. Swerved off the road for reasons no one would ever know, managing to careen down an embankment and into a tree with such force that Molly was thrown out of the car completely and Matty… Well, Matty managed to dislodge some part of the fuel system on his way down the hill, and the car went up in flames. That it was a nearly impossible convergence of events — tragic mishap on top of tragic mishap — made it even harder to accept, especially for my parents.

It had all happened so long ago — nearly a dozen years now — that I could drive this road sometimes and not even think of it. And then, of course, there were times when I could see the burned-out wreck of Matty's car imprinted on the backs of my eyelids with every blink.

And tonight, as I navigated my truck around the final bend toward O'Leary, my headlights glinted off something shiny sticking out from the trees on the far side of the road that made me wonder if I was having some kind of flashback.

It was a car, goddammit. A little blue Toyota with out-of-state plates. And by the look of the skid marks, it had crossed the lane before wrapping itself around a huge-ass tree.

I put my hazard lights on and pulled across the road, right behind the car, then climbed out and ran over. I hadn't realized I'd been holding my breath until I saw the car was empty and I exhaled shakily. Doors and windows locked, no sign of the driver.

I grabbed my cell phone from my pocket and called Marci while I climbed back into the truck.

"Marci, you had any reports of an accident on the Camden road in the last couple hours?" I knew for a fact that car hadn't been there when I'd driven past earlier.

"Not a one. Why?"

"I found a car wrapped around a tree about a mile east of the town line."

"Animal hit? Or drunk driver?"

"No sign of an injured animal," I told her. "And no sign of the driver at all. Car might be totaled. Airbag deployed."

She whistled. "Want me to ring Joe Cross and see if he got a call for a pickup?"

Joe was pretty much the only tow truck driver in the three-town area that included Camden, O'Leary, and Rushton to the west. "Do that," I confirmed. "And if he hasn't gotten one, ask him to come get it." I gave her the make, model, and license number.

"You got it. Oh, and I did manage to talk to Mitch finally, just a minute ago." She sounded apologetic. "He said he'd head out to Frank and Myrna's, so…"

So, *nothing*. I spared Reggie one last thought and then waved him goodbye. Now I had to find the damn Toyota driver.

Turned out, it didn't require much investigation. I found the asshole half a mile down the road, carrying some suitcase-thing and lurching along in a kind of shuffle-step, like he was three sheets to the wind.

Anger clogged my throat.

The guy stopped when he saw my headlights and turned around to watch me, shielding his eyes from the glare. He looked younger than one of Marci's kids, barely out of his teens. An arrogant, entitled tourist who thought he was invincible, and could have taken out any number of innocent people when he found out differently.

I shoved the truck into park when I was about ten feet behind him and jumped out.

"What the fuck do you think you're doing?"

"Huh?" The kid straightened, trying to meet my eyes, and honest to God, he practically fell at my feet. It was a wonder he'd managed to climb out of his Toyota in the first place, let alone make it a quarter mile down the road.

I grabbed my badge from my pocket and flashed it at him. "O'Leary Police. How much have you had to drink?" I demanded.

"Pardon?" The kid's voice was high, like he was scared. Scared he'd gotten *caught.*

"You heard me. That was your car back there, wasn't it?" I hooked my thumb behind me. "Blue Toyota? Wrapped around a giant oak tree?"

"Y-yes," he agreed, frowning.

"And you were the driver?"

"Yes, I was driving." I couldn't make out much in the glare from my headlights, but his eyes looked red and bleary, his face scraped raw from the airbag.

"Uh-huh. Wanna explain to me how you went sailing all the way across the road to accomplish that feat of automotive gymnastics?"

He glared at me for a moment, then licked his lips nervously and set his jaw. "No."

*No.* What a punk.

"Right," I said. "Well, step this way, kiddo. You can take a breathalyzer, and I'll be able to solve that mystery without your explanation." I grabbed him by the elbow and pulled him toward my truck.

"Breath-a… Wait." The kid shrugged out of my grasp. "Wait! Do you think I was drinking?"

"Are you saying you *weren't?*"

"God, no," he said, so vehemently that it actually gave me pause. "What the hell made you think that?"

I suddenly couldn't remember what *had* made me think that. Standing next to the truck, out of the glare of the lights, he didn't seem to have any trouble focusing on me. His balance seemed much steadier. His words were well-articulated. I couldn't smell any alcohol on him.

*Shit.*

"I…" I stammered. "It's common when there's an accident involving a teen driver."

"A teen driver?" he repeated, his eyes narrowing. "You cannot *possibly* be talking about me. I'm twenty-nine, you idiot!"

Once more, I was caught on the back foot. Yeah, the guy was maybe five-seven, tops, and lean along with it, but the cut of his jaw made it clear that he was no teenager. Plus, the look in his eyes — bone-weary and enraged simultaneously — wasn't one I'd ever seen on a kid.

Detective work like this would have gotten my ass kicked out of any police force in the world, even that of tiny O'Leary, New York.

"I'm sorry," I said, rubbing my palm over my chest. I expected to feel the starched cotton and buttons of my uniform, but I didn't. I glanced down and winced at my casual summer date-wear: shorts, sneakers, and a fitted polo.

I was driving my own truck, and not a marked car, too. Jesus, no wonder the guy looked scared. Other than my badge, I had nothing identifying me as a police officer.

"*Christ.*" I ran my hand through my hair. "I jumped to conclusions. I apologize."

His eyes were green. It was dark as fuck out here, making it almost impossible to differentiate between shades of color, and yet I knew without a doubt that his eyes were an impossible bright green, and would be even in sunlight. They locked on mine with stunning force.

"You *apologize?*" he whispered, his voice trembling. "Let me explain something. I have been driving for the past six hours. I was on *your* fucking ink-black roads, heading for *your* godforsaken town, to stay with my grandfather, when a ma… moose, or something," he faltered. "Popped out of the fucking woods and ran at me. I turned my wheel so I wouldn't hit it and ended up destroying my car and banging the hell out of my knee. And then I've had to hike approximately fifty-thousand miles down this road *on that injured fucking knee*, with only a half-dead cell phone to light the way, because no one out here believes in streetlights or telephone reception, wondering if the movie of my life is going to look more like *Deliverance* or an episode of *Criminal Minds*!"

By the end of his tirade, he was jabbing his finger into my chest and had me arching backward over the hood of my own truck. It was impressive.

It was hot.

*Down, boy*, I instructed my cock, which must've still been on a hair trigger thanks to Reggie.

"I, uh, have given you no actual reason to believe this," I said, straightening up and grabbing the wrist he'd pointed at me. "But I am not actually crazy. It's been a frustrating night, and I was keyed up, and I don't like this road, and… well. I really hate car accidents."

His pulse raced beneath my fingertips. He looked at me for another second, then nodded. He seemed to shrink back in on himself once the anger had leached out of him, like a deflated balloon.

I felt a surge of sympathy. God knew, I'd felt that. Still felt it, sometimes.

"I'm Si Sloane," I said, turning our hand clasp into a hand shake.

He took a deep breath. "Everett Maior. Ev." The words were like a sigh. "Henry Lattimer's my grandfather." He pulled his hand away.

"Oh, yeah? You the artist or the runner?"

"Pardon?"

"Before she passed, your grandma used to brag about

her two grandsons. I remember one of you went to art school and the other was a track star."

"Oh. I'm the artist, I guess." He paused. "More or less."

"Got it. Well, climb in, Ev," I told him, nodding toward the passenger side. I smiled. "I'll drive you to my *godforsaken town.*"

I could almost swear he blushed as I repeated his words. It was weirdly cute… and *God*, it really should not have been. I needed to get laid even worse than I'd thought.

"That's not necessary," Ev argued. "If you could just call…"

"The police?" I suggested. "Done." I spread my arms to my sides. "There aren't many of us to choose from around here, and the others are all busy. You're stuck with me."

He sighed and lifted a hand to rub his forehead. "A tow truck?"

"Already called. Joe Cross will come and get the car."

"Well, then, I'll just wait for…"

"I should say, he'll come *at some point*," I continued, rocking on my feet. "There's a preseason game on tonight."

"A… what?"

"Preseason. Football?" I added, when he continued to look confused. "Pats and Jacksonville. Joe's a Patriots fan, but we like him anyway."

Ev nodded, a little bewildered. "Okay."

"You like football?"

"I… guess?" he said. He shook his head. "Listen, fascinating as this is, I…"

"You need to get off your injured knee," I surmised. I

reached out a hand toward him. "All the more reason to let me help you into the truck."

He stared at my hand for a second, and then his narrowed eyes met mine. He was trying to decide if he could trust me.

I snorted. "This isn't *Criminal Minds*, and it's sure as fuck not *Deliverance*. You hear any banjos?"

Everett's lips twitched reluctantly, and he shut his eyes for half a second. "No," he admitted. He exhaled loudly. "Fine, let's go."

When he set his palm in mine, I felt a rush of protectiveness that nearly bowled me over. I told myself it was because his fingers were icy and his hand felt so small in mine; because I felt bad I'd practically accosted him, and I was still horny from the *hookupus interruptus* earlier.

Still, I had the irrational desire to make him smile, full-on. To see what his face looked like when it was unguarded.

"Remember that you're in O'Leary," I told him as I guided him to the door.

"Oh, I'm well aware." His teeth were clenched like he was in pain, but it didn't stop him from being snarky.

"So, when you're considering a theme for the movie of your life, think less psychological thriller and more… Hallmark."

"Like the cards?"

"Like the movies."

Ev snorted. "Right."

"No, seriously," I told him. "White picket fences. Apple trees. *Pumpkin Festival.*"

"*Pumpkin Festival.*" He blinked. "Not really?"

"Oh, so *very* really," I promised him, swinging the door open. "Foliage. Arts and crafts. Costumes. Jack-o-lanterns. Cable-knit sweaters. Hay rides. A disgusting and disproportionate number of happy couples." I leaned in closer like I was imparting a secret, and caught the faint hint of his cologne, something citrusy and warm. "We have pie contests."

"Eating or making?" he asked with narrowed eyes, like he was intrigued despite himself.

I raised one eyebrow. "Both."

"Yeah, well, I'm only here until the spring," he said, waving a hand. "I will observe your strange rituals from a distance."

I chuckled, charmed, as he climbed into the seat. "Be careful," I warned. "You might just drink the Kool-Aid, too." I tapped my chin and studied him thoughtfully. His curly hair was a dark, coal black that seemed to absorb the light from the truck, but his eyes were every bit as vibrant green as I'd thought. "I betcha you'll be calling this home by Halloween."

"Ha! Nope. Pretty sure your wholesome little cult doesn't include queer guys who vote liberal."

I grinned. "Actually, pretty sure those are my *favorite* kind of guys."

"*You?*" So damn suspicious.

"O'Leary might surprise you, Everett," I said with a wink. "Wait and see."

# Chapter Three

## EVERETT

*WAIT AND SEE*. Jesus Christ. Maybe it was just this fucked-up night, or my lingering hangover, or the way I was freakin' primed to see ghosts popping out all over the damn place, but his throwaway comment had unsettled me.

Unsettled? Hell, it had made shivers dance down my spine like he'd been a sideshow fortune-teller whispering portents of the future.

Si collected Daphne's carrier from the side of the road and tucked her into the back seat with a whispered, "Welcome to O'Leary, Daphne," I wasn't sure I was supposed to hear and I was positive I shouldn't find so charming. Meanwhile, I sat in the cab of his gigantic truck, mulling over his words while my leg throbbed in time to the country song playing low on the radio.

*Wait and see.* No, thank you. I was tired of surprises. And if Officer Sloane had outed himself to me for a reason, he was barking up the wrong tree.

He was good-looking, yes. One could objectively call him *hot*. And yes, he was kind. Funny, too. But right now, I wouldn't care if he was the love child of Jason Momoa and

Chris Pratt, and his dick was magic. I had no need of friends and even less of a lover.

"The cat is a shitty conversationalist, and the more you try to charm her, the more she'll ignore you," I warned him as he climbed into the driver's seat and buckled his belt. My voice was defensive, and I didn't care. "Don't bother making an effort."

Si chuckled. "Eh. She might be cranky, but she's pretty. Maybe the effort will be worth the reward."

I tilted my head to study him. His eyes were focused on the road, but his lips were quirked like he found me amusing and I wondered — because I was so thoroughly out of the game, I couldn't say for sure — if this was his way of flirting with me. I should probably feel more outrage.

I faced forward, folding my arms over my chest. "I'm not sure where you learned about cats, Officer Sloane, but sometimes they don't want to be friends."

I felt his gaze on my face. "Sometimes," he agreed. "And sometimes they're just prickly when they're injured."

I hadn't been paying attention to where we were going, since all the damn woods looked the same in the head-lights, so I was confused when he pulled over behind the remains of my Toyota. The mangled metal looked even worse from this angle than it had from inside, and I shuddered.

If life worked the way it was supposed to, I shouldn't have walked away from the crash, but then, it generally didn't. Win some, lose some.

Before I knew it, Si had turned off the truck, walked around to my side, opened my door, and was holding out his hand to me again.

"What are we back here for?" I demanded.

He rolled his eyes — eyes that were very patient, very

blue, and on a level with mine even while I was sitting in his truck. "I figured you'd want to get stuff out of your car. You know, clothes? Phone charger? Toothbrush?"

I looked at the ground. I was an idiot. "Yeah. Yes.… Thank you."

He nodded and tipped his head toward his hand, which was still outstretched. With a sigh, I grabbed it and let him help me down.

I pulled out my keys and unlocked the trunk, then reached for a suitcase. He pushed my hand aside. "You're hurt," he said, like I might have forgotten.

"So? I can still do it," I protested.

"Sure you could," he said, grabbing the heavy case like it weighed nothing and swinging it into the cargo area of the truck. "But why?"

Uh, to prove I could? To make sure I never again forgot *how*? Duh.

"Suit yourself," I told him, like it didn't matter either way. I hefted the other suitcase awkwardly and hissed as I stumbled under the weight of it.

With another eye roll, Si grabbed that bag too and set it next to the first. "Christ, you're stubborn." He frowned at me severely. "Listen up, Everett: if you even touch those boxes, I'm strapping your ass in the bed."

I blinked at him in shock, and against my will, my stomach flipped.

Si made a choking noise.

"The bed of the *truck*," he stammered, his face turning beet red. "Jesus Christ. I meant, I'd strap you in the…" His horrified eyes came to mine. "Wait! I meant *strapping*, like I'd tie you up! Not like I'd use a belt or a… a…I mean…" His voice was strangled and he ran a hand through his hair. "Oh, God. There's nothing I can say without making this worse, is there?"

The noise that came out of my mouth was a cross between a giggle and a snort, a bubble of sound so rusty and unexpected I clapped a hand over my mouth to stifle it. But it was all so ridiculous and impossible; not just Si hurling himself over a conversational cliff, but everything else, too — the 'ghost' in the road, the accident, exiling myself to fucking O'Leary in the first place, ending up in the woods with this unrelentingly friendly man, and making a noise like a fucking pig being violated. I couldn't stop laughing at the absurdity of it, and every gasp for breath made me snort even louder.

Si stared at me, likely wondering if I was having some kind of fit, but when he realized the sound was laughter, he started laughing too, doubling over on himself with the force of it and burying his face in his hands.

And that made me laugh harder still.

When the worst had subsided, I propped my ass against the open trunk of my car and wiped my eyes, watching Si try to get himself under control. The man was so capable, but looked helpless in that moment. Vulnerable in his laughter. I felt something inside me crack a tiny bit.

Maybe I did have need of a friend, after all.

"God, if you only knew how smooth my game was earlier tonight," he moaned. "You wouldn't believe it."

"Your game?"

"I was on a date. At a bar." He lifted his head and gave me a rueful smile. "Guy was hot, totally into me. I'd almost locked things up." He came over and leaned on the car beside me with a sigh. It was comfortable, companionable, and I found myself relaxing for the first time in… well. A while.

"Almost," I snickered. "Sure."

He knocked his shoulder gently into mine. "Believe what you like. It was *this close*."

"The guy must have been easily impressed."

Si turned his head to glare at me in mock outrage. "I'll have you know, lots of guys are into *this*." He waved a hand up and down his body.

"Uh-huh. So what happened?" I demanded, still smiling. "How'd your destiny get derailed?"

Si snorted. "Destiny doesn't exist, Ev. Everyone makes choices. And sometimes you have to live with the consequences of other people's choices."

"Okay." I put my hands up in surrender at his unexpected lecture. "Whatever you say."

"Like, in this case, my date got derailed because a sweet old lady heard gunshots and decided to report it. And then further derailed when some dumbass got scared off the road by a deer or something." He shook his head at me in reproof. "We don't even *get* moose this far west."

No kidding. The moose had been about as real as my hallucination.

"So, kind of a wild night in O'Leary, huh?"

"Pretty much."

"And your date wouldn't wait for you to finish your business?"

He sighed again and tilted his head back to look up at the sky. The moon had risen, and there was a smattering of stars just visible through the canopy of trees. "Most guys don't like coming in second to the job. Kinda kills the vibe."

I nodded. "Well, I'm sorry," I told him. "For my part in the derailment."

He shook his head like I was crazy, his eyes still trained on the sky. "Not your fault."

I tilted my head back so I could appreciate the view, too. I had to admit, it was kinda pretty. The night was mostly silent around us, but it didn't seem so terrifying anymore.

After a while, my stomach grumbled, reminding me I hadn't eaten since… Damn. *Yesterday.*

Si turned his head and raised a teasing eyebrow. "We'd better get you to Henry's before your stomach starts digesting itself." He reached into the trunk for the largest of the boxes.

"Don't bother with that one," I told him, giving up on the idea of carrying them myself. "Just the other two."

"The big one has all the incriminating evidence?" he joked, lifting one of the smaller ones into the truck.

"It has art supplies," I said dismissively. "I haven't used them in ages."

Over a year, to be precise.

Si looked at me curiously, hands on his hips. "Why not? Doesn't it drive you crazy if you go too long without… doing whatever kind of art you do?"

"Painting," I said, frowning. "And yeah, it used to. Do you paint?"

"Oh God, no." He shook his head ruefully as he grabbed the other small box. "I can't draw a straight line with a ruler. But Matty — my brother Matthias — he was a whole other story. Always had a sketchbook in his hand."

He broke off and turned to look at me, his body tense like he'd accidentally opened a conversational door and now he wasn't sure he wanted me to walk through it.

*Was*, he'd said. *Had.* Past-tense.

I felt a stirring of sympathy.

"That was me when I was younger." I turned to slam the trunk lid and lock the car again. "I used to draw cartoons all the time, anthropomorphic cars, and squirrels, and cans of soda. Half of them weren't even funny. But it gave me something to do in social situations. An outlet for my random thoughts." I was babbling, and his soft smile told me he appreciated it.

I cleared my throat, profoundly uncomfortable, and hobbled back to the truck. "Do you, uh, know where my grandfather lives?"

*Stupid.* Of course he did. My grandparents used to live in an old Victorian on the outskirts of town, with a huge front yard where Grandma Anna had grown roses and I'd played under the sprinkler. But Grandpa had gotten rid of the house after she died, and now he lived in the two-bedroom apartment above the hardware store, which was pretty much smack in the center of O'Leary. Unmissable.

Si opened the door and handed me up. "I'll get you where you need to go, Everett." He winked.

For once, I kept my mouth shut.

———

"How's Hen doing with his leg?" Si asked a few minutes later, when we were back on the road. "I haven't been by to see him like I should have."

"My mother says he's complaining about the doctor putting him in a cast when any fool could see it was just a bad bruise, and that the kid who's been helping him in the shop is *incompetent* and *weird*." I shrugged. "Sounds like he's pretty much the same as ever."

Si winced. "Theo's a good kid."

"Oh, no doubt," I agreed. "I'm sure I'll love him. We incompetent, weird kids have to stick together."

"Uh. Your grandfather is…" Si began, in the careful, diplomatic tone people had used my whole life when trying to explain or excuse my grandfather's behavior. But I was old enough to know some things couldn't be explained or excused away.

"Is stuck in a time warp? Where girls are girls, and men are men? Where Adam and Steve are a crime against nature, and for the love of all that's holy, don't dare call their relationship *marriage*? Yeah. I know."

Si frowned. "So why are you here?"

That was a damn good question. One I'd asked myself a million times.

"He needed someone to take care of him. Apparently, he'd had a lady helping him out, but he's refusing to let her help him anymore. Maybe she's incompetent and weird, too? Who knows." I traced patterns on my leg with my index finger. "But my mother freaked out because he was all alone, and she can't get away from work, so she basically guilted me into helping. She, uh, called some old friend of hers and found out there was an opening for an art teacher at the elementary school, then called Grandpa and told him to expect me."

I debated saying more, mentioning Adrian and how my life had suddenly become so rootless and portable, but I never knew how to bring up the subject of Adrian, especially now. So instead, I turned my head and watched the little houses of O'Leary pass by.

Si whistled long and low. "So you were *voluntold* to come."

"You might say that. But if Grandpa's the worst I have to deal with, I can handle it. I accepted a contract with the school until June, and then I'll head back east."

"Marking days like a convict?"

*Well… yes.* I glanced over, worried I'd offended him, but found him smiling.

"I'm telling you, the town might grow on you."

"Like a fungus."

"Exactly."

He pulled to a stop in one of the diagonal parking

spaces right in front of my grandfather's store and hopped out, but this time I was too quick for him. I opened my own door and eased myself down before he could help me. He smirked like he knew what I was thinking and shook his head at me, then continued around to the back of the truck to get my stuff while I looked around at the town that was going to be my new — *temporary* — home.

In the darkness, it looked almost exactly as I remembered it.

O'Leary Hardware was a two-story clapboard building, located almost in the center of Weaver Street, right between Marybeth's Salon and Spa and a store that used to be simply called Nickerson's Books, but was now called Nickerson's Books *and More*, maybe as a nod to the town having climbed out of the nineteenth century somewhere around the turn of the twenty-first.

But I had to admit, I was curious what the *more* was.

Nothing about the hardware store was different. The front door was flanked by enormous, lit-up picture windows bearing ancient, hand-lettered signs that read, "Tools and Fixtures!" and "Hardware and Gifts!" Beneath one of the signs sat the giant model train set that Grandpa Hen's father had first constructed back when dinosaurs roamed the earth — a miniature locomotive chugging in endless circles around a tiny, unchanging O'Leary.

"Don't s'pose you have a key?" Si appeared on the sidewalk in front of me, carrying both of my suitcases.

I shook my head.

He looked up at the windows on the second floor, where golden light was spilling out between black shutters. "Well, maybe Hen's got company with two working legs. Otherwise, we'll figure something out."

He walked to the small door set to the right of the building and knocked loudly, but nothing happened.

*Shit.* I hadn't even considered how Grandpa would be able to let me in from upstairs with a broken leg. Apparently, there were a lot of things I hadn't considered before embarking on this trip.

But eventually, we heard muttered curses and thumping, then the door opened to reveal my grandfather, red-faced, sweating, and leaning heavily against the banister of the staircase behind him.

He was a bleached-out version of the man I remembered — his bushy mustache more salt than pepper now, the thinning hair on his head decidedly whiter, his eyes a lighter version of my own green, and his right leg swathed in plaster.

He looked directly at me for the first time in years and said, "Everett, you're late."

Which was about the reception I'd expected.

Like his store, Henry Lattimer's personality hadn't changed at all.

"Ev ran into some trouble with his car, Hen," Si interjected mildly, drawing Grandpa's attention. "On the road in from Camden."

Grandpa gave him the grin he hadn't given me. "Silas Sloane! Good to see you. You been up Lake Loughton recently? I heard it's the best summer for trout in near on fifty years."

If Si was surprised at this change in conversation, his smile didn't show it. "I can't comment on what it was like fifty years ago, Hen, but I can say my dad and I caught ourselves a pair of two-footers last weekend."

"How about that!" Grandpa slapped the door frame with his open palm, then pointed his finger at Si. "You tell Jack I owe him a drink and he can tell me all about it."

"Yes, sir," Si replied with a chuckle. "Just don't let him convince you it was anything over two feet."

"I know better," Grandpa agreed. "And you tell your mother I said hello."

"I will, sir. She's got the council meeting coming up."

"Oh, *that*," Grandpa scoffed. "Why they need a meeting to deal with that eyesore of Rena Cobb's is beyond…"

Christ. They could go all night, and my knee was officially killing me. I cleared my throat and shuffled forward. "Si, we don't need to keep you any longer. I can take care of the suitcases. Thank you."

Grandpa looked at me reprovingly. "Don't be rude, Everett."

But Si looked chastened. "Shit," he said, all concern. "Your knee must be killing you. Let me drop these upstairs and then I'll help you up and take a look at it."

"Uh, no," I said, with what I hoped was finality. "I can manage, and I don't need a doctor."

"What'd you do to yourself?" Grandpa said, frowning. "Your legs look alright."

"They are," I agreed. I shuffled forward until I stood next to him, waiting for him to move to let me in. But when he didn't, I realized he likely *couldn't*. I turned to Si. "If you're going to help anyone up, it should be him. I have no idea how he got down here on one leg."

Grandpa's face darkened. "Strength comes from will, Everett."

"Inspiring." I rolled my eyes. "I'm gonna go ahead and embroider that on a tea towel, but in the meantime, unless you can *will* yourself back up the stairs, let Si help you."

"Too fresh by *half*." Grandpa scowled. "I will *not* be treated like an invalid in my own home."

Si cleared his throat. "Ev's right, Hen," he said matter-of-factly. "I'll help you up the stairs, and…"

From above came a buzzing, like a smoke detector going off.

"Goddamn it! The pie!" Grandpa said. He used the banister to turn himself around, but when he tried to lift his casted leg to climb, he paused. I could imagine the scowl on his face. "Fine! Help me up, Silas."

Si left the suitcases on the sidewalk, then ducked through the door and under Grandpa's arm, wrapping his hand around Grandpa's waist, then proceeded to mostly carry the shorter man up the stairs.

It would have been amusing if I wasn't dreading my own climb.

But I hadn't taken more than two halting steps up when Si jogged back down the steps to me and held out his hand.

"I'm fine," I told him, holding the railing with two hands. "But on second thought, if you *could* maybe get Daphne and the suitcases…"

I barely registered Si's huff before he grabbed me over his shoulder and hauled me up the stairs.

I shrieked. "What the hell are you doing?"

"Being efficient," he said. He set me down at the top of the stairs, in the tidy living room where my grandfather was already sitting in his ancient, green recliner in front of the football game. "We *could* have had a whole drawn-out argument, and in the end, you would have agreed because you're a reasonable person. But I've only known you an hour and I swear we've already had that conversation twice, Ev. So, you know." He shrugged and gave me a smile. "Efficient."

It was mildly mortifying that his smile — ten times more devastating now that I could really see him properly — made me hesitate. But by the time I'd regained my wits enough to argue, he'd already moved into the kitchen, which was the next room back from the street.

"Pie's out!" he said. He strolled back into the living room with an ice pack in one hand and a dishtowel slung over the other. "And don't you tell me you made that delicious-looking thing, Henry Lattimer, or I'll call you a liar."

Grandpa's cheeks, which had already been red from either his climb down the stairs or the way Si had hauled him back up, blushed a deeper red. "Diane Perkins brought dinner," he said. He gave Si a defiant look. "She knew Everett was coming."

"Ah," Si said. His eyes found mine, and he grinned. Then he seemed to realize that I was still standing next to the stairs. "Let's get you to the couch."

But when he approached me, I slapped his hand away and belatedly hobbled across the room to sit down on the plush burgundy couch that used to be in my Grandma Anna's living room.

I didn't need to be manhandled *or* coddled. And I was wary of the strange closeness that seemed to spring up fully formed between Silas and me. I'd never been that way with anyone before, sure as hell not within an *hour*. I didn't trust it.

Si held out the ice pack wrapped in the towel. "At least put ice on it," he said impatiently.

"I don't have a broken leg, Si, I bruised my knee. I'm perfectly *fine*."

Grandpa Hen sighed. "That's what *I* tried to tell the doctor," he said plaintively. "It's just a bruise! But nobody believed me."

I glanced at Si, then at Grandpa, then back to Si. His blue eyes were mocking. "Runs in the family, then?"

I knew he wasn't talking about bruises.

"Fine." I snatched the ice out of his hand and set it on my knee. I *was* reasonable. Just apparently not in O'Leary.

"I'll just bring up Daphne and the suitcases," he said way too cheerfully, then he took off down the stairs, whistling.

From across the room, I studied my grandfather. He was watching the football game avidly, the remote control gripped in one hand. It seemed he'd forgotten I was there.

"O'Leary, New York is going to make me a murderer," I grumbled.

"Let me go ahead and embroider that on a tea towel," Grandpa said. Then he turned the volume up before I could reply.

## Chapter Four

### SILAS

It was dark and silent in the woods, but I knew I wasn't alone. Ev was right next to me, close enough that I could reach out my pinkie finger and touch his cold hand.

"You were lying earlier, weren't you?" he demanded. His voice was husky, private, and I turned to look at him. His eyes were green as summer, glowing in the dark. He was beautiful, and he scared me to death.

"I wouldn't lie to you," I said around the sudden dryness in my throat.

"But you did, Silas." He stretched out a finger to touch the hair at my temple, then slid it down across my cheek, and I realized that I'd been wrong. His hands were so, so warm. "You said you meant to strap me to the bed of the truck, but you didn't. Not really. You pretended it was a joke, but it wasn't."

The knowing look in his eyes made my cock swell instantly. I'd had no ulterior motive when I'd blurted out my threat the day before, but I couldn't lie; the way his eyes had fixed on mine after I'd uttered it, wide and maybe just a little *excited*, I'd suddenly realized I'd meant it in a whole other way.

"Would you like that, Ev?" I asked softly, and maybe a little menacingly too. "You want me to tie you down?"

"Maybe." His hand brushed down my chest then lower, tracing gently over my cock. "I like that you'd want to," he whispered. "I like that you want *me*."

"I do," I whispered back, and in the moment I said it, I knew it was true. I wanted him, more than any hookup I'd ever had. The man was a prickly, snarky challenge, but being with him felt *right*, and choosing him was by far the easiest thing I'd ever done.

I ducked my head to kiss him, wrapping my arms around his waist… but he evaporated before my lips touched his.

I woke up and growled at my empty room.

Even my fucking dreams were cockblocking me now, and I was hard as a rock for a guy who seemed to like me and hate me in equal measure.

I threw a hand over my eyes and chuckled in the pre-dawn gloom of my bedroom at the ridiculousness of it all. I didn't dream of guys I *had* fucked, let alone guys I hadn't and likely never would. I was horny. That was all. At that point, my dick would have reacted to any stimulus, whether it was a hot, new guy or a warm breeze.

And when I stroked myself to a hard and dirty orgasm in the shower and imagined it was Ev's hand instead of mine, that was just simple biology, too.

When I was clean and more-or-less sated, I flopped back down on my bed in my towel and stared out the window. The sky was pink-gold, the sun not even risen. I had a whole day off and no plans at all for once.

No last-minute phone calls from my parents, wanting me to come over and do yard work, or help my mother redecorate, or endure yet another uncomfortable dinner at their house. No calls from Marci diverting my day. It was like the hookup gods were giving me this consolation prize; I could bring up the hookup app on my phone right now and have my dry spell broken by lunchtime.

But I didn't get further than swiping my phone to unlock it before I started wondering what Everett Maior was doing right now. I threw my phone on the bed in frustration and scrubbed a hand over my face.

I liked him. I really did. He was hot as hell, with a tight little body, black curls, and fierce green eyes. He was darkly funny, too. As prickly as his cat and twice as suspicious. But I was not a guy who liked a challenge for the hell of it. I wasn't into conquests and I sure as hell wasn't into complications. Ev had complicated written all over him, just by the very fact that he would be living in O'Leary, and hooking up with him could provide exactly the kind of fodder for town gossip that I'd always avoided like the plague.

So why the hell, after just an hour's conversation, had he become a lodestone, drawing my consciousness toward Henry Lattimer's place like a needle pointing north?

Maybe it was because Ev was only here until the spring — he'd admitted he was practically counting down his days of captivity in O'Leary with hatch marks on a wall — and that was *exactly* what I wanted. Hot, fascinating, and *temporary.* Maybe the very fact that he was safe — that he wasn't going to fall in love with me, or expect some kind of false permanence, the way every other person in this town seemed to — was what made him so attractive.

This was a theory that made sense.

O'Leary was a permanent sort of place. A Pumpkin-Festival and Christmas carols sort of place. A "*Silas Sloane, I'm still waiting for you to return that library book on Jackie*

*Robinson you took out in 1993*" sort of place. And for what-ever reason — heteronormative culture or poison in the water, take your pick — folks around here were all about meeting their One True Love and settling down. I'd seen it happen to all my high school football buddies — every one of them had found a nice woman and gotten down to the business of churning out babies. I'd watched it happen to the LGBTQ couples in town — Rena Cobb and her wife, Paul Fine and his partner Quinn. And I'd even watched it happen to my friend Caelan James, the most curmud-geonly man I'd ever met and the person I'd have voted least-likely to ever fall in love… until he'd met his boyfriend Ash Martin. Hell, commitment had become a freakin' cottage industry in this area, ever since it was named one of the top wedding destinations in the Northeast.

I mean, I couldn't imagine living anywhere but O'Leary, but just living here was about all the commitment I could handle in my life. I'd been born without whatever genetic component made people want to stare at another person the way Paul and Quinn's pug stared at bacon, or made them want to parade the streets with their lover hanging on their arm. The very idea of Marci and her friends discussing my love life in the cereal aisle of Lyon's Imperial — linking my name with some other man's, becoming an item of gossip that people would still be discussing at my retirement party — made me twitch.

But I was pretty sure none of that would be an issue with the town's new art teacher. We could hook up for as long as he was in town, and he'd never expect me to hold his hand as we walked down the street. It would be perfect. It would be friendly. It would be *casual.*

Assuming I could convince him, of course. We'd had a friendly conversation in the woods the night before, but things had been decidedly tenser after we'd gotten to

Henry's, and by the time I'd left, after bringing his suitcases to the little guest room where he'd be staying, he'd been acting decidedly chilly.

Remembering the way he'd smiled made me think that I could work with chilly.

I took my time shaving and dressing in faded jeans and a t-shirt, but even so, the sun had barely crawled over the horizon by the time I closed and locked the door of my little house on the corner of Lobelia and Crescent, just a few blocks from town. Since showing up at Hen's at the literal ass-crack of dawn did not say *casual*, I climbed in my truck and headed to the police station.

Marci's car was already in the lot — since her son went to college and her husband left town a few years back, she spent more hours here than not — and surprisingly, so was Mitch's. I parked next to his SUV, strode up the ramp to the front door, and pushed it open with a jangle of bells.

Marci's cubicle was empty and so was the rest of the small squad room, not that I expected any different at this hour. I stopped at my desk to check my email and found a confirmation that Joe Cross had picked up Ev's car and taken it to his repair shop in Rushton, along with a copy of Mitch's report about the incident at Pickett Campground.

I frowned as I scrolled through the report, then headed for his office.

Marci opened his office door and stepped out just as I approached. Her dark blonde hair was falling out of her ponytail, and her severe white blouse was wrinkled, like she'd slept at her desk.

"Marci," I greeted her. "Late night or early morning?"

"What?" She smoothed her hair back and her eyes darted around the empty room. "Neither."

"You okay?" I asked, putting a hand on her arm. "Are you getting enough rest?"

She twitched her arm away. "Perfectly. Yes. I mean…" She drew a deep breath and gave me a small smile. "I'm fine, Si. Thank you."

"Alright," I said, unconvinced. "But if Mitch is giving you a hard time, you let me know and I'll beat him up for you, okay? Everyone needs time off, even O'Leary's best dispatcher."

She blushed crimson. "O'Leary's *only* dispatcher, except when Constantine's on duty. Which he was supposed to be last night, but he called in sick."

I frowned again. "Constantine called in sick? He seemed fine Saturday." Constantine Ross was young — only twenty-four — and Mitch could only afford to have him on part time, but he was as dedicated to this place as Marci or Mitch, or even me. "Everything okay with his family?"

Marci shrugged. "I haven't heard anything to the contrary. He's still helping his mom with the landscaping business whenever he's not here, though now Micah's Blooms is giving them a run for their money, I'm guessing he's run ragged."

I frowned and nodded. "Well, listen, don't be afraid to talk to Mitch if you need more time off. I can cover for you myself if need be, yeah?"

She blushed further. "I, uh… I'll be sure talk to Mitch. Thanks, Si." She hurried off to her desk without another word, which was so surprising I turned to watch her as she walked away.

No rants about Rena Cobb's sculpture? No gossip about Constantine's family's business troubles?

"That's odd," I told Mitch, striding into his office a second later. "What's gotten into Marci?" I threw myself into the chair in front of his desk.

Mitch glanced up from his screen and raised one

eyebrow. "Good morning to you, too. You're up early. Hot date last night?"

I grinned. Mitch Turner was as disorganized as his brother Dare was tidy, which had always amused me as we were growing up. The only thing messier than his desk was his unruly gray hair. But just like Dare, Mitch's brown eyes missed nothing. And likely Marci had already given him an earful about my interrupted hookup.

"Sadly, no. I got called to Pickett Campground before anything could happen, and then I found a car wrapped around a tree on the way."

"Oh, yeah. Marci said something about that. Single-vehicle?" Mitch frowned. "Who?"

"Everett Maior. Henry Lattimer's grandson."

"Ah, right. Going to be the new art teacher at the school," Mitch said, leaning back in his chair. Two buttons on his shirt were done up incorrectly, and I had to fight a smile. The guy knew every fucking thing about the town, but couldn't manage to dress himself. "He okay?"

"Yeah. Banged up his leg pretty good, but otherwise alright. Car's likely totaled, though."

Mitch grimaced. "That sucks. Think he'll be able to take care of Henry with no car?"

Of course Mitch knew Ev was here to take care of Hen. I wasn't sure why his superpowers surprised me anymore. "How do you know all this?" I demanded.

"Having a sister who's the principal at Garnett Elementary helps," he said. "Hen's daughter called Janice to ask if they had anything open." He shrugged. "I guess the kid's had a hard year and she and Hen were worried about him."

"Ev's not a kid," I said without thinking. I remembered how weary his eyes had looked, the triumph I'd felt at making him laugh, even if it had been at my own expense, and how shocked he'd seemed by his own laughter. "What kind of hard year?"

But Mitch's eyes had lit up. "He's not a kid, huh? *How* not a kid?"

"He's twenty-nine." Information I'd learned the hard way. I squirmed under Mitch's bright gaze. "What?"

He tipped his chair back further. "You like him."

Damn it. "I gave you his age, Mitchell."

"It's not the data, it's the manner in which it's delivered, Si. You said *Ev's not a kid* like I'd been insulting him or something. It was oddly proprietary."

I snorted. "How long have you known me? I don't *do* proprietary. He's Henry's grandson, and he seems like a nice guy. I drove him to Hen's house and called a tow truck for him, same as I would for anyone in this town."

"Is he hot?"

"*Christ.* As Dare and I have explained to you a billion times, just because I'm gay doesn't mean I'm attracted to every man I meet, okay? Just like you're not getting it on with… with *Marci*," I chuckled, inserting the first woman's name I could think of, "just because she's a woman."

Mitch's smile fell and he cleared his throat. "No. Of course not. Sorry. What were you saying before that?"

I blinked at this easy change of subject. "You were going to tell me what kind of hard year he's had."

Mitch shook his head. "I don't know. I don't invite gossip if I can help it." He tapped his finger on the arm of his chair thoughtfully. "Maybe you should go and see if you can give him a hand sorting through the accident business. Single-vehicle collisions can cause a bunch of red tape."

"Hmm." I frowned, pretending the idea of seeing Ev again had never occurred to me. "I guess I could, if you think it's a good idea. And, uh, your report about the campground said I should stop by to follow up with Frank and Myrna?"

"Doesn't have to be today," Mitch said. "I know you're off-duty. Tomorrow's fine. But I want to follow up on the missing camper." He nodded at the report in my hand. "John Carpenter. Guy was in his twenties, said he was from the Philadelphia area, but paid cash so we have no credit card or address on file. Told Myrna he was here to get over a bad breakup. Completely green — all brand-new gear, still with the tags, and Frank had to show him how to build a fire."

I snorted.

"Exactly," Mitch agreed. "So the guy wasn't planning on doing anything adventurous, just sticking pretty close to the campground. Some easy-to-intermediate hikes. It's entirely possible the dude just got bored and went home without realizing he should even tell Frank. I'm gonna have Carmen try to track down his home address today, and more than likely we'll find him sitting at home in his pajamas watching TV. But in the meantime, I sent Grace out with Carpenter's description, to see if anyone in town's seen him. And tomorrow you can talk to Frank, see if he's heard anything."

"Will do."

He smiled hugely. "And FYI, your *thoughtful, reluctant* face needs work, Si. Practice that poker face if you don't want everyone in O'Leary to know you're into Hen's grandson."

"Great." I sighed. "Thanks a bunch."

I drove down to Fanaille, Caelan's bakery, grabbed two cups of coffee and a few muffins from his assistant, Maura, then headed diagonally across the street to O'Leary Hardware.

"Theo?" I called pushing open the door with my hip as I juggled the coffees and bakery bag. "You around?"

"Oh, hey, Si," Theo said, coming out from the back room. At eighteen, Theo Ross had the same dark hair as his brother Constantine, but he was tall and lanky, with none of Constantine's bulk. "What can I help you with? You ready to start that apartment conversion project yet?"

I sighed. The large, open attic above my garage was currently packed with mementos and memorabilia, just as it had been when my grandparents left me the house in their will seven years before. My plan to convert the space into a rental, which I'd dreamed up and blurted out one night after a couple of beers at Goode's Diner, had become almost a joke around town. So had my plan to restore my grandfather's Porsche, which had been sitting half-assembled in the garage for just as long.

It was pretty lowering when teenagers were dragging me for my procrastination.

I forced a smile. "Funny. One of these days, kid, that place is gonna be a goldmine. But today, I'm just looking for Henry. Or, his grandson, really. Mitch told me to follow up with him about his accident."

"Ev. Yeah, I met him this morning, and I think the guy's my new hero." Theo looked around the empty store before saying in a hushed whisper, "Dude, I heard them sniping at each other from down *here.* And I've gotta say, I don't hate hearing someone giving Mr. Lattimer a taste of his own medicine."

I remembered Ev's words from yesterday, his unlikely solidarity with the other incompetent, weird kid, and my forced smile became real.

"Grab a muffin, Theo." I nodded toward the plain, white bag in my hand.

His eyes widened. "Oh, sweet. From Fanaille?" He

removed a blueberry muffin from the bag before handing it back. "Thanks, Si."

A loud *crash* came from above, followed by an annoyed bellow. I exchanged a glance with Theo. "What was that?"

He shrugged. "Mr. Lattimer's pissed. As usual. Maybe about *that demon cat.* Or maybe that he *doesn't need help wiping his ass yet, goddamn it.* Or maybe that *he'd have thought Ev's kind would be able to brew a cup of coffee that didn't taste like swill.*"

"Ev's kind?" I repeated.

Theo shrugged again. "I dunno. A city boy, maybe?"

Or a gay man.

I'd never gotten a homophobic vibe from Hen Lattimer before. There were no secrets in O'Leary, so he knew I was gay, and he'd never said a derogatory word. We talked hunting and fishing, town politics and football prospects. He even teased me about my inability to put the Porsche back together, without ever adding a snide comment about *my kind* being incapable of auto mechanics. Maybe being a cop protected me from that kind of thing. I found myself wanting to protect Ev from it, too.

I told myself I'd feel the same way about anyone, but I wasn't sure that was true.

And oddly enough, I still felt no desire to back off.

"Okay if I head up the back way?" I asked Theo, nodding toward the stock room, where a second staircase led to the apartment above. "Ev hurt his leg on his way into town, and I don't want either of them to have to come down and let me in the front door."

"Sure," Theo mumbled around a huge bite of muffin. "Just knock, I guess. Although, the way they were stomping around up there a minute ago, *someone*'s using their legs." He took another big bite and seemed to think for a moment. "Or maybe they've just been throwing shit."

I looked up at the ceiling. "Great," I muttered.

I hurried through the store, past row after row of perfectly organized appliances and tools, and out to the back room where a narrow staircase led directly to the kitchen above. I sprinted up, two at a time, bakery goods in hand, and kicked at the bottom of the door with my boot.

"Go away, Theo!" Henry bellowed.

"Do *not* go away, Theo!" Ev countered. "Get in here and help me before this man kills himself *or me*."

There was another loud thump, followed by the sound of breaking dishes.

I juggled the coffees into one hand and pushed the door open, rushing forward to protect Ev…

And found Ev standing over Henry, who was seated at the kitchen table, the two of them struggling over a knife. What the *actual* fuck?

"Let go. Let go or I'll do it!" Ev cried. "I swear to God, just give me a reason, and I'll do it, old man. Hell, I'll *enjoy* it."

Training kicked in immediately. I moved another step into the room and put the coffees down on the counter. "Ev," I began in the placating voice I'd first been taught in hostage negotiations. "Maybe you could…"

"You wouldn't *dare*," Henry taunted, glaring up at his grandson from his seat at the kitchen table. He was still in his pajamas and bathrobe, his white-gray hair combed perfectly. And on the table in front of him was what appeared to be a bowl of oatmeal and a nearly empty juice glass. The shards of a coffee cup lay on the kitchen floor next to his casted leg. I moved around the table, positioning myself behind Ev.

"Oh, wouldn't I?" Ev said menacingly. "If you don't stop being ridiculous, I'm *calling my mother.* We'll see how you like it when your firstborn comes to O'Leary and starts *crying* all over you. Now, drop the knife!"

Henry's eyes narrowed, he released the knife, and I stopped in my tracks.

Ev was threatening to… call his mother?

"What the hell is going on?" I demanded.

Ev turned to look at me, then walked around the table to return the knife to its spot in the knife block on the counter. A snug blue t-shirt was stretched across his chest, and well-fitting khaki shorts highlighted the curve of his ass. He looked both well rested and seriously pissed off, but fortunately not at me. "Good morning, Silas."

"Everett. Henry." I pulled out one of the unoccupied kitchen chairs. "Either of you mind explaining what I just witnessed?"

Ev snorted and nodded at his grandfather. "This one pretended to have an allergic reaction to the oatmeal I made him, and when I left the room to get his Epi-Pen, he attempted to cut off his cast with a steak knife."

I looked at Henry, who was sulking like a toddler. "I hate oatmeal. Everyone knows I hate oatmeal. Diane Perkins never makes oatmeal."

"Then why the heck isn't Diane Perkins here, one wonders?" Ev rolled his eyes and took another seat at the table. "I don't do *dishes* like Diane Perkins, I don't make *coffee* like Diane Perkins, I don't *cook* like fucking Diane Perkins." His gaze came to me. "Who is this saint, and how can I meet her?"

I grinned. "She's a waitress over at Goode's Diner. Been working there since… God, before I was born?"

"She's not just a waitress," Henry protested. "She's a damn good cook! Better than that idiot Shane Goode, who likes to pretend the pumpkin pie that won the contest last fall was his own recipe! Bullshit, it was." He wagged a finger at me. "That one has criminal stamped all over him, mark my words. If you'll steal a pie recipe from a beautiful woman who's been nothing but good to you, what *won't* you stoop to?"

I nodded sagely. "Fair point. I'll keep that in mind. Now, why the heck were you trying to cut off your cast?"

"I don't need it!" he fumed. "What I need is to be downstairs running my shop. Theo's head's so far in the clouds, he'll recommend a hammer to tighten a screw. And this one," he jerked his head to Ev. "Wants to poison me in my own home. *Oatmeal*," he said, pushing the bowl further away from him.

"Uh-huh. The nerve of me, trying to lower your cholesterol," Ev retorted. "Just wait until I stop by Lyon's Imperial and grab some quinoa and salmon for dinner."

Henry opened his mouth, no doubt to give some blistering response… but then spied the goodies from Fanaille I'd left on the counter. He shifted in his chair to smile widely at me.

"Never mind our piffle, Silas. So, what really brings you by this morning? Come to bring me breakfast?"

I cleared my throat, a little ashamed. I'd gotten coffees for Ev and me, already planning how I was going to turn this morning into Operation Make Ev Want Me. I'd forgotten Henry entirely.

Damn.

"Yeah," I said. "Yup. Coffee and muffins for you and Ev. From Fanaille."

Henry leaned back in his chair slightly. "Ah! You see, Ev? Silas knows what proper food is. A man needs more than nuts and twigs to recover his health… *if* he's in need of recovery, which I'm not."

"Uh-huh. I'm taking notes here," Ev said dryly. "Just so I understand, you're in perfect health? The leg doesn't bother you at all? Is that why you practically sobbed when Daphne brushed up against your cast this morning?" He folded his arms over his chest and returned his grandfather's glare.

"Brushed up!" Henry scoffed. "That *creature* rubbed herself against me like I was her personal scratching post. I was… annoyed."

"You were crying out of annoyance." Ev nodded. "I see."

"That's not… I wasn't *crying*, Everett." Henry looked at me for help, but it was far too entertaining to watch them baiting each other. As far as I could tell, they were as opposite as two men could be, while somehow managing to be exactly the same, from their eyes to their scowls. Even their posture exactly mirrored one another. "I was trying to hold in my anger."

"By leaking water from your eyes." Ev nodded again. "I've experienced this phenomenon myself. I call it… *crying*."

His voice was dry as dust, and I had to fight laughter once again. Ev wasn't just hot, and my attraction to him wasn't just sexual. I liked the guy, more than I could remember liking anyone I also wanted to hook up with.

"Silas, hand me a goddamn muffin," Henry said, breaking the standoff.

"Yes, sir," I agreed, fetching the food for him mostly so I could hide my smile.

After placing a coffee cup in front of each of them and setting the bakery bag in the middle of the table, I grabbed a broom to clean up the shards of pottery on the floor.

"Oh. Thanks," Ev said, sounding surprised. "My knee is mostly better this morning, but it still hurts when I bend it."

"You can walk on it fine?" He nodded. "So, no need to go to the doctor, then?"

"God, no." Ev shuddered. "Not unless I'm dying." He swallowed. "Not even then."

"Okay," I agreed. "And what about Daphne?"

"What about her? I shut her in the bedroom when Grandpa started calling her Demon Cat." He shot his grandfather a glare.

"Well, I was thinking…" I began, making this up as I went along. "You should probably get her checked out, just to make sure she's okay."

"You think?" Ev frowned. "But she seems fine."

But if she was fine, Ev would have no reason to take a scenic tour of O'Leary with me this morning.

"I'm no vet," I said. I dumped the broken shards of crockery in the trash bin next to the counter. "But Julian Ross — my friend Constantine's older brother — is. His practice is literally across the street, so it wouldn't be out of your way." I hooked my thumb over my shoulder to show him. "You wouldn't want to take any chances."

Ev bit his lip and looked at his grandfather, then back at me. "I guess. But who'll watch Grandpa?"

"*Watch Grandpa?*" Henry chortled around a bite of muffin. "I've been watching out for myself for seventy-eight long years, my lad, and you haven't visited me for fifteen of them."

"Roads run in both directions, you know."

"Not when you have a business to run," Henry replied. "Besides, you'll be starting school in a couple of days. You take care of your demon feline, and I'll take care of myself."

Ev still hesitated.

"Ah, youth is wasted on the young," Henry sighed mournfully. "You know, Everett, back in my day…"

Ev stood abruptly. "I think it's a great idea," he told

me. "Let's have your friend examine Daph. Just give me five minutes to bribe her to get back into the carrier."

"Great! Henry, if you want, I can help settle you in the living room before we go."

"Check his pockets for more knives," Ev said from the doorway, looking back at his grandfather with narrowed eyes. "Easy capitulation is never a good thing."

Henry hmphed. Then he removed a pocket knife from his robe and slapped it on the table with a scowl.

"Uh-huh," Ev nodded. "Figured."

"Go summon your demon, Everett!" Hen sniffed, removing a second muffin from the bag. "Leave a lonely, old man to enjoy the few pleasures he has left." He paused with the muffin in his hand and his gaze turned crafty. "And if you run into Diane Perkins while you're out, you could mention that you're planning to serve me fish and *dirt* for dinner. Maybe she'll have mercy on me."

# Chapter Five



Sɪ ɪɴsɪsᴛᴇᴅ on carrying the cat carrier. It was a measure of how tired and messed up my brain was that I didn't even argue beyond a perfunctory eye roll. I'd had a terrible night's sleep, filled with weird dreams I couldn't quite recall, except I knew Silas Sloane had been in every single one of them. And when I'd tried to quiet my mind the way I sometimes did, imagining a bubble of protection around myself, I couldn't seem to get Silas outside of the bubble.

Instead, he was in there with me, hot and kind and *easy,* in a way that nothing had been easy since Adrian's death. Easy to talk to, easy to trust (more or less), and easy to find really, really attractive, which made me feel pretty shitty.

I mean, Adrian had been gone for fifteen months and thirteen days. I wasn't cheating on him for finding someone attractive. And honestly, if he was still alive, we'd have been checking Si out *together*. But since Adrian's death, that part of my brain had shut down completely and, I'd assumed, permanently. I hadn't considered what I'd do if I was ever attracted to someone else, because there'd been nothing to consider. I wasn't sure how I felt about the fact that I apparently wasn't as dead to the outside world as I'd assumed I was.

It felt wrong that Adrian's death was a thing I might *heal* from.

But when Si ushered me down the stairs ahead of him, all I could think about was how good he looked in the faded jeans that clung to him in all the right places, and how his tan skin made his blue eyes seem electric in the light of day.

"Which way?" I asked him as we reached the sidewalk. It was warm outside, and even more humid than it had been back in Boston.

"Just there," he said, pointing to one of the many store-fronts across from O'Leary Hardware, their windows gleaming in the morning sun.

In the light of day, I could see the subtle signs that Weaver Street actually *had* changed from the place I remembered as a kid. Back then, I'd spent as little time in town as possible. My grandfather's store had been the most uncomfortable place I could imagine — an endless variety of pointy tools and dangerous machinery I wasn't allowed to touch, coupled with the assessing stares and too-firm handshakes of Grandpa Hen's customers, who'd seemed disappointed to learn that hardware knowledge hadn't been passed down to me genetically. "Ev's an artist," Grandpa would tell them apologetically, and they'd nod and shuffle their feet, glancing away like this was somehow embarrassing.

But now, the street seemed more human. The air smelled delicious — vanilla and cinnamon, probably from the bakery, bacon from the diner, and flowers from the huge display that an older man was setting up outside the shop directly across the street — a shop with an actual *rainbow flag* hanging outside, just below the awning.

Well, damn.

"Ev?" Silas called. "Jaywalking's not okay, even in O'Leary."

"What?"

"Ev, honey," he said again, and the endearment made me stop my inspection of the storefronts to glance at him. "You're in the middle of the road. This isn't Boston, but if you stand there long enough, at some point a car is going come."

And I was. *Jesus*. Standing in the middle of the street staring, like some person who'd been raised on a deserted island and had never seen civilization before.

If O'Leary could be called civilization.

"Sorry," I said, catching up to him on the sidewalk. "It just looks different than it did before. I haven't been here since I was in middle school, other than the day of Grandma Anna's funeral."

Si's forehead wrinkled, and he looked at me skeptically. "You think it's changed a lot?" He looked up and down the street, like he was trying to see what I saw, then shook his head. "All I see are the same things I've ever seen."

"Makes sense." I shrugged. "You look in the mirror all the time, but you don't really see yourself change day to day."

"Or even year to year," he agreed. "But I guess that doesn't mean it's not happening."

I frowned, filing this away to think about later.

Silas stopped outside of a small glass door set between a bridal store and the bakery. He pushed it open and ushered me in front of him. *Again*. I wanted to call him out on this, to remind him that I was capable of opening doors for myself like a grown-up, but I figured that would be rude. Plus, it mostly made me uncomfortable because I liked it too damn much.

"Well, hey, Si!" A heavily pregnant brunette in purple scrubs stood by a filing cabinet behind a high counter, and flashed Si a wide smile as he came in. She gave me a curious glance. "You must be Hen Lattimer's grandson. Everett, right?"

"Uh… Yes?" I looked at Si, who didn't seem to notice anything odd in someone I'd never met before knowing my name, but it made me feel as exposed as if I'd left the house naked.

"I'm Kathy Chang," she said, slamming the file drawer closed and coming forward to offer me her hand over the counter. "Welcome to O'Leary."

"Thanks," I mumbled, shaking her hand.

"Hey, Kathy, is Julian here?" Si asked.

She chuckled. "Where else would you find him? He's here day and night! But he's busy looking after a fox kit Daniel Michaelson brought in." She rolled her eyes. "Because he doesn't have enough paying clients, so he needs to tend to the entire woods, obviously. Why? What's up?"

Si lifted the cat carrier and placed it on the counter. "Ev has a new patient for him. Meet Daphne."

"Oh!" she said, bending down to peer at Daphne. "Aren't you the most beautiful?" she crooned.

"She's cranky," I corrected. "Even more than usual. She spent most of the day in the carrier yesterday, and Her Highness is displeased."

"Awww, and who wouldn't be cranky, stuck in one of these things? Hmm?" She reached for the zipper.

"Be careful!" I warned. "Daph scratches when she's pissed off. Maybe I could…"

But Kathy either didn't hear me or didn't care. She reached right into the carrier and pulled out my cat. And honest to God, the traitorous little fur ball practically leaped into Kathy's arms, curled herself up against Kathy's chest, and glared at me like *I* was the cause of all her misfortune.

Did I mention she was a shithead?

"Oh, so precious," Kathy sang, petting Daphne's thick, white fur. "What a good girl you are."

The look Daph shot me was positively smug, and she swished her long tail at Kathy in apparent delight.

I groaned.

"I just wanted to get Daph checked out," I told Kathy. "Make sure she's fine. We were in a bit of an accident last night."

"Hit a tree head-on. Likely totaled his car," Si interrupted.

I huffed. "I really hope not. But I called the insurance company this morning and they're sending someone out tomorrow or the next day, so I guess we'll see."

"Aw, poor thing," Kathy said, still talking to the cat who, I almost wanted to point out, wouldn't have to go through the ordeal of handling an insurance claim or replacing a car out in the middle of nowhere. "We can take care of you." She looked up. "Just leave her to me and stop back in later this afternoon."

I blinked. No paperwork or intake forms, no need to prove that I'd be able to pay for the checkup, let alone whatever her treatment cost? What strange land was this?

"Great! You're a star, Kath. Come on, Ev," Silas said, heading for the door.

*Come on, where?*

"Uh. Right. Okay," I said, following him, but it felt weird leaving Daphne behind. She wasn't my favorite creature in the world, but she'd been Adrian's pride and joy. It was strange to leave her in someone else's care, even temporarily.

"So the insurance company isn't giving you any trouble?" Si asked, turning to face me when we were back on the sidewalk. The sun made his brown hair glint gold and his eyes crinkle at the corners as he squinted.

Silas wasn't young, I realized. And damn if that didn't make him even *more* attractive.

"Um. Not yet, no. But the woman I spoke to had actually heard of the road where I crashed. Apparently, accidents there are pretty common." I wasn't sure why I felt the need to prove my driving competence to Si, but I was definitely still spooked by the phantom I'd seen the night before. It had seemed incredibly real. I wanted to blame anything but my own broken brain.

"They are," he agreed. "Too common." But now *his* eyes were troubled and *his* voice was hard. I remembered him saying he really hated car accidents, and it occurred to me for the first time just how many he must have seen in his line of work, with outcomes far more tragic than mine.

*Could you be more selfish if you tried, Everett?*

"Maybe we could lobby the town council for some lights out there?" I suggested.

He snorted and dropped his head to rub at the back of his neck. "Yeah, I doubt it. My parents are both on the council. They, uh… they definitely know how dangerous that road is." He shrugged. "The state had some studies done about impact to the wildlife, and it was determined that the risk *fell within acceptable parameters* or something."

"Well, that just sucks." It wasn't precisely comforting, but there were some things you couldn't make better with words.

He lifted his eyes to mine and grinned. The simple gesture should not have made me feel as good as it did.

"It does. But I guess the silver lining is that the road

keeps O'Leary kind of insulated," he said. "We don't get a lot of crime."

I snorted. "You also don't have Starbucks."

He laughed. "Honey, you don't need Starbucks when you've got Fanaille." He pointed over his shoulder at the storefront next door. "Come see."

I frowned. "I should really be getting back…" Who the hell knew what kind of mischief my grandfather had gotten in during the last few minutes? He'd probably hacked off a limb along with his cast.

"Nah," Silas said. He moved to stand beside me and slung an arm over my shoulders. "Hen seems to enjoy riling you. He's less likely to cause trouble when you leave him be."

Si probably wasn't wrong about that.

"Alright, but I can't say long," I warned him as I let him pull me a few feet down the sidewalk and in the door. "I have things to unpack, and a staff meeting at the school tomorrow, and… and…"

*Holy shit.*

If the place smelled good from outside, it was nothing compared to the absolute fragrance *wonderland* inside. It was buttery, sugary perfection. And I barely noticed the cute little tables and chairs arranged in front of the lace-curtained windows, because my attention was caught by the dizzying array of baked goods in the glass case at the front counter. There were intricately decorated cakes, muffins as big as my head, and rows of cupcakes in different flavors. A tray of cookies sat atop the counter, so fresh they were still *steaming*.

My empty stomach gave an embarrassingly loud rumble. I hadn't even thought I *liked* sweets anymore.

"I can't quite tell if you like me, Everett Maior," Si said, his voice a joking whisper in my ear and his arm still firmly around my shoulder. "But I know your stomach does. Did you ever remember to eat before you met me?"

I tried to pretend the shiver that went down my spine was purely from hunger and that I wasn't as much of an attention whore as my cat.

"So we're thinking Bronwyn for a girl and Blakely for a boy!"

I looked away from the baked goods with difficulty—*my preciousss!*— and finally noticed the other people in the shop — two men behind the counter, talking to a man and woman standing in front of the cash register. The woman — who wore sky-high heels and a dress that stretched around her tiny baby bump, flicked her long, blonde hair over her shoulder.

"The good thing about the last name *Martin*," she said, "is that any first name sounds good with it." She clutched the arm of the man next to her and beamed up at him. "That's why I married you!"

I waited for one of them to laugh, but no one did. The men behind the counter — a ginger who was about my height, and a dark-haired, broad-shouldered giant — exchanged a speaking glance. The other man — Mr. Martin — smiled down at her adoringly.

The redhead turned his attention to Silas with something like gratitude. "Hey, Si. I thought Maura said you'd already been in today."

"You know I can't stay away," Si joked. His hand drifted from my shoulder to my back and he pushed me forward slightly. "This is Everett Maior, Henry Lattimer's grandson. He busted his car on his way into town, so I'm helping him out by showing him around. Ev, this is Cal James. He owns the bakery."

The redhead lifted his chin in greeting. Not unfriendly, but not particularly warm and fuzzy, either. I approved.

"That's his boyfriend Ash Martin," Si continued, pointing at the giant, who gave me a broad grin I couldn't help but return.

"This is Ash's younger brother Mackie." Si lifted a hand to the man on our side of the counter, who gave a short, good-natured wave. "And that's Mackie's wife, Karen."

Karen stepped forward. "Karen *Mitchener*-Martin," she said, holding out her hand palm-down, like maybe she expected me to bow and kiss it. I shook it instead.

"Nice to meet you. Call me Ev," I told all of them.

"You're here to teach, right?" Karen said, rubbing a hand over her belly. "Art or something?"

Were they all briefed on my birthday and shoe size, too?

"Yes, art," I agreed. "At Garnett Elementary."

"And what are your qualifications?" she demanded.

I blinked. Was this a job interview? "I have a Master of Fine Arts from Tufts."

Cal whistled. "Impressive."

But Karen was not impressed. "And your *teaching* qualifications?" she insisted.

"Uh, well. The principal helped me qualify for a transitional teaching certificate. I have to take some classes over time and…"

"So, you're really not qualified to be teaching my child." She rubbed her stomach again.

I would be long gone from this town by the time Karen's child was ready for finger paints, but for some reason, I was hesitant to say so.

"Not unqualified," I informed her. "Possibly overqualified. And you can take your concerns to the principal."

"Karen," Ash interjected. "Maybe we could finish

planning Bronley or Blakewyn's baby shower before you start worrying about their education, hmm?"

"*Bronwyn*," she corrected, narrowing her eyes at him. "*Blakely*."

"That's what I said," Ash agreed. "Do you want to go sit down and I'll come over in a second to talk about the cake you'll be needing *in January*?" He pointed them to a table, and when they moved away, Si and I stepped up to the cash register to take their places.

"Sorry about the inquisition," Ash said. "Ignore her. I try to."

"She's a little… high-strung?" I suggested.

"She's a raving bitch. But she's good for Mackie and murder is illegal, so here we are." Cal shrugged.

Ash laughed and wrapped his arms around Cal's waist from behind, dropping a kiss on the side of his head. "That's the sweet man I fell in love with."

Cal cracked a smile for the first time. "If you thought I was sweet, you were deluded."

"Oh, you're sweet," Ash insisted, squeezing him harder. "Just not *vanilla*, baby."

Cal snorted and relaxed against Ash for a second. I looked up at Si, feeling like I'd missed a joke somehow.

"Fanaille," Si said. "The name of the bakery. Means vanilla in Irish."

Oh. I frowned again.

"Anyway," Cal said, stepping away from Ash. "What can I get you gents?"

"One of everything," I told him. "And coffee. The biggest coffee you've got." I would need it to get through this day.

Ash grinned. "A man after my own heart. But if you're going to be living here, you'll need to pace yourself. Start slow. Go for the blueberry lemon bars, since they're seasonal. Next week, we're bringing out our fall stuff."

"Enough pumpkin spice and apple pie to induce a diabetic coma from across the street, so be wary," Cal confirmed.

Si leaned against the counter, making the muscles beneath his t-shirt bulge in a disconcerting way. "Ash speaks with great wisdom," he said solemnly. "I can confirm that the lemon bars are an excellent gateway drug."

"Fair enough," I said. I was a little shocked by the reappearance of my sweet tooth, but I figured I had to make up for lost time. "Bring me two. And…"

"And a vat of coffee," Cal said. His mouth tipped up on one side in what felt like approval. "I'll bring the same for you, Si. You guys can go sit down and I'll bring your stuff over." He turned to his boyfriend and said with less enthusiasm, "And we can go sort out Karen's shit."

"Oh, I feel like that might take more than a morning," Ash sighed. He squeezed the back of Cal's neck in a reassuring gesture, then walked over to his brother's table.

By unspoken agreement, Si and I took a table as far from the others as possible.

"So… they're totally out?" I asked Si, nodding at Cal, who was preparing our order.

"Cal and Ash? Yeah, of course," Si replied. "Kinda hard to hide it when a twenty-foot-tall former Navy SEAL suddenly starts baking cupcakes and moving into Cal's place upstairs."

I nodded. "And people don't… care?"

"Oh, they care." Si's eyes widened dramatically. "If a day passes when one of them doesn't get asked how much longer until their wedding, I'll give up baked goods for a year. And your grandfather was in here a few months ago, explaining to Cal that he and Ash can't possibly raise their children in that tiny apartment upstairs, because kids need room to roam."

"*My* grandfather?" Grandpa Hen hadn't even attended my wedding. I couldn't imagine how he'd have felt if Adrian and I had children. "Wait, are Ash and Cal having a kid?"

Si snorted. "God, no. They just got together last February. One of those love-at-first-sight deals. I wouldn't have believed it if I hadn't seen it. No, the people of O'Leary just assume that everyone wants a spouse, and a house, and a kid or twelve." He shook his head.

"And you don't," I surmised.

He shrugged and gave me a half-smile. "I have a house. So, one out of three isn't bad."

I chuckled. "No babies for you?"

"Nope! I like other folks' babies just fine. Never felt the need to have one."

"Same," I told him. "We used to talk about it, but it was always a distant-future kinda thing."

"We?" Silas asked.

I swallowed. I'd walked into that one.

I didn't talk about Adrian, not if I could help it. And it wasn't just because it hurt, though it made my chest get tight just thinking about it. It was more like I didn't know *how* to talk about him — how to deal with the instant sympathy and embarrassment, how to assure people that I was fine when I wasn't. Over the past year, Adrian had gone from a flesh-and-blood man to a sacred duty; memories of him should only be discussed in reverent tones and never in casual conversation.

Fortunately, while I was sitting there like a deer in headlights, Cal came over with our order, and I quickly stuffed my mouth with too much lemon bar to hold a conversation.

Ash was right — this was *fucking amazing*.

*Un*fortunately, the silence at our table meant that we could hear every word Karen was saying on the other side of the room.

"We'll arrange the tables like we did at my wedding," she said. "With a head table for just me and Mackie in the middle, and then two other tables coming off of each end like this to make a horseshoe. Our mothers will sit on the ends closest to Mackie and me, and then my girlfriends will take up this table, and the other table will be for the uncles."

"That's us," Ash said proudly. "Uncle Cal and Uncle Ash."

"*Oh*. Oh, not you, Cal," she said. "Not until you're married."

I gave Si a look and he tilted his head to the side as if this had proven his point.

"Then who are the uncles, plural?" Ash demanded. There was a dangerous undercurrent to his voice, like his earlier calm was gone. I had to force myself not to turn around and stare.

Karen sighed. "You and Rhett, of course."

"Rae," Ash corrected. "And they are not an uncle."

"Well, they're not an *aunt* either," Karen sniffed. "So how the heck am I supposed to list them when I write up the announcement for the *Gazette*?"

"There are several nonbinary terms. One is Ommer," Ash informed her.

"*Ommer*!" Mackie repeated, nodding. "Hey, that's cute. The kiddo can have uncles and an ommer."

"No one will even know what that *means*," Karen insisted. "I'm going to have to explain it to people!"

"Yes, and then re-explain it when they insist on using the wrong term," Cal said dryly. "How inconvenient for you."

Karen sighed. "You'll understand someday, when *you* become a parent, Cal," she said, as though this explained anything.

I looked at Si and nearly choked on my coffee when he rolled his eyes to the ceiling.

"Mackie, I can't do this today," Karen announced. "I feel stressed. I need to go home and rest."

"Of course! Do you want me to handle the arrangements?" Mackie asked, all concerned.

"No! God, no. I need you to take me home. It's not safe for me to be alone."

"Afraid she might open a hellmouth if left unsupervised?" I whispered. Si snickered.

"Is everything okay with you and the baby?" Ash asked. He didn't sound as friendly as he had been, but I could hear a real note of concern in his voice, and my opinion of him was confirmed. Ash Martin, Good Guy.

"Yes, we're fine!" Karen said. "But there's a murderer on the loose. It's not safe for a woman to be alone, especially not if she's expecting."

Once again, I looked at Si, and he shook his head, confused.

He coughed. "Pardon me, Karen. I couldn't help but overhear. There's a murderer I don't know about?"

"You *do* know about it!" she said, and I swiveled in my chair to look at her. "Or the other officers do. Carmen Purchase was in here earlier telling us *all about* the missing camper! Have you found his remains yet?"

I had no clue what she was talking about, and still the eagerness in her voice made my stomach clench.

Ash sighed. "Missing and murdered are two different

things, Karen. Which is exactly what Carmen told you when she was in here."

Si nodded. "We're investigating it as a matter of course, but we have every reason to believe…"

"What about the shots Myrna heard?" Karen demanded. "Gunshots *and* a missing camper."

"We're not sure what she heard," Si said placatingly. "I'm going to speak to them today. The fact remains, it's extremely unlikely that a random camper with no ties to the area, staying in a mostly deserted campground, would wind up shot. Especially outside deer season. And it doesn't do any good to be spreading…"

"Unless we have a murderer right here in town," Karen whispered. "A serial killer. I've seen stuff like this on TV. It can happen literally *anywhere.*"

All three men at her table burst out laughing.

"Think it was David Siegel?" Cal demanded. "I saw him give me a dirty look when I stole a grape from a premeasured bag over at Lyon's Imperial, and he seemed ready to commit violence."

"You should have heard the way Quinn threatened me when he caught us whispering during the Marilyn Monroe retrospective at the Fine last month." Ash shook his head sadly and held out one rock-steady hand. "To this day, I'm petrified to meet him on the street."

"Ms. Dorian at the library scares the crap out of me," Mackie admitted. "I wouldn't be surprised if she snapped one of these days. Every time I check out a book, I feel like she's peering into my soul."

The men were silent for a second, and then Si said, "Actually, Mack, I kind of agree with you there. I have the *opposite* of a hot-librarian fantasy. Dragon Dorian ruined that for me."

"You guys are disgusting," Karen huffed.

While they were distracted, I dropped my voice to a husky whisper. "You have a librarian phobia? So if your date from last night had said, 'Silas Sloane, you need to *pay your fine…*'"

Si looked at me for a long moment, then shivered. "No, okay, I *do* have a hot librarian fantasy. I think you've cured me."

I laughed out loud.

"Hey, what about that dude my grandfather was warning us about this morning?" I joked to the others. "The one who shamelessly stole Diane Perkins's pie recipe?"

"Oh, right." Si shook his head. "Shane Goode, pie thief!"

"Poor Shane." Mackie sighed. "He's a good kid."

"Not a kid. The guy's around my age. Hasn't been the same since Molly died, though," Cal said. "He was really in love with her. That was a long while back. Ten years ago? Eleven?"

"Twelve," Si said. "Twelve years in October."

"Oh, shit." Mackie's eyes widened and he smacked his own forehead. "I wasn't thinking, Si. I'm sorry, man."

"It's fine," Si said, waving a hand. "It was a long time ago."

I frowned. "What happened a long time ago?"

But before he could answer, Karen interrupted. "You all think you're hilarious, including *my husband*, but you just remember I called it first! There is something going on here. I can feel it. And remember, not every person in this town is someone you all grew up with. You need to be cautious of people you don't know."

She looked at me when she said it, and I blinked. "What? Me?"

"You did arrive last night," she reminded everyone.

"Well, yeah, but… I didn't kill anyone!" I was too busy having visions and nearly killing *myself*.

"Of course you didn't," Silas soothed, putting his hand on my wrist.

"There's that Daniel Michaelson," Karen said. "He lives over by the woods, and never has two words to say to anyone. Same with that guy that looks like Hagrid from Harry Potter and lives up near the State Park. What's his name?"

"Francis," Si said hotly. "Francis Goode. He's Shane's uncle, and he's a great guy!"

"If *you* say so, Si, I guess we have to believe you." Karen pursed her lips as she stood. "But in the meantime, I'm taking precautions, and I'm advising other people in town to do the same."

She swept out of the bakery and after a quick, apologetic glance at all of us, Mackie followed after her.

"I'm beginning to doubt that she's good for Mackie," Cal said, gritting his teeth as he watched her exit. "Or for anyone."

Ash stood and walked behind Cal's chair to rub his shoulders. "I know, babe." He bent to kiss Cal's cheek, but Cal stood before he could.

"I'm not sure I'm comfortable making our relationship public until we're married, Ashley. You understand, right?"

Ash shook his head and grabbed Cal by the arm, pulling him close. "What I understand is that I couldn't love you more deeply or permanently if we were married for a million years. And little Bronson or Banger is going to fucking love you, too, almost as much."

Cal took a deep breath and softened against Ash's chest. "Yeah?"

"Yeah."

Cal lifted a hand to stroke Ash's cheek. "I made a batch of that cold vegetable soup you like. I'll get you some."

Ash nodded and gave him a smile that suggested the soup was more precious than rubies.

"Caelan James, you are fucking *domesticated*," Si said with a grin. "I didn't think you knew how to *eat* vegetables, let alone cook them."

Cal raised one middle finger in the air but didn't look away from Ash. "I'd do a hell of a lot more than that to keep him happy. Not all of us are commitment-phobic, Silas."

"Hey!" Si scowled. "I'm not commitment-phobic. I'm commitment *cautious*. If I ever fall for someone, I'll shout it from the mountains. But until then, I don't need O'Leary speculating about my life any more than they already do." He turned to me and explained, "The town's memory is longer than an elephant's. At the Summer Picnic, Nessa Corcoran asked me why I'd ever broken up with *that nice Asa Liu*, because we made such a *cute couple*. Asa moved away ten years ago!"

I smiled wanly.

"You used to be the same way, Cal," Silas insisted. "Remember?"

"Not really," Cal said, shaking his head and smiling tenderly at Ash. "I can't really remember that at all anymore."

Si made a gagging noise.

"All you have to do to keep me happy is be happy yourself," Ash said in a low voice.

I stood abruptly. "Listen, it's been so great meeting you all, but I really have to..." I hooked a thumb over my shoulder. "Thanks again for the..." I motioned at my plate.

"Ev? You okay?" Si asked, frowning at me.

I nodded. "Oh, God, yes. Fine. Just, you know…" And I bolted out of the bakery as fast as my injured leg could carry me.

I was *not* okay. Watching Cal and Ash together — talking with their eyes, joking and offering one another comfort in a language only they understood — I was jealous. Disgustingly, viciously, chest-meltingly jealous. And as I hobbled across the street and climbed up the stairs to my grandfather's apartment, I found myself crying harder than I had since… well, since two nights ago.

What the fuck was wrong with me? No tears for months and then suddenly, *whoosh*, my tears were overflowing like a goddamn river and I was drowning in them.

And the worst part, the most terrible, shameful part, was that I wasn't crying because Ash and Cal had something I'd *lost* — hell, I couldn't remember Adrian and I ever having that effortless shorthand. Maybe we hadn't been together long enough, or maybe we'd communicated in different ways.

Instead, I was crying because they had something I *wanted*. Wanted for myself, in a future that wouldn't, *couldn't*, include Adrian. And that simply wasn't right.

Someday, I would be the last person on earth who remembered Adrian's laugh or the curve of his cheek when he smiled. He'd died, and I'd lived, and I owed it to him to never forget all the things I'd loved about him, not to let anyone else usurp him in my mind.

I could fucking feel that very thing happening already. Silas Sloane, with his gorgeous smile and his kind blue eyes, with his snarky humor and his full mouth that twitched up at the side when I said something ridiculous, was *dangerous*. He could make me forget; he certainly made me wish I could.

Which meant somehow I had to avoid Silas Sloane for the next ten months in a town the size of a prison cell.

I sat down on the step and held my face in my hands.

*How hard could that be?*

# Chapter Six

SILAS

I FUMBLED for the phone on my nightstand in the half-darkness of my room, and answered without checking the caller. "Yeah?"

"Hey, Si. Did I wake you?"

Dare sounded surprised, and I didn't blame him. I wasn't really the kind of person who answered the phone on the first ring at sunrise on a Saturday morning. Then again, I didn't usually spend most of a Friday night staring at my ceiling, so this had been a week of unusual experiences.

Two weeks, more like.

I cleared my throat. "Nah, I'm awake. There a problem? Need help?"

Herriman-Sizemore State Park, where Dare worked, was relatively small as state parks went and didn't get a lot of tourists in the shoulder season before peak foliage hit. But every year, there were at least one or two people who wandered off a trail and were too tired, disoriented, or injured to make their way out again. When that happened, the state conservation folks, like Dare, would call in rein-forcements from local police departments.

It was a sad thought that I actually wouldn't mind if he was calling me out for something. I needed a distraction, and none of my usual methods were cutting it.

"Kinda. Actually, I was calling to see if I could talk you into grabbing breakfast with me this morning. I've been having a craving for the pancakes at Goode's. Early bear season starts on Monday, and I feel the need to load up on carbs before I have to deal with that shit."

I chuckled. "And to think, you could be working for the FBI right now if you'd just picked the right track out of college."

"Yeah, right." Dare sounded amused. "Then I'd be hunting serial killers. I doubt I'd be sleeping better at night."

"Any word on the missing camper?" I asked.

"Meet me at Goode's," Dare insisted. "I'll fill you in on what I know. And you can tell me what the hell is going on with you."

I frowned and ran a hand through my hair, which was overdue for a cut. "There's nothing going on with me."

"Really? That's not what I've heard."

I grimaced, though Dare couldn't see it. "Pretty sure I don't want to know what you've heard."

"I heard you haven't made plans to come back to Camden and reschedule your date with Reggie Carbury."

*Carbury.* That was his name. Like the chocolate, but not.

I'd considered calling him. Once. Last Saturday night. And then it had occurred to me that maybe I shouldn't mess around with a guy if I couldn't remember his last name, so I'd deleted Reggie's number.

Look who was developing standards.

"It wasn't a date," I informed Dare. "I met Reggie for a hookup… and it wasn't even that, in the end."

"Pardon me," Dare said. "I forget that for you *dates* and *hookups* are vastly different things. So, why haven't you had a hookup redo? Reggie's cute. I see him around town sometimes. Seems like just your type."

"My type?"

"Cute. Short. Smart. Interested in sex."

This assessment felt vaguely insulting somehow, though it was accurate enough. "I just wasn't into it, that's all," I told Dare. "There's no deep secret here. We just didn't mesh."

"That's not what I heard," Dare said. "Carl was at the Dark Horse a couple weeks back and saw you and Reggie, quote, *making eyes at one another like they was ready to fuck over the table*."

"Jesus."

Dare chuckled. "And since the tables at the Horse are really fucking high, and that would not be remotely comfortable, I can only assume that means you two were *very much* into each other."

I snorted. "Reggie was cute, like you said. But he got pissy when I got called out, and then… well. I realized I just wasn't interested."

"You," Dare said skeptically. "*You* weren't interested in a hot young teacher who's interested in you? Because word around town is that he's tried calling you several times and you haven't returned his calls."

"Fuck me," I muttered. "And who told you that?"

"Jessica — she's a teacher at Camden-O'Leary High — she heard it from Reggie himself, who was bitching in the break room about how you'd led him on."

"What?" I was faintly outraged. "I did not!"

"*She* told Coach Simms," Dare continued relentlessly,

"and *he* mentioned it to his wife, Peggy, who's one of our visitor's center volunteers, so *she* mentioned it to me, likely because she assumes that every gay man knows every other gay man and can divine their inner thoughts and motivations." He paused for air. "Which in this case, I'm pretty sure I can."

"Stop, please. You remind me of my mother," I grumbled. It was not a compliment. I sometimes forgot that Camden had its own gossip network that was at least as fast — and inaccurate — as O'Leary's. "You were in the Air Force, you carry a gun, and you just managed to sound like Carolyn Sloane when she's at MaryAnn's getting her hair fixed."

"I've always liked your mother," Dare said sardonically.

"And what do you mean *in this case you can?*" I demanded. "I haven't talked to you in almost two weeks." Not since the night before Ev came to town. "What the hell do you think you know?"

"Goode's Diner. Half an hour. Wear something pretty for me," the asshole who used to be my friend said. I swore I could hear his smirk through the phone.

He disconnected the call, and I flopped back on my pillow in the wrought-iron double bed, staring at the ceiling of what used to be my grandparents' spare room and was now mine. Ceiling-staring was pretty much my hobby these days. It had gotten so that I knew where every tiny crack and bump was, even in the dark.

A chill breeze blew in through the open window, bringing with it the comforting smell of wood smoke, and I ran a hand idly over my bare chest. One of the neighbors had started up their wood-burning stove to combat the early autumn cold snap — probably the Daleys across the street, since Mrs. Daley said the cold aggravated her arthritis, and Mr. Daley lived to keep his wife happy.

My grandparents had been like that. When my grandmother had stopped being able to bend down to weed her garden bed, my grandfather had done it for her. And when his cataracts had acted up, she'd gone out and gotten her license for the first time ever, at age seventy, so she could take over the driving. When I got old, would anyone care enough to step in and…

Oh. *Oh, God.* Ew. *No.* Vomit. I *refused* to sit and fret about fucking dying alone. I was thirty-eight, not eighty-three.

I had just reached a new low in a week of all-time lows.

Closer to two weeks, really.

*Whatever.*

I threw the faded quilt off me and forced myself into the bathroom to shower.

The whole *cry-and-whine-because-the-cute-boy-doesn't-love-me* thing had never been my style, not in high school and sure as fuck not as an adult. I could honestly say I'd never wondered what they were doing when we weren't together, or worried about whether they were happy, or gave a shit why they weren't returning my many, many, *many* phone calls.

I'd never had a guy I'd been so hung up on, I'd been unable to swipe right on a hookup for over a week.

Nearly two.

If a hot guy wasn't into me, which happened often enough, I'd simply find another one. Thanks to modern technology, my next hookup was only a swipe and a click away, after all. No wedding announcements, no broken promises, no matter what Reggie Chocolate-name said.

Then, I'd met Everett Maior, and suddenly, I *was* the guy who was pining for someone. I didn't fucking like it. Not one bit. It was goddamn inconvenient.

It wasn't that I had feelings for Ev, obviously. I was still the same commitment-cautious person as ever, and I barely knew the guy.

What I felt for Ev was a very specific craving. I mean, if a person planned to have one of Ash Martin's famous tequila-lime cupcakes, and spent days fantasizing about *exactly* how that cupcake might taste and how delectable that cupcake would smell, it would be reasonable for them to be disappointed if they got to the bakery and found it was closed… for a fucking week. Or two. Right?

And would it make sense for that person to just go across the street to Goode's and get a baked potato? Hell, no. Potatoes were tasty, and they might curb your hunger, but they wouldn't be *satisfying*. You'd be thinking of the cupcake the whole time you were eating the potato, and that wouldn't be fair to the potato, so…

Wow.

I was comparing men to potatoes.

Okay, maybe *this* was the new low.

I lathered my hair and turned the water up hot enough to scald the thoughts out of my brain.

I had no idea what had made Ev decide that I wasn't a person worth knowing anymore. At first, I'd thought maybe he was horrified by Karen when he ran out of the bakery — not an uncommon reaction — or overwhelmed by so many new people, or genuinely concerned about Henry. But I'd tried to talk to him later that afternoon when he'd stopped by Julian's clinic to pick up Daphne (after spending most of the day hanging out in Julian's waiting room just for that purpose), and Ev wouldn't even meet my eyes. He was back to being the same closed-off guy I'd found on the side of the road, only worse because this was a conscious retreat. He'd walled himself off from me, thoroughly and effectively.

I'd stopped by the hardware store. I'd taken to standing

outside Fanaille every morning like a fucking stalker —
and yes, I know just how uncool that was. Still, no dice.
He'd nod and smile pleasantly enough, but he wouldn't
look *at* me, he looked *through* me. I had no idea how I'd
pissed him off, and no clue how to make it better, or if I
should even try.

So, as August had eased into September, as the nights
had turned cooler and the kids being in school had
brought a different rhythm to the town, I'd found I was
really good at finally cleaning out my grandparents' stuff
from the attic above the garage, sorting it into a manage-
able pile of memorabilia, and a much larger bunch of
furniture and shit that Marci had helped me cart off and
donate to the charity rummage sale for the Pumpkin Fest.

I was good at working until my eyes bled, trying to
track down what leads we had to find the missing camper
— who seemed, indeed, to be really missing, given that he
hadn't contacted his family — and covering shifts for
Constantine, who seemed to be out sick more than he was
working these days, which was a worry of its own.

I was good at ignoring Reggie's countless calls and
replying with terse, negative answers when he'd texted to
reschedule our date, even though the poor guy couldn't
help being a potato.

What I was not good at, though, was ignoring Everett
Maior. He'd become a fucking squatter in my brain, and I
wanted to evict him.

I pulled on jeans, a t-shirt, and a Henley, along with my
hiking boots, then made a slow walk down the driveway to
start my truck. While the blowers took care of the early
morning condensation on the windshield, I looked back at
my house and for maybe the first time ever, I really *saw* it.

It was a small house — a Cape Cod style, with white-
painted shingles, black shutters, and dormer windows

peeking out of the sharply slanted roof that my grandfather had built by hand back in the '50s. It had a white picket fence surrounding it on two sides, and a giant sugar maple out front that my grandmother planted right after my father was born. If you didn't know the history of the place, though, maybe it'd be easy to assume it was hopelessly traditional. Mired in the past. I wondered what Ev saw when he looked at O'Leary.

*God.*

I was disgustingly into this guy, and I was *never* this way. *Evict. Exterminate. No más.*

I pulled into a spot outside of Goode's and physically restrained myself from looking two doors down at O'Leary Hardware. Wherever Ev was and whatever he was doing, it was none of my business.

I yanked open the diner door a little more roughly than I'd intended and stepped inside. Dare was already there, and he stood up to wave me over to his booth in the back.

I couldn't help but smile as I got closer. The man looked like he'd walked out of a sporting goods catalog. His dark brown hair was perfectly combed, and the sharp blade of his jaw was perfectly smooth — nothing less would do for Darius Turner. He wore a light-blue wool-blend t-shirt, ancient khaki cargo pants —the kind that would dry in ten seconds — and a huge black hiking watch strapped to his wrist.

"What's up, man?" he said, giving me a brief hug before sitting down again, facing the door.

"I love the look," I told him, sliding onto the bench opposite him. "It's very Boy-Scout-Den-Master-Daddy."

He looked down at his t-shirt, pulling it away from his body, and lifted an eyebrow at me. "It's *hiking gear.* Why do you always have to make it sound kinky?"

I shrugged and bit the inside of my cheek. "Some of us

manage to hike in our sneakers and t-shirts, that's all I'm saying. Low-key, you know?"

"Yeah, and it's low-key people like you who make my life hell," he said, pointing an accusing finger at me across the table. "Getting hypothermia and breaking your ankles in the backwoods."

This argument was as old and familiar as the bacon-coffee scent of Goode's, and I hadn't realized how badly I needed to ground myself in this reality.

"I mean, if you *need* the gear, by all means, wear it," I allowed. "It's just that some of us are… natural woodsmen, I guess?" I blinked innocently. "We don't need all the extra accessories to do the job?"

"Well, as it turns out, that's really convenient," Dare said. He grinned broadly. "Because I have just the job for a natural woodsman such as yourself."

"I knew it!" I gasped in mock outrage. "I knew you wouldn't offer to treat me to breakfast for nothing."

"First off," Dare laughed. "I didn't offer to treat you. And second…" He paused as Shane Goode stopped by our table with a pair of mugs and a carafe of coffee. "Oh. Hey, Shane."

"Dare. Si." Shane nodded and a strand of long, dark hair escaped the short ponytail at the back of his neck to fall across his face. "How's it going?"

"Pretty well," I said as Shane filled my mug and then Dare's. "Except Dare's about to rope me into a favor."

Dare sighed. "The kind of favor that's actually his job, so don't feel too bad for him." At Shane's puzzled frown, Dare explained, "We had a camper go missing a couple of weeks back. I'm sure you heard about it. We're heading up a little search party."

Shane nodded. "Oh yeah. I heard. Kid from Philly, staying up at Frank's place?"

"That's the one," Dare agreed.

"Karen Mitchener says he was murdered," Shane said dubiously.

I groaned and rubbed my forehead. "Karen says a lot of things," I reminded him. "There is absolutely no evidence to indicate that. Okay?"

"Yeah." Shane gave me a relieved smile. "Yeah, okay."

"I keep hoping we'll get a call from his people saying he's turned up somewhere, but time keeps passing and no one's seen him."

Shane's mouth twisted. "Woods are dangerous," he said with a shake of his head. "People who don't know better shouldn't be thundering around out there. They should mind their own business."

I shrugged. "Frank wouldn't earn much of a living if tourists didn't come to town, though. Or Scarlet Maple Inn, with their weddings. Or Crabapple B-and-B."

Shane looked totally unconcerned at that prospect. "Upsets the balance," he insisted. "People leaving, people coming. Sometimes don't it seem like it'd just be better if everyone stayed where they were *meant* to be?"

I blinked at his vehemence and exchanged a look with Dare, whose eyes had turned sympathetic. "Yeah, Shane," he said carefully. "But sometimes people aren't born where or *who* they were meant to be, and it takes time and a change of perspective to get them to the right place."

"Or maybe they were in the right place all along and didn't know it," Shane countered. "Maybe they went looking for something they never needed at all." He shook his head and smiled. "Anyway, I'm just rattling on. What can I get you? Molly's got a gingerbread pancake recipe she's been working on, or there's a real nice hash and eggs."

"You mean Diane?" I clarified.

"Uh, *yeah*," he drawled, like this was obvious. "That's what I *said*."

I nodded slowly. "Right. Well, I'll be adventurous today and try the gingerbread pancakes."

"And Dare, you'll have your usual? Four eggs scrambled with spinach, double bacon, and sausage?" Shane guessed.

"You've got it," Dare agreed.

I wasn't sure if they had menus here at the diner; if they did, I'd never seen them. But it hardly mattered when Shane had been working here long enough that he'd memorized orders for every person in town. He couldn't have been more than thirty-two, just a little older than my brother would have been, but he had a sort of agelessness about him, a combination of childlike innocence and ancient weariness. He was an old, grief-ravaged soul in a young body.

"Gotcha. Be right out with them," Shane said, giving us that same forced grin as he walked away.

"Poor bastard," Dare said. His finger traced the edge of his coffee mug as he watched Shane retreat. "This time of year is always hard for him. And for you. What day was it again?"

I picked up my coffee and took a long sip. "The fourteenth," I said. "Couple more weeks." A couple of weeks until the twelfth anniversary of the car accident that killed Shane's girlfriend Molly Burke and my little brother.

Dare nodded. "I sometimes forget it's coming," he said apologetically.

I huffed once. "You wanna know something terrible? So do I," I admitted. "Last year, I didn't remember until my mom called and asked if I was planning to meet them at the cemetery."

"Meet them at the cemetery? Do they still do that?"

"Oh, you know it. Every year. She's called me twice already about this year's tear-fest, but I haven't called her back."

Dare grimaced. "She shouldn't guilt you into it, if you don't want to go."

"Eh. It's fine. I'll do my duty." I laughed shortly. "Besides, guilt is the cornerstone of our relationship."

"Sounds healthy."

"I'm joking." Mostly. "Losing Matty was hard for her. Different than it was for me. He was their great, shining hope, you know?"

Dare frowned. "And you weren't? High school quarterback, Eagle Scout?"

"Gay," I reminded him. "Determined to be a cop and not a financial analyst like my father." I waved a hand in the air. "Not worth talking about that shit, though. Over and done now."

But Dare's frown didn't subside. "Not if it's still eating at you, it's not. You think your parents care if you're gay? I thought they were pretty cool?"

I shrugged. "We don't talk about it. *Ever*. But I figure there's being pretty cool with the concept of people being gay, and pretty cool with *your only son and legacy* being gay. Two different things."

"And they're not okay with you?" he asked. "Because I think it's bullshit to be cool about a hypothetical and then treat your own kid like…"

"Can we please drop it?" I interrupted.

"Fine." Dare held up his hands in surrender. "Tell me about the guy."

*Excellent job exploring the full range of topics I do not want to discuss, Darius.*

"What guy?" I hedged.

Dare sighed. "We're gonna do this? Really? Henry

Lattimer's grandson Everett. *That* guy. The guy I'm pretty sure is the reason Reggie Carbury is never gonna hear from you again. The guy Ash Martin said you were laughing and flirting with at Fanaille a week ago."

"Nearly two," I corrected.

Dare smiled triumphantly and I winced.

"Uh-huh." He lifted one eyebrow. "Spill."

I rolled my eyes and ignored him.

Dare rested his chin on his hand and stared at me.

I stared at the smooth tabletop.

Dare kicked my ankle *hard*, forcing me to look at him again.

"Fine!" I said, my resistance dissolving like chalk in the rain. I massaged my sore ankle and glared at him. "Fine. You win. Ev's a decent guy. He's hot as fuck. Seems nice. I was into him. He's not into me, though, which is sadly *not* a crime in New York State."

Dare frowned. "You sure?"

"I know, right?" I widened my eyes. "Seems like it should be, but I looked it up just in case."

Dare groaned. "Not that, asshole. Are you sure he's not into you?"

"Given the number of times I've called, visited, and accosted him over the past two weeks? Yeah, it's a safe bet." I grabbed a napkin from the silver dispenser on the edge of the table and unfolded it in front of me. "Short of arresting him and locking him up, I've exhausted all options to get him to talk to me."

"Interesting," Dare said.

"What?"

"I dunno." Dare shrugged. "Cal said the guy was putting out a strong *interested* vibe. Maybe he's fighting it."

"Oh, and now Caelan James is an expert on these things?" I rubbed a hand over my forehead. "And people seriously wonder why I take steps to keep my personal life personal? *Cal says he's into me, Ash says I'm into Ev.* Jesus. It's like being in high school, but with legal booze and no summers off."

Dare looked down at the table and pursed his lips like he was trying not to smile.

"So, okay, given that I'm already getting chewed up by the O'Leary gossip mill, tell me. What's his deal?" I tore my napkin into rectangles and then the rectangles into squares.

"Who, Ev?"

My turn to raise my eyebrow. Dare chuckled.

"I haven't the first clue. If he has a deal, it's not something the fine folks of O'Leary know about. Yet." Dare narrowed his eyes at me speculatively. "You could always ask him."

"Uh, you recall the part from a minute ago where I've been trying to talk to him and he's done everything but get a restraining order to avoid me?"

My asshole friend snickered. "That bad, huh?"

I wadded up my napkin and threw it at him so it landed on the table like so much confetti. "Yeah. That bad."

"Never thought I'd see the day." Dare gave me a soft smile like I'd done something cute. "Si Sloane, falling for someone."

I scowled. "*Please.* It's not that. Dude, I barely know the guy. It's just annoying when someone seems like they might be into you one minute, and the next, they're just… *gone.*"

"Ahhh, so it's the mystery you like," Dare said, nodding. "This makes more sense. It's rare that you have to work for it."

*That's because I never wanted someone enough to work for it,* I thought but didn't say.

I sipped my coffee so I didn't have to answer and leaned back in the seat, staring at the wall over Dare's head and pretending I couldn't hear him chuckle.

The bell above the front door chimed behind me and Shane greeted some newcomers.

"Explain to me about the search party for the missing camper," I said, changing the subject. "I'd think at this point it'd be more like a recovery operation? Unless you think he's lasted out there for two weeks somehow?"

Dare shook his head, but before he could speak, a sight behind me caught his attention and he studiously looked down at the ground, fighting laughter.

"No, I will *not* sit near the front door, Everett, and I will *not* sit at the counter. I didn't just come here for the damn pancakes, I came here to *socialize*. That's an ancient custom we used to practice in the days before your FaceThing."

I turned around, eyes open wide and mouth open wider.

Henry Lattimer was hobbling toward the back of the restaurant on one crutch and Ev — red-faced and unhappy — trailed behind him. Hen's face lit up when he saw we'd noticed him.

"Ah! There we are! Silas and Dare!" He thumped closer, which seemed to involve him planting the crutch and leaping in a way that couldn't be healthy for a man his age. "Just the men I wanted to speak to."

"Hen," I said. "Doing better?"

"Better?" He waved this away. "I'm fine. *Been* fine." He glared at Ev. "Just need some bacon and pancakes."

I looked up at Ev because it would have been rude not to.

It *would*.

Similarly, it was only because I was a trained law enforcement officer that I noticed the way his dark curls hung over his forehead, all sexy-messy, and how his tight jeans and t-shirt hugged his body, making him look even leaner and more supple than I'd remembered.

"Ev." I said it low and friendly, trying to make it an acknowledgment and not an invitation, but he sucked in a deep breath like I'd attacked him or something.

I couldn't win with this guy. I turned my attention to Dare, who was scratching his forehead and studiously not looking at us.

Henry grabbed a chair from a nearby table and turned it around to place it at the open end of our booth. He seated himself with a sigh and propped his foot up on the seat next to me. "Ahhh. That's the ticket."

I glared across the table at Dare, who was fighting laughter and failing miserably.

"Dare, this is Everett. Henry's grandson," I said pointedly, since it was clear no one else was going to perform introductions. "Ev, this is Dare Turner. He's a conservation officer."

Dare smiled. "Welcome to O'Leary, Everett."

Ev lifted his chin. "Nice to meet you." He looked around at the dozen empty booths in the restaurant. His shoulders slumped.

"Don't just stand there like a bump on a log, Everett. Sit down, sit down. Dare doesn't bite."

Dare took the hint and pushed over. Ev gritted his teeth and sat, giving Dare an apologetic smile.

"Football tomorrow, boys?" Henry asked without preamble.

"Yep. Like every Sunday," Dare confirmed. "This week we're meeting at the bar. Be at Hoff's at one."

"I will. Ev will too, not that he's a football fan. Gotta make sure I don't eat anything delicious, you know," Hen grumbled.

"Yes, the fun police never take a day off." Ev rolled his eyes. "Football. That's the one with the black and white balls and the nets, right? Where they run, run, run and kick, kick, kick?" He mimed the motions with his fingers while the three of us stared at him. "*Goooooooal!*" he whisper-yelled, shaking his hands like a jazz performer.

Hen groaned in disgust and Dare snorted, but I noticed the way Ev's mouth twitched as he tried to control his laughter, and damn if I didn't like him more for the way he baited his grandfather... and the rest of us.

"So!" Hen's eyes flared. "Tell me all about this missing camper! John Whatshisface."

Dare and I exchanged a look. The trick to police work in O'Leary, or any town around here, really, was that nothing stayed secret for very long. The town was too tight-knit for that. It also meant that crimes didn't stay hidden either, so kind of a double-edged sword.

"Carpenter. His name's John Carpenter. And we're getting together a search party today," Dare said. "Volunteers." He smiled smugly at me. "And volun*tolds*."

"Searching for what?" Hen demanded. "A body? If the kid's out there, he's dead."

Ev made a soft noise of discomfort.

"What? It's true," Hen said. "Ask them."

Dare sucked his teeth. "Based on what Myrna and Frank reported, and what we heard from John Carpenter's family down in Pennsylvania, the kid wouldn't have survived long in the backcountry on his own. We found his car parked up north of Herriman Wilds — a wilderness area on the eastern edge of the park," he explained to Ev. "There's a sizable parking area and a campground there, but it's not uncommon for people to just hike the five miles or so through the woods to one of the other, smaller campgrounds."

Ev nodded. "And that's where the camper was staying?"

"Yeah. At Pickett's Campground," Dare confirmed. "Just south of town."

"Is it possible he grabbed his gear and hiked back out the way he came in?" I asked. "Or went up to Lake Loughton for a while?"

"Possible he headed out to do that," Dare said. "But he never made it. I've had the folks from our department combing the trails for any sign. Hiked to and from the Wilds myself last week and again this week, just in case. Had Jonas and Rachel doing the same up by the lake, and I even had Elliot Marks go halfway up Jane's Peak. No luck. I'm thinking what I need is a bunch of people who'll check closer to Carpenter's last known location. See if we can find any of his equipment or a sign of where he might have left the marked trails."

Diane Perkins sashayed up to the table, her red hair coiled in a bun atop her head and her arms overflowing with plates. "I've got your pancakes, Si, and eggs for Dare. The usual pancakes and bacon for you, Henry. And Ev, honey, I took a guess that you might like pancakes, as well."

Ev smiled softly, like he was surprised she'd thought to bring him anything at all. "Thanks, Diane."

She nodded, smiling down at all of us. Her gaze seemed to linger extra-long over Henry, though. And the man who couldn't keep his damn mouth shut suddenly seemed to find the platter of pancakes *fascinating.* He fiddled with his fork and said nothing, not even a thank you.

Diane sighed. "Well. You need anything else, you holler."

"Coffee?" Ev said. "Please?"

"Sure thing," Diane said. "Cup for you, Henry?"

Hen blushed and nodded without looking up, and Ev's amused eyes met mine across the table before his gaze skittered away.

"So when you say you want the search party checking out Carpenter's last location, you mean out by the campgrounds?" I asked. "Just spreading out in a radius?"

"Well, mostly inward toward the park," Dare said. "Since I doubt he headed toward O'Leary. But yeah."

"You're starting a search party?" Diane interrupted. "You need volunteers?"

"Yeah," Dare said. "Later today. You free?"

Diane smiled. "Oh, not me, kiddo. But I'll let Shane and Jamie know."

"Great." Dare turned to Ev. "How about you, Everett? Wanna volunteer?"

Ev coughed on a bite of his pancake. "I wanna say yes, but I'm pretty sure you'd end up with a missing camper *and* a missing art teacher," he said. "I'm pretty hopeless at orienteering, or whatever you call it."

God, he was so fucking cute when he wasn't trying to be cute.

"Best way to learn is by getting out there," Hen said. "Gotta be brave. Can't live your life being scared."

Ev's cheeks flamed, and he stared at his grandfather incredulously. "You want me to *get out there* and get lost in the fucking woods? As a test of my *bravery*?"

I bit into a slice of bacon with more force than necessary.

"No, of course not," Hen barked, like that wasn't what he'd just implied. "Si will go with you."

The bacon became stuck in my windpipe and Henry had to lean over and thump me on the back before I could stop choking. "I don't know if…" I croaked at the exact same time Everett said, "Oh, I wouldn't want Si to have to…"

But Dare, my *former* best friend, spoke over both of us.

"I think that's a great idea, Henry! Best way for Ev to really get acclimated to the town. Plus, it's supposed to be a real pretty day."

"And who'll be watching *you* while I'm out proving my manhood in the woods?" Ev demanded. He turned to me and scowled, pointing at Henry. "Do you know what I've already caught him doing this morning? Climbing a fucking ladder in the shop. *On his crutch.* And yes, that's *one* crutch, *singular*, because unlike a normal human, he won't *baby himself* by using two."

"I don't need you smothering me."

"Then why did you have me come here?" Ev demanded, brandishing his fork in the air. "Why the hell did you want me to uproot my whole damn life to come help you if all you want is for me to leave you alone, or to listen to how Diane Perkins does everything right?"

Henry's eyes narrowed and he looked around like he wondered if Diane might have overheard. "I said *help*, Everett. Not smother. I appreciate you coming here, but I don't need you watching me twenty-four hours a day. I've got a *life* to lead. You'd best go out and get your own."

Ev's face blanched. He put his fork down on the edge of his plate with a *click*.

Henry floundered, his mouth opening and closing for a moment like a fish. He scowled. "Now, you know I didn't mean it that way, Everett. Don't take it wrong."

I didn't get exactly how Hen's words had hurt him, only that they had. Ev looked so vulnerable in that moment, as if he couldn't decide whether he should kill or cry. Seeing him like that made me feel protective in a way I never had before.

"How about you make the effort to say things the right way, then, Henry?" I said it mildly enough, but the look I gave Henry wasn't mild at all. "How about you man up and do better than a half-assed apology, if you misspoke?"

Henry's head went back and he looked at me appraisingly for a second. Then he nodded slowly.

"Si's right," he said. Ev lifted his eyes, but not to his grandfather. Instead, that bright green gaze locked on *me*, and I couldn't move. "I'm sorry, Everett. I just meant that I want you to get out and do things for yourself. Don't worry about me so much."

Ev nodded, then took a deep, shuddering breath. "Alright," he said softly. Then he gave me a small smile that shocked the shit out of me. "And I'll go with you, Si. If you'd like the company."

"Yeah," I said. "Of course."

Just like the first night we'd met, seeing Ev's smile was like winning a prize. It was a chink in the wall he'd built between us, which was thrilling. But I was glad no one at this table could read my mind, or know how monumental this felt, because I was also scared as fuck.

Getting something you really wanted was always such a let-down that way. I liked focusing on the goal of attaining a thing, putting in the work, thinking of the whys and hows. All the calm, logical bits I could survey like *The Terminator* and figure out how to attack and destroy. All the parts I could control.

But once I'd attained something, it became… I dunno. Terrifying, really. How did you *keep* a thing? How did you *hold* it? And when you inevitably lost it, how did you deal with the shitty feeling of being reminded daily, by the whispers and kind looks of the people all around you, that you'd once had it and now you didn't anymore? Sometimes it was just better not to want things.

But I wasn't sure how not to want Ev.

The little seed of attraction had sprouted into a fucking tree of fascination, like all of my attempts to shut it down and deny its existence had acted like water and sunlight, just making the roots burrow deeper.

And that smile…

Well. That smile made the terror nearly worthwhile.

"So, I'll pick you up at eleven?" I said, super-casual, like I didn't give a shit either way.

"Sure," he agreed.

"It's a date," Dare said, giving me a way-too-knowing glance over the edge of his coffee cup. "Isn't it, Si?"

A date, not a *hookup*, Dare meant. An important distinction.

"Yeah," I said, giving Ev what I hoped was an easy smile. "It is."

# Chapter Seven



ANOTHER DAY IN O'LEARY, another moment of utter lunacy on my part.

I'd never been endowed with much common sense — my tendency to see deeper meaning in cloud formations, or to believe the universe communicated deep messages through the irrational yelling of a panhandler on the street were quirks that both my grandfather *and* my husband had rolled their eyes at, and I swear I'd tried to break myself of those habits since Adrian died — but I was clearly a special kind of stupid these days.

Stupid, confused, and *weak*, as evidenced by the fact that I'd somehow consented to go hiking with Si Sloane, after two fucking weeks of doing everything in my power to avoid him.

Maybe the reason O'Leary was so isolated wasn't due to simple geography, but because it was a black hole, like the Bermuda Triangle. Good judgment went in but never came out.

I kicked at the packed suitcases still sitting on my floor and threw myself on the guest room bed with a sigh.

Daphne, seeing an opportunity to get affection without implying that she needed or wanted affection, jumped from her spot at the end of the bed and curled in the crook of my arm, just where a patch of fall sunlight was streaming in the window.

My stomach was full of pancakes, my head was full of doubt, and my heart was thrumming like a hummingbird's wings even though I wasn't capable of fighting or fleeing at the moment if my life depended on it. I threw my forearm over my eyes and groaned.

Anxiety was such a bitch.

Avoiding Silas this long had been no easy feat. He'd been persistent in a way that might have screamed *stalker* but instead came off as really sweet. Sweet enough to nearly make me forget why I was avoiding him in the first place, especially since the reasons all tended to sound stupid when I tried to articulate them even to myself.

Fear that I might be attracted to him? Was that really the best I could do? Because honest to God, that ship had sailed so far out of the harbor I couldn't see it from the shore.

It wasn't just that Si was handsome, though. Simple good looks, I could have ignored. This tiny, backwoods town had a disproportionate number of hot guys, and strangely enough, I'd gotten more flirtatious looks while taking my shift in the hardware store the past few evenings than I'd ever gotten walking down the street in Boston. I had no problem tuning them out.

It wasn't that Si was friendly, either. Si wasn't one who carpet-bombed people with friendliness, unlike the rest of the appallingly friendly people in this town. Given that Adrian and I had referred to most of our neighbors by the cars they drove — like, *Ms. Silver Mercedes and her husband better clean up after their damn dog* — the culture shock of having perfect strangers who'd seen yearbook photos of me greasy-haired and pimple-faced was a very real thing, and I approved of the way Silas stayed a step removed. If I lived here, I'd shy away from town gossip too. People assumed they knew you when they really knew only one part of you… and maybe not even that.

No, the attraction to Silas was because being with him was the closest to human I'd felt in a really long time. I liked his sense of humor and the way his eyes crinkled. I liked the way my stomach got warm when I felt his gaze on me, even from across the bakery in the mornings. I liked the way his lips twitched like he was fighting a smile when he saw me, even when I wasn't doing anything bright or funny or amusing at all; like maybe just seeing me made him happy.

Si had spoken my name in the diner today and made my spine tingle like he'd uttered a command in a language I couldn't fully process but instinctively understood. And Silas had defended me. That had been the real nail in the coffin of my resistance right there. I'd known him for, like, *a day*, before retreating into my shell like a turtle, and I was pretty sure he didn't even get why Hen's comment had been hurtful, and *still* he'd come down on my side and made Hen apologize.

I didn't want to be attracted to that. I was pretty sure it ran contrary to the whole self-reliant, stand-on-my-own-two-feet thing I'd been so determined to attain after Adrian's death. But there was a difference between requiring something and liking it.

He made me feel *special*, important, understood. And that, right there, was pretty damn impossible for me to resist.

I'd had a really shitty revelation earlier in the week, while rinsing dinner dishes after a long day of teaching, stocking shelves at the store, and preparing dinner for a man who seemed determined to hate everything I cooked: I wanted someone I could talk to who would really understand me. Just that. And if that someone came attached to a pair of strong arms that could wrap around me, and gorgeous blue eyes, and a mouth with a perfect little scar right beside it that could distract me from all the piddly shit that made me spiral? Well, that would be pretty fucking excellent too.

I'd spent so long just wanting Adrian back that I had no frame of reference for wanting anything else. I couldn't decide if it was normal that I should want more out of life than memories, or if I was the shittiest lover in the history of love, because I couldn't remember the way my name had sounded on Adrian's lips anymore.

How much was too much to let go? How much of myself could I give Si without forgetting Adrian entirely?

I stroked a hand over Daphne's soft fur and focused on the rhythm of her breathing, letting my own heart rate calm.

Last week, the insurance company had gone out to inspect my Toyota at the repair shop and declared it a total loss, which was pretty much what I'd expected. But the adjuster had sent me pictures of the damage, too, and I'd felt this rush of leftover adrenaline sing in my blood at the reminder that *I could have died.* The night of the accident, I hadn't cared very much either way, but now I was pretty damn glad to be alive, and right or wrong, wanting Si, who made me feel very much alive just by watching me from across the floor of the hardware store or texting me some lame joke I wouldn't reply to, was all caught up in that.

"Everett! Are you nearly ready? Silas will be here soon."

I rolled my eyes as Grandpa Hen's voice bellowed

down the hall. Since we'd left the diner, he'd been acting like I was a teenager and Si was my prom date. He'd suggested I pack a picnic; he'd asked me *what shirt I was wearing*. I'd sort of imagined he'd try to warn me away from Si, or any man actually, but instead, he was all but pimping me out. *Just be nice to the gentleman, Fancy*.

"Yeah," I yelled back, dislodging Daphne, who gave me a disgruntled look. I muttered under my breath, "Ready as I'm gonna be."

I had no idea how to act, what to wear, what to think. I'd been out of the game longer than I'd ever been in it.

Lucky Silas had no idea what he was in for.

I rolled off the bed and appraised myself in the mirror over the wooden chest of drawers. Same jeans I'd worn at breakfast. Cotton button-down over my t-shirt because I'd read somewhere that layers were good outdoor wear. Either I'd do, or I wouldn't. I was *not* going to dress up.

I pulled on my sneakers and grabbed my old backpack, which I'd filled with water bottles and protein bars in lieu of a picnic, then made my way down the hall to the living room, leaving Daphne shut in my room.

Grandpa sat in his recliner and looked me over before nodding once. "You need a haircut, Ev."

I snorted and patted a hand over my unruly curls. "Grandpa, I'm going hiking to find a missing camper. I don't think anyone's gonna be looking at my hair."

"Hmmph." He regarded me steadily. "You know, I've known Silas Sloane since he was a baby."

I nodded. He'd known practically everyone in town since they were babies.

"He's a good man," Grandpa continued. "Reliable. Smart."

"Okay."

"Steady job. Kind heart."

"Healthy teeth. Strong back. A fine specimen?" I pushed my luck a little, still pissed off at him basically telling me to *get a life* back at the diner. "If he proposes, I'll accept. It's legal now and everything."

Grandpa flushed a satisfying beet red. "I'm just saying that you could do worse than Silas Sloane, that's all."

I frowned down at him. "I don't get it. Is this a change of heart? Have you decided to accept that I'm gay suddenly?"

"Didn't realize it was a thing that required my acceptance," he shot back. He looked supremely uncomfortable. "But since *you* are, and *Silas* is, then… He's a good man to… date." He cleared his throat. "That's what I'm saying."

I shook my head, still baffled, but before I could question him further, the doorbell rang downstairs.

"You sure you're going to be okay here by yourself?" I demanded. "Need anything before I go?"

"Of course not! I'm capable of…"

"Yes, yes, I know," I sighed. "You're capable of taking care of yourself, capable of vaulting the building with the aid of your crutch, capable of taking down an armed intruder without leaving your recliner." I rolled my eyes. "But when you're out saving the world, avoid the shop, okay? Theo's got everything under control and when you're there, you fluster him."

Grandpa scowled. "Fluster him? Sort him out, more like. He doesn't do things right!"

"He doesn't do things the way *you* do them," I corrected. "They're not wrong."

"Hmph. Well, I'm watching college football today anyway," he informed me, which was as close to capitulation as I was likely to get. "If you happen to see Diane on your way out, send her up?"

I blinked. "*Am* I likely to see Diane? She didn't say anything about it earlier, and God knows *you* didn't say anything at all to her. And for that matter, why does she still come around three times a week when I'm here to take care of you? Doesn't she have her own things to do?"

"Never you mind, Everett." He waved a bony hand through the air. "Go on with you. Enjoy the sunshine. Live while you're still alive."

I stared at him for a minute, but he was busy tracing the patterned fabric in the arm of the old recliner and wouldn't look back.

The bell downstairs rang again, and I hefted my backpack higher. "I'll see you later, then?"

Grandpa nodded. "Off you go," he commanded.

So, off I went.

Si was standing by the door when I got downstairs, wearing the same outfit he'd been wearing earlier, except now the sleeves of his maroon Henley were pushed up to his elbows to reveal lean, muscled forearms lightly sprinkled with dark hair.

I stopped in my tracks.

Bizarre but true fact: I am a *forearm* guy. Don't get me wrong, biceps are great. Thighs, asses, pecs, all wonderful also. But back when I was still drawing regularly, I had notebook after notebook filled with sketches of forearms in all different shapes and sizes. I'd sprung wood for my junior high track coach's forearms — and lifted weights religiously during that period since it meant that he would stand behind my head and spot me with those arms on prominent display. I was a forearm connoisseur, and Adrian used to tease me mercilessly about it.

And so *of course* Silas Sloane's were the epitome of forearm perfection, and I could barely breathe in that first minute, with the way his pulled-up shirt sleeves highlighted his lean strength.

I didn't know what the right thing to do about Si was, but I knew what felt good and necessary. I was attracted and I didn't want to fight that anymore. Maybe for today, that would be enough.

"Hey," Si said, not realizing that in my mind we'd already dispensed with the greetings (along with the whole damn hike) and I was already feeling his arms around me. Considering we hadn't exchanged more than two-dozen words in two weeks, I might have been moving a teensy bit fast.

"Hey. How, uh… have you been?"

He grinned, and his blue eyes were as warm as the summer sky when they landed on mine. "You mean, since breakfast?"

I cleared my throat. "I mean, since the last time we talked." *Since I ran away from you and ignored you because you made me want things I shouldn't want and thought I was strong enough to resist.*

He frowned, like he was considering his answer, before finally deciding on, "It's been a long two weeks." He grinned again. "Annoyingly productive. I cleaned out the attic over my garage and got caught up on my paperwork." He opened the passenger door of his truck for me and held out his hand for my backpack, then laid it gently in the back seat. "What about you?"

"Uh…" I waited for him to walk around the hood and climb in before answering. "It's been good, I guess? Classes started."

He nodded. "You settling in at the school?"

"Yeah."

We drove on in silence for a minute but God, there were

so many things I'd been thinking about these past couple of weeks, so many silly stories and surprising experiences, that it felt like my brain might overflow if I didn't share them. My friends in Boston had been great about staying in touch, but they might as well have been on a different planet for all that our lives had in common right now. And I realized that Si was maybe the only person in the world who might understand.

"I thought teaching kids was going to be one of the harder aspects of moving here, but it's actually been great."

Si glanced at me and smiled. Warm, comfortable. "I can see that. Sometimes they're really funny. It's relaxing to be around them."

"Exactly! They're young enough that they say what they mean most of the time. And they make me see things differently."

"How so?"

"Well, I had them do self-portraits last week. Draw yourself doing something that makes you happy, I told them."

"Self-portraits?" He whistled low as he started the car and backed out of the parking space. "Just jumping right in the deep end, eh? And next week they're carving statues out of marble with mini chisels?"

"Shut up." I slapped his arm lightly. "I'm not expecting mini-Van Goghs here, Silas! It's mostly just a baseline to see what they already notice about form."

His expression was dubious. "Form?"

"Like, kindergarteners draw bodies as sticks, you know? Older kids make them two-dimensional; one big rectangle with four smaller rectangles attached." I waved my arms in illustration. "And then eventually they get that there are fingers attached to hands attached to arms, and *hey*, we actually exist in three dimensions with shadows and light. That kind of thing."

Si glanced at me again. "Okay, first of all, I feel very judged right now, Everett. Some thirty-eight-year-olds draw bodies as sticks as a stylistic *choice*."

I bit my lip. "I... I'm sorry. Of course, you're right. Well, Frannie and Sivan Siegel are identical twins, and..." I caught myself and rolled my eyes. "I mean, obviously you know that."

"I do," he agreed. "Can't tell them apart, though. They're mirror images."

"Right?" I was usually pretty good at spotting differences, but as an outsider, it seemed these girls were identical down to their expressions. "So I'm expecting, you know, some variation of lines and rectangles. Not that there's anything wrong with that," I added, leaning over to pat his arm. "But they're both actually super talented. And the coolest part was that the way each girl drew herself was completely different."

Si made an encouraging noise, like he was really interested, and I found myself spilling my guts. We had pulled away from the buildings in town and sped up, flying past acres and acres of open land and pretty little houses. There was something freeing in that, too.

"Frannie drew herself with her sister and parents — one, two, three, four, in a row like stair-steps. And even though she and Sivan are the same height in real life, she drew herself bigger. Her smile was wider, her eyes more open. She's the bigger personality of the two, the more protective one, and she knows it on a deep level."

"And did Sivan draw herself smaller?"

"No." I laughed. "She didn't draw her family at all. She did this incredibly realistic portrait of herself in the woods petting a deer. The color of the deer's pelt was spot-on. The bark of the tree was, like, ten different shades of brown, all intricately blended. And then her own face was basically a sphere with brown circle eyes and a red smile. That was the part *she* cared about."

He looked over at me, his gaze slipping over my face and catching on my mouth. "And you didn't mind," he guessed. "Because you know what it's like to get caught up in something. Your anthropomorphic… squirrels, was it?"

I nodded. I had no clue how he remembered that, but he did. "I loved that she got passionate about something. Probably means I'm a crap teacher," I allowed with a chuckle. "But maybe they'll get someone better next year."

"She'll remember you her whole life," he corrected me. "All it takes is one awesome teacher to inspire an artist."

Si was somber, just a little bit, and I wondered if he was thinking of the brother he'd lost. I both wanted him to talk to me about it and didn't. I wasn't sure how much of myself I wanted to share, or how much of him I was ready to handle.

It didn't matter, though. A second later, Si slowed the truck to a stop and pointed at three tall, metal structures set side by side, high up on a hill.

"What do you think of those?" he asked, pointing with barely suppressed glee.

"What are they?"

The structures were just a bit taller than the two-story house next to them, slightly different in width and height, although that might just have been a matter of perspective. They were all hollow and sort of cylindrical, but topped with pointy ends, like giant watchtowers surveying O'Leary. The one in the center was dark orange, while the ones on either side were blood red and yellow-gold. There appeared to be a fourth one, half-constructed, on the end.

I tilted my head to the left. Maybe crayons?

I tilted my head to the right. Nuclear missiles? Some kind of claws?

"Are they… carrots?" I guessed.

"*Carr*… Wait, are you kidding?" he demanded. He looked at me with this expression of arrested laughter on his handsome face, like he'd been so sure I was giving him shit. But I wasn't. Not even a little.

"I have no clue what it's supposed to be," I told him honestly. "I'm sorry. Is it a local history thing?"

He stared at me incredulously. "Come on," he said. "It's obvious."

I shook my head. "Oh, pencils?" I guessed.

"They're… they're cocks, Ev." He looked at me pityingly. "Giant cocks."

I stared at the sculptures again. I mean, they *could* be cocks, if you only had the most basic understanding of what a penis looked like.

"Huh. Well, that's interesting. And did the artist say why they did it?"

"No, Ev!" Si laughed again. "No one's cornered Rena Cobb and asked her why she erected — pardon the pun — three enormous dicks in her front yard. It's not exactly the kind of conversation folks have around here."

"So you don't even really know if they're meant to be penises?" I surmised. "You all just assumed?"

"No! I mean…" He frowned. "I don't think so."

It was *my* turn to laugh. "Oh, my God. What is wrong with this town? Freud could have set up shop here and never had to leave."

Si sat up a little straighter and eased his foot off the brake to get us back on the road, but that little pucker between his eyebrows stayed in place. It was hilarious. It was sexy.

"You know," he said a moment later. "I think you could be really good for this town, Everett Maior."

I wasn't sure how to respond to that. My stomach flopped painfully, soaking up the validation like sunshine, and my heart also thrummed with very real fear because… damn, I liked that way too much.

He pulled the truck off the main road onto a rocky dirt path and drove us under a wooden sign that read *Pickett's Campground*. His mood changed with the road, becoming quieter, more reserved. Focused on his job. And goddamn it, *that* was appealing too.

I chuckled, running a hand over my face.

*God.*

I liked when he focused on *me*, I liked that he was dedicated to something *else*. I liked the efficient way he breathed and how he managed to have ten fingers and two eyes. If I found out he had six toes, I'd wax rhapsodic about how six-toed men were so much more compelling than their five-toed brethren.

Essentially, I was deep in lust and everything about the man was appealing.

I laughed again, and Si glanced my way. "Everything okay?"

I waved a hand dismissively. "Yeah! Yeah, totally. This is, uh, the place where the camper was staying?"

"Yep. Frank and Myrna Lucano's campground. Don't ask me how it got the name Pickett's," he said. "Not sure if anyone remembers anymore, even Frank and Myrna."

I forced myself to look around at the scenery — trees upon trees upon trees, with peeks of red and gold among the green, and a tiny clearing visible just a little ways ahead. "It's pretty."

"Wait till the fall colors really catch," he said softly. "Frank always closes down at Labor Day, and I've told him he's crazy. If he kept the place open, he could make as much in October as he does in June."

"But he doesn't?"

"Nope. Says autumn is a time for him and Myrna to enjoy the place. Sometimes their kids come home for the weekends. And of course, the locals are always parking here for a hike, stopping in to say hi. Faster than driving all the way around Lake Loughton or over to Camden to the nearest public lots." He made a circular motion with his hand, like he was drawing me a map in the air. "But he and Myrna bought the place because they loved these woods so much, and for a few months a year, he'd rather not share it."

"That's really cool," I said sincerely. Enjoying things while you could sounded like a hell of a philosophy. Maybe one I should adopt.

"Yeah, well." Si winced. "Not so much anymore."

Before I could ask what he meant, he pulled to a stop outside an actual, honest-to-God log cabin set in the small, grassy clearing. The house was small but clearly well-tended, its wide front porch set with a pair of white rocking chairs and at least a dozen pots of orange chrysanthemums that were too bright to be anything but plastic. The shutters on the windows had cut-outs shaped like maple leaves, and there was a giant purple-and-orange welcome sign hung on the front door.

"It looks like something out of a fairy tale," I whispered. Si lost a little of his melancholy and grinned.

An older man, bald but for a border of white curls around three sides of his head, appeared immediately at the front door, like he'd been stationed there waiting for our arrival.

"That's Frank," Si said. He waved at the man, then climbed out of the truck, and I followed.

Frank rattled down the porch stairs and over the path to greet us. "Silas!" he said, clapping Si on the bicep. "Heard you boys were doing an organized search today." He looked at me while he spoke, though, like my presence was way more exciting news.

"You heard right," Si said. "And this is Everett Maior, Hen—"

"Henry Lattimer's boy! Of course!" Frank shook my hand. "Haven't seen you since you were waist-high, but I heard you and Si were at the bakery together the other week! Myrna will be real excited too… *Myrna*!" he called. "Myrna? Get out here, honey! Si's brought Everett with him!"

Si looked down at his hiking boots and scratched the back of his head. He looked so bewildered by Frank's excitement, I had to bite the inside of my cheek to keep from laughing, and I couldn't help but admire the way his arms flexed as he moved them.

The door slammed and a tall, thin woman with gray-blonde hair came striding out of the house, her slippered feet *slap, slap, slapping* down the porch stairs and her bright-pink blouse floating behind her. She even looked like a Myrna.

"Good morning, Si!" she said. But she, too, looked at me as she said it. "Everett Maior! You sure have grown!"

From waist-high? "Yes, ma'am." I held out my hand. "Nice to see you."

Myrna ignored my hand and gathered me up in a two-armed hug. "Nonsense! I knew your mother back when we were girls! You're like a nephew or something."

She held on tight, rocking me from side to side, because no one in this town had any sense of personal space.

I hugged her back anyway.

"You boys are here for the search, eh?" She nodded to herself without waiting for a reply. "You're the first ones to come in this way, but I guess the rest'll be coming soon. You're welcome to take a peek at the poor man's campsite, if you'd like, but I don't think there's much to find."

"Thanks, Myrna," Si said. "I know Mitch already came out here, but it might help."

She nodded. "Mitch and Dare, both," she said. "New eyes are always good though, I guess. He was staying at site ten, the one closest to the river."

"Told John Carpenter he might as well stay there now, since it wouldn't be a campsite at all next year," Frank said gloomily.

I frowned and looked at Si, who scratched his cheek with one long finger before answering. "The State of New York is taking a small part of Frank's land."

"Small? Big enough!" Myrna corrected.

"Right," Si agreed, he shot me a tiny smile, lightning-fast, that managed to convey amusement and sympathy all at once. "I just meant, they're not taking the part with the house or the majority of the campsites, but a part up back there. They want to build a new, expanded visitor center and parking area."

"Eminent domain," Frank spat, shaking his head angrily. "Bastards."

"They're paving our paradise," Myrna sighed, resting her head on Frank's shoulder.

"Did you fight it?" Looking around the clearing, I was strangely moved. This place was beautiful. I understood the desire to want to keep all of it close, to protect it.

"Oh, sure. Our daughter Regan is a criminal attorney down in the city, and she got a friend of hers to look into it," Myrna said. "No dice."

"But we're not gonna let it go quietly! We'll keep

fighting until the trucks move in." Frank wrapped his arm around Myrna's waist.

"You two make sure you stay *safe*," Si cautioned. "Don't go looking for reasons why Dare will have to arrest you."

"Darius Turner," Frank sneered. "Mighta thought he was on our side, given how long he spent here as a kid."

"He *is* on your side, Frank. He works for the state, but he doesn't set policy," Si said, folding his arms across his chest. I could tell this was a discussion they'd had more than once. "Dare cares about both of you, and no one's sorrier than he is."

"Maybe," Frank allowed. "But maybe intentions don't matter as much as actions. Maybe there's right and wrong, and you need to stand up for things you care about because some things can't be undone."

Frank's words made my stomach jangle, and I frowned. I'd grown up steeped in superstition on my father's side of the family, and I wondered if this was some warning from the universe to stay away from Silas before it was too late, even as the pull of him throbbed like a toothache — insistent and impossible to ignore.

"Maybe there isn't one right answer," Si told Frank gently. "Maybe once you've fought the good fight and things didn't work out, it's okay to let it go and to be happy with what you still have. You don't have to stay angry forever."

*Whoa.*

The problem with superstition, of course, was that once you allowed it to catch hold of your brain, it was impossible to control. Once you opened yourself up to the possibility that the universe was sending you a *warning* disguised as two men discussing an eminent domain case, you had to accept that that same conversation could be the universe sending you some sort of tacit approval.

Even when you weren't sure you wanted it. Even when approval was by far the scarier option.

My cheeks flushed, and tears burned the backs of my eyes. I tried to suck in a breath, but my lungs stuttered, and I couldn't quite level out. *High-strung*, Grandpa Hen used to say. All that Romanian blood. All that artistic temperament.

"Ev? You alright?" Si asked. When he put his hand on my lower back, the warmth of him burned through all my layers and left my skin tingling. "You need anything?"

I needed very badly not to cry in front of strangers, and I was about to. I needed to stop the seesaw of emotions because I couldn't *hold them*, and I was drowning. I needed to be kissed, because it had been so damn long. I wanted to figure out how to get Si to make a move, since that seemed beyond my capabilities at this juncture, and I needed to let him know I was interested, since the man seemed to have finally gotten the message and backed off, just as I changed my mind. I wanted to hear him say my name again, just to feel the shiver of it flow through me in a way I'd never felt before, reaffirming for me that there *were* more things for me to experience and I was alive to experience them.

I wanted to just *be*.

Si studied me for a second, then nodded like I'd somehow managed to convey with a look, some fraction of what I couldn't articulate. We said our goodbyes to Frank and Myrna, with Si not seeming to care how strange it was that the high-strung freak of nature at his side was struck mute and on the brink of tears. He simply grabbed my backpack, took my hand, and led me into the woods.

# Chapter Eight



Ev and I walked deeper into the campground in complete silence. The path was narrow — barely wide enough for Frank's four-wheeler, let alone the two of us side by side, but I didn't let go of Ev's hand and he didn't ask me to.

I felt like this should be weirder than it was.

I'd more or less just held hands in front of Frank and Myrna — no, not *more or less*. That was exactly what I'd done — and the tale of it was one-hundred-percent making its way across O'Leary right now, growing with each re-telling. Sometime this weekend, my mother would hear that I'd been kneeling in the mud of Frank's driveway pledging my troth, and wouldn't *that* be a fun conversation to navigate?

But I hadn't considered that in the moment, and I really couldn't be bothered about it now. Ev was upset; I had the ability to take away some portion of that by making him feel less alone. And on a totally selfish level, I really liked the feeling of his smaller fingers laced with mine. It made my breathing come a little faster, both from the thrill of being close to him and... pure fear at how *thrilled* I was to be close to him. I didn't know if I'd ever held a man's hand unless I was holding him down to fuck him or cuff him.

I studiously avoided looking at Ev, though I was dying to. I didn't want him to be self-conscious about getting upset, and I didn't want him to have to explain things to me unless he wanted to. But I was pretty sure I wanted him to, which was a new sensation.

*Note to self: google the definition of casual.*

"So! Looks like the maple trees are starting to turn," I remarked, my gaze darting around like I'd never seen fall foliage. I had literally no experience in pretending to be casual because I'd never had to *play* at it before.

Ev made a noise of agreement. "The, uh… the yellow ones are maple?" He bent down to pick up a leaf by the stem and squeezed my hand for balance as he stood back up, and still neither of us commented on our hands at all.

"No, those are sycamore. The red ones over there are sugar maple."

Ev nodded and twirled the leaf between his fingers, seemingly fascinated.

"I'm super outdoorsy, as you can no doubt tell."

"It was clear to me from the first time you called it *orienteering*, back in the diner. That's pretty next-level," I agreed, and he snorted.

Suddenly, we were an awkward pair of teenagers who couldn't talk about anything that mattered, but maybe that was okay.

"I'll have you know, I was a Cub Scout," he said.

"Me too! I was an Eagle Scout in the end. How far did you get? Wolf, tiger…"

"Ah, right. I was a, um… dragon?"

"That's not a thing," I said sadly, though I swear the

sun shone hotter and brighter as I watched him smile mischievously. "Alas."

"Maybe not for *you*." He looked me up and down. "I mean, you weren't an *Advanced* Scout."

"Advanced!" I whistled. "I didn't even know there *was* such a thing."

"Well, first rule of Advanced Cub Scouts is…" Ev broke off. He gasped. "Damn. I've said too much."

And I squeezed his hand a little tighter because *goddamn*, I could spend the whole day just listening to this guy.

The path forked four ways, and I directed us to the one all the way on the right, which forked again a short distance later. We took the one that went uphill.

"This is it," I said when we'd crested the rise. "This is the site where John Carpenter was staying."

Ev frowned and shivered despite the warmth of the day, studying the clearing. Just like I'd done with my own house, I tried to imagine what *he* saw when he looked at it. Likely not ten years of scout campouts and teenage parties. Not a familiar little patch of well-trod ground.

"It's really open," he said, glancing at me, then at the blue sky visible beneath the thin branches above us. "But peaceful. A good place to think." He stood in total silence, letting the sun shine on his face and the breeze mess with his dark curls, so I stood there quietly too, memorizing the cut of his cheekbone and the tiny brown freckle in front of his ear.

He was so damn beautiful.

It was almost too much. My brain was buzzing, and I knew if the moment spun out any longer, something stupidly *real* would come spewing out of my mouth. I wasn't sure which of us would be more horrified if that happened.

But Ev pulled his hand away before I could ruin anything and tilted his head like he was listening for something. "D'you hear that?"

I frowned in concentration, but I couldn't hear anything but the *whoosh* of the wind and the creak of the tree branches. "Nope."

He shook his head. "Me neither, anymore. I would have sworn I heard *bells*. God. Add hallucinations to the list of symptoms that undiluted O'Leary might cause."

"Undiluted O'Leary?" I repeated.

"Mmm. Like on those medicine commercials? Exposure to undiluted O'Leary may cause chills, Ebola, prickly heat, increased appetite for sweets, sudden interest in football, and… hallucinations."

"Whoa. What the hell does it *cure?*"

Ev gave me a wry look. "I haven't figured that out yet." He sighed. "And this isn't even the first time I've imagined something. I thought I saw a ghost the night of my accident."

"What?" I hadn't realized he believed in that kind of stuff. It was weird in the most adorable way.

"Yeah." He grimaced. "When I said I saw a moose I actually, um… maybe… meant… a man?"

I frowned. "There was a man on the road?"

"No! No, that's what I'm saying." He shook his head. "It was a trick of the light or something, but it happened so fast, I'd already swerved to avoid it… him… *whatever.* After I crashed, I grabbed my flashlight and searched the road, but there was no one." He grimaced. "Total. Hallucination."

"God, Ev. That's… scary," I decided.

"I know. I mean, in my own defense I was exhausted and a little hung over, but…"

"But you blame undiluted O'Leary."

"It's a hell of a drug," he deadpanned. "You're probably immune to it by now, but trust me."

Something about the cement-block fire pit Frank had laid in the middle of the clearing caught his attention and he crouched down to look. "Hey! River rocks." He picked up a stone from a pile on one side of the pit. "Wonder how these got here."

"No shortage of rocks in the woods, Ev."

"Yeah, but these are smooth. See?" He held one out to me and I took it, startled by the warmth of the thing as it landed in my palm. He stood and took my hand in both of his, guiding my thumb to stroke the flat surface of the rock. It was one of the most erotic things anyone had done to me in thirty-eight years on this earth.

I needed to get *laid*. Jesus Christ.

I cleared my throat and closed my hand, trapping the stone.

"People collect them for good luck sometimes," I said hoarsely. "There's a river not far from here. Maybe half a mile east? We've even got ourselves a waterfall."

His eyes lit. "No way! A big one?"

"It's not Niagara, but yeah. Unfortunately, access is on the part of the property that's going to the state."

His mouth curled up in a rueful frown. "No wonder Frank and Myrna are upset."

"Yeah. Sucks for them, but it's good for visitors. And Frank and Myrna will still be able to hike there anytime they like."

"But it won't be theirs." Ev shrugged, picking up another of the rocks and smoothing it under his thumb. "It's not selfish to want something that's yours, is it?"

It sounded like an honest question, so I answered it

honestly. "There's not a thing wrong with wanting that. But like I told Frank, you have to play with the hand you're dealt. There's no… I dunno, higher moral ground, or whatever… in staying angry all the time. Not everything in life has to be a struggle, Ev. Sometimes you can just let go."

He sucked in a breath and stood abruptly. "Can we see the waterfall?"

"Uh. You want to? It's a bit of an uphill climb."

He shrugged and tossed his stone back to the ground. "I mean, I'm guessing we didn't come out here just to poke around this empty site, right?"

I nodded. "I was gonna pick some flatter terrain, but the waterfall trail is great. Definitely one of the more likely places John Carpenter could have headed." Then because I was maturing in reverse, I added, "Betcha the view beats anything you had back East."

Ev smiled and crossed his arms over his chest. "Says who? You?"

I nodded solemnly. "I know things, Ev."

"Absolutely," he laughed. "You know every cylinder is just a penis in disguise."

I rolled my eyes and assessed him, from his gym shoes to the light shirt he'd thrown over his t-shirt. His body was compact and spare; sexy as hell, but not helpful when you were walking uphill. "You sure you're up for a challenge?"

Everett gave me the same look he'd given me the first time I'd met him, the one that dared me to insinuate *again* that he wasn't up to a task. "I'm not incapable of hiking, Si." He slapped his thigh. "Quads of *steel.*"

I wasn't sure which part of this I liked more.

I grinned. "Alright then." I hooked a thumb at the path we'd taken. "We've gotta head back down so we can head up." Without thinking, I held out a hand for Ev, and he took it.

"You said your brother liked to draw, right? Did he come out here?" Ev asked a few minutes later. "The light is just incredible."

I hesitated for a second. I didn't mind talking about Matty. I *loved* to. But everyone in town remembered him as a tragedy, a thing we talked *around*. I couldn't remember the last time someone wanted to know anything about the person he'd been, or even said his name without expressing pity.

Ev likely mistook my silence for reluctance. "I'm sorry. Forget I asked. Gosh, these maple trees are really…"

"Matty painted out here all the damn time," I blurted. "He'd fill a backpack with art supplies and disappear for a whole day." I glanced down to find Ev concentrating on the trees which to me seemed utterly unremarkable. They were pretty uniformly green, still. "Would you want to bring your stuff out here? I think Matty had a portable easel-thing, if you need one."

His attention snapped to me and he frowned. "Thanks, but no. I told you before, I haven't painted in a long while."

"Sure, but if you wanted to do it again, you could."

"Just that easy, huh?" he demanded, his eyes sparking with annoyance.

"Well, no, but…"

He waved a hand through the air, cutting me off. "No, I'm sorry. That's not… I just haven't felt inspired in a while," he said.

"Oh."

"It's not something I know how to call back, and that's frustrating. But I don't really know if I want to, either? I think it'd be a little like, I dunno, blood coming back into your foot when you've been sitting on it too long." He grimaced.

"Painful? Scary?"

"Little of both." He blew out a breath and changed the subject with so little finesse it almost made me smile. "Seems like a peaceful place, a great place for solitude."

"Maybe. But more often than not, Matty used to come up here with Molly Burke. They were thick as thieves. They, uh, died in the same car accident on their way back to school. Out on the Camden road, not too far from where you had your accident. Twelve years ago this month."

"I'm sorry." He hesitated. "God, I really hate saying that."

"It's okay. Thanks. It was a long time ago. It gets easier."

"Do you ever feel like… I dunno." Ev squeezed my hand tightly. I wasn't sure he was aware he was doing it. "Like you need to be *more* because he can't be here too?"

Wow. That wasn't a thought I'd ever articulated before, but it settled over me comfortably.

"For myself, it's gotten easier," I said eventually. "I can have a shit day without feeling like an ungrateful bastard for not enjoying every extra minute I get on the planet. But it's a little harder when I'm with my parents. Like, they don't remember Matty as a person as much as a dream they had for the future. He was a total shit," I said, grinning. "Used to draw naked caricatures of me with my hair up in this fabulous pompadour and sell them to kids in his class for a dollar."

Ev laughed out loud. "Well, you do have fabulous hair."

"Thank you so much for noticing."

He laughed again.

"I don't think my parents remember that stuff, though,

you know? They lost this smart, sensitive kid who was going to set the world on fire, and give them a daughter-in-law and grandkids to spoil. That's the tragedy for them. And I mean, it's not that it's less sad to lose that than to lose your sidekick, it's just not the same thing I lost." My smile faded. "I can't relate. And I can't mitigate that loss for them, even if I wish I could. No daughters-in-law here. No kids." I shrugged.

"Right, and they can't relate to you losing your brother, either. Which is doubly hard for you."

I frowned. "I guess that's true. I hadn't thought of it that way." Which was pretty much the thing I thought most often when I was with Everett Maior. He made me think differently about so many things, and *I liked it.* "I mean, O'Leary lives to remember the tragedy."

"But that's not the same either. Your parents are grieving the future, and O'Leary's remembering the past, but you just miss your brother. Right? You want to remember him as he was, and not the way they think of him."

My heart squeezed painfully tight. "Yeah."

Ev closed his eyes and sighed like he totally understood. We kept walking.

"Part of the problem is that his best friend died at the same time he did," I said a moment later. "I mean, if there was anyone else who got him the way I did, it was Molly. I miss her too."

"I can see that."

"You know, she used to work out here at the campground. Technically, she was supposed to handle summer bookings for Myrna and Frank, but I don't know how much time she ever spent in the office." I tried for a smile, but it felt foreign on my face. "She was a brilliant photographer. You can see some of her stuff over at Frank and Myrna's place. She'd take a picture of something and I'd suddenly see it in a different way. Just like you were talking about with the kids at your school."

Ev smiled. "I love that."

"Yeah. It's funny. They were way younger than me. Eight years. Which is, like, a hundred lifetimes when you're young."

"How old are you?" Ev asked. "Thirty-eight?"

"Uh-huh. Matty would have been thirty this year." My chest tightened around the words.

"Well, remember I'm twenty-nine," Ev teased. "Does that make me *more* than a hundred lifetimes younger than you?"

I hip-checked him lightly, and he chuckled.

"And he drew?" Ev prompted carefully. "Caricatures and other things?"

I laughed. "Yeah. Yeah, he just..." I broke off and shook my head, feeling the smile fall from my face. "I've never been as good at anything as he was at drawing. Everyone said he *had* a gift, but I thought... I thought he *was* a gift. I walk through these woods and I see *sugar maples*, and squirrels, and chipmunks, but he saw *light* and life and color. He could make things dance in two dimensions."

I chanced a glance at Ev and found that his eyes were closed and he wore a small smile. "Sorry," I said. "I get carried away."

His eyes popped open, and they were shining. "Don't be sorry. Don't ever be sorry. I sometimes wish I could talk..." He shook his head. "Never mind. That was beautiful. I think anyone would be proud to be remembered that way."

I cleared my throat. "Yeah, well. I try to see things the

way he saw them now, but I don't have the same talent. It's a little bit like looking at one of those hidden-image pictures, you know? The ones where you try to look *through* the shapes and colors and hope something pops out at you in 3-D?"

Ev chuckled. "I know what you mean."

"I have a fifty-fifty success rate." I shrugged, then admitted, "It was easier when he was alive." A lot of things were easier when Matty was alive.

Ev's hand tightened on mine to the point of pain, but I didn't protest. "You loved him. Both of them," he said.

"Of course. My brother and my honorary sister." I paused. "Not that they were involved romantically, though. People used to speculate — that's O'Leary's favorite pastime, if you hadn't noticed — but there was nothing there. Molly dated Shane Goode from the diner forever. I bet she would've married him after college."

Ev frowned and shook his head. "I don't think I've met Shane."

"He was at the diner this morning. Tall, thin, long dark hair, probably said hi when you came in? No? Well, he's easy enough to overlook. He's a good kid. Moody, sometimes, but I get it. He didn't have anyone in his life but Molly, really. Now he goes to work every day and his manager is Molly's older brother, Jamie." I winced. "Not easy to live with those reminders constantly."

"Yeah," Ev said softly. "It's not easy."

The path through the woods was steep and covered with slippery pine needles. I gave Ev a little push, letting him go in front of me so I could catch him if he fell. But he surprised me by turning right in the middle of the path and looking at me defiantly.

"My husband Adrian died last June. I mean, a year ago June. Fifteen… no, sixteen months ago?" He frowned like he was surprised it had been that long. "I don't… I don't talk about it. But I thought you should know."

My jaw dropped. He'd lost his *husband*? When Mitch said he'd heard Ev had a hell of a year, I'd imagined… I dunno, a job loss or something. The kind of tragedy a twenty-nine-year-old *should* have to handle. Pretty dumb of me not to remember that life handed out shit regardless of age or station.

"Ev," I said. "Fuck. That's just…"

"Yeah," he said softly. "Yeah, it is."

He turned around and started climbing again, and I trailed behind him. My brain was whirling, trying to reconnect the snippets of the Ev I'd thought I knew in light of this new information. I had so many questions, things I was dying to know, like what had made him pull away from me two weeks ago, and was he even remotely in the right place to consider falling for someone else?

But I wasn't sure I had any right to ask those things, and it was pretty clear he wouldn't answer them if I did.

I was still stunned at how much Everett had understood about *me*, though, and I thought… well, maybe I could offer the same to him. Even if I'd just been projecting all of my own hopeless attraction onto him, even if he only wanted to be friends.

Friends who held hands.

"You know, if you ever wanted to talk, I'd really like to hear…"

A branch cracked sharply to my left, and I whirled to face the possible threat. A vaguely familiar blond figure about my height emerged from the dense scrub with his hands up.

"Just me," the man said, voice low and calm, like I was a startled animal. "Sorry for disturbing you."

My heart still racing madly, I nodded and tried to

relax. "Yeah. No problem. My fault for not paying attention. Daniel Michaelson, right?"

The man nodded. He was dressed for hiking in a moisture-wicking t-shirt and nylon pants Dare would've approved, and I recognized the logo on the strap of his backpack as a high-end brand. He scratched the back of his head, clearly uncomfortable with my perusal.

"I'm Si," I reminded him. "Si Sloane. And this is Everett Maior. He's new to town."

Ev offered his hand, and Daniel shook it. "Same here," Daniel said. "Maybe been here… seven months now?"

"So there's more than one of us. Excellent. Nice to meet you," Ev said.

"Were you just out hiking, or are you here for the search party?" I asked.

Daniel frowned. "Search party? Someone's missing?"

"Same camper went missing a while back. Did you hear about that?"

"Yeah." Daniel nodded and threaded his thumbs under the straps on his backpack. "Someone mentioned it. In town."

I nodded slowly. "Well, we're mostly looking to see if we can find any sign of where he might have disappeared or maybe even spot his gear."

"I haven't seen anything out of place, but I wasn't really looking." Daniel glanced back in the direction he'd come. "I was just at the overlook south of the falls, and it was the same as ever."

"Beautiful?" Ev said.

Daniel smiled, a small fragile thing on a man his size. "Always is. Nothing like a waterfall to clear things away, you know? Reminds you of your place in the universe."

Ev smiled back, the way I'd only seen him smile at me — soft and real. I was unreasonably jealous about that. "I know that feeling," Ev said. "I've gotten it at the beach before, when the waves are really whipping."

Daniel's grin widened. "Exactly like that. Like just before a storm. Wild and unstoppable." His grin fell away as he glanced at me, and he went back to being nervous. "I can, ah, stick around? If you want help?"

"No," I said quickly. "No. I think Dare Turner had a bunch of people interested. But thanks."

"Sure." Daniel nodded. "Nice to meet you, Ev. Si." He gave a tiny wave and continued down the trail.

I found myself frowning after him.

"What's that look for?" Ev said.

"Huh?"

"You're scowling. He seemed like a nice guy."

"I dunno. Seems a little odd to me," I said, though I'd honestly never thought anything about Daniel Michaelson one way or another before Ev smiled at him. "Wandering around out here. Alone."

Ev snorted. "Watch out. You sound like my grandfather. Or that Karen person," he warned. "Which way to the falls?"

I pointed right, and he moved off quickly, not waiting for or wanting my help.

I sighed as I watched him walk away, and tightened the straps of Ev's backpack on my back as I followed him.

He could hardly get lost now. Within a minute, the hiss of rushing water filled the air, growing louder and louder with every step. The air was thick here, humid and chilly, thanks to the thick tree canopy and the kicked-up spray from the falls. In winter, the tree branches in this area got coated with ice and the whole damn place sparkled in the sunlight like something from a fairy tale. Today it wasn't nearly that pretty but the sun was shining brilliantly, and I had an idea.

"Hold up," I yelled. "Everett! Hold up!" When I grabbed his arm and turned him, his face was set mulishly.

"What?"

"This way," I said, pointing off to the side just slightly, where there was no broken trail through the underbrush.

Ev hesitated. "Why aren't we staying on a trail?"

"Because this is a secret spot," I told him seriously. "And you have to pinkie swear never to reveal it to anyone." *Especially Daniel Michaelson*, I thought but didn't say.

His eyes narrowed. "Is this a trick? Come check out my van by the river, I have candy? And meanwhile, I get stuck in a giant vat of mud?"

I barked out a laugh. "Geez, you're suspicious. Not a trick. Not *Deliverance*. Just a… a cool thing," I said lamely.

His eyebrows lifted just a tiny bit. "A cool, secret thing."

I inclined my head. "A place where Matt and I used to go when he was a kid. Our secret spot."

He bit his lip and his eyes went soft. "Fine. Lead on."

I reached for his hand and he let me take it, let me guide him over the slippery ferns and fallen leaves that formed the forest floor. The rush of water became overwhelming as we got closer to the source. And then suddenly, the trees around us were just… gone, and we were standing on rocky outcropping forty feet above the river, just a few feet away from the most dramatic part of the falls.

"Holy shit," Ev breathed, as he came up beside me. "This is…"

"Cool?"

He laughed, his green eyes shining up at me. "Yeah," he agreed. "Definitely cool. This is a *great* secret spot."

The sunlight refracted off the millions of tiny water droplets that hovered in the air and clung to Ev's hair and eyelashes, making them shimmer like diamonds. Everything around us seemed impossibly clean and new. Ev's fingers twitched in mine.

We stared at the water for long minutes. I found it soothing, hypnotic almost, the white noise and utter power of the falls making my brain fall quiet. But I wished I knew what Ev saw. I wished I could see it the way he did.

"I don't even know how I would paint this," he whispered, like he could hear my thoughts. His voice was hushed, broken. "But I kinda want to try." He looked up at me, like he'd shocked himself. "I do want to try."

I nodded. "That's good. Someday, if you want, we can…"

"No, Si. You don't get it." He pulled me away from the edge of the world, back into the safety of the trees, and grinned up at me. His smile was a feral thing, wild as this place, and nothing I'd ever seen or imagined on Everett Maior before. "I haven't felt this way since… God, long before Adrian died. And when I saw this, my fingers itched for a brush and… I don't know. It's not painful at all. It's fucking amazing."

"Oh." I grinned back at him. I couldn't have resisted that smile even if I wanted to. "That's great, Ev. That's…"

Ev kissed me with the force of a heavyweight boxer, a sucker punch that literally sent me reeling into a giant oak tree.

"Wait," I said, lifting a hand to my bruised lip and another to his shoulder. "Ev, what…"

But Ev didn't seem to want to talk… or think, or breathe, or any of those mundane things. He lifted both hands to my cheeks, stood on his tiptoes, and dragged my face down to his. "Just kiss me, Silas," he breathed. His eyes were alive with excitement and more than a little pleading.

I wasn't sure what alternate universe I'd entered, that Ev was begging me to do the thing I'd been trying to stop myself from doing since the minute I'd met him, but I didn't hesitate. I wrapped a hand through the back of his damp curls and hauled him more firmly against me.

# Chapter Nine

## EVERETT

HOLY *SHIT* COULD Si Sloane kiss.

It was a beautiful thing, hotter and sweeter than I'd ever imagined, not that I'd ever allowed myself to imagine *this*. If imagining him putting his arms around me was a betrayal of Adrian, this would be…

*No. Not today, Satan.* For once, I was just going to enjoy something.

I ran my fingers through the short, dark hair at the nape of his neck that felt like silk between my fingers. I concentrated on the slide of his tongue against mine, and the way his arms were braced around my waist and shoulders, pressing us together from chest to belly. I inhaled the sharp tang of pine and the warm, clean scent of Si that had roughly the same effect on me as that goddamn waterfall, erasing every other memory and every other smell.

I wanted to lose myself in him, and I let it happen.

I pulled back, breathless, to study his face. I traced the curve of his eyebrow and the tiny, fascinating little scar at the edge of his lip.

"Fistfight?" I whispered.

"What?" He sounded drugged, and I loved it. "No. Uh. Football. Cut it with my tooth."

"You played football?" I demanded. This seemed like crucial information somehow, something I needed to know *now*, in this moment when I had him backed up against a tree at the edge of a forest.

When he nodded, his nose bumped against mine, making this stupid conversation almost unbearably intimate. "Wide receiver."

I didn't give two shits about football on any given day, but now all I could think about was Si, with his shoulders already as big as the other guys even without his pads, his muscular legs bulging out of his tight pants, and that hyper-focused, predatory look in his eyes.

The look he was giving me now.

I pulled his head down and kissed him again and swallowed his groan.

It was the easiest thing in the world to trace the side of his neck with my lips, to tease the edge of his shirt with my chilly fingertips. His whole body jerked like I'd electrocuted him, and it was insanely powerful to know I'd caused it. I let my palms coast down the hard planes of his chest, pull the shirt from his waistband, and then coast up again, feeling each individual muscle of his stomach contract as I grazed it.

My tongue found his earlobe and the salty taste was so real that I bit down on it, hard.

"Fuck, Ev! *Fuck*. What should we…?"

But this was not a time for questions, because the easy ones led to the hard ones, and I had no answers for any of them.

"Shhh," I said, pulling back just far enough to catch his

eyes, which were nearly black in the shadows. I stroked my thumb over the scar on his lip again, then tasted it with my tongue. "Shhh."

I sank to my knees and my hands went to the waistband of Si's pants. He frowned down at me. "Ev, wait…"

But I didn't want to wait any more than I wanted to talk. For once, I wanted to break the rules, because following them hadn't helped me anyway. I wanted to feel, I wanted to make *him* feel.

I unzipped him quickly, pushing his pants down to his thighs and nuzzled my face against the soft cotton of his boxer briefs. He was only half hard, but he hissed like he was already on the brink of something. He reached down and grabbed two handfuls of my hair like reins, a move I'd always hated but which right now set me on *fire*.

"Everett. Talk to me," Silas demanded, yanking on my curls, and I groaned loudly.

*Fuck*, that felt good. If Si thought that pulling my hair was going to be a deterrent, he was so, so wrong.

I ran my nose along the front of his underwear, my breath blowing warm against his cock, which was perking up with gratifying speed. "How about less talk, more action?" I whispered against him. He frowned, but his eyes had glazed over and I was pretty sure he had no clue what I was talking about. "Do you want me to stop?" I teased.

He shook his head, probably purely out of instinct, and before he could change his mind, I grinned up at him and curled my fingers under the waistband of his boxers. "Good," I said, and then I yanked.

His cock slipped out and whacked me in the face, which was apparently the hottest accident that ever could have happened, if the predatory look in Si's eyes was anything to go by. His mouth firmed, his frown disappeared, and this time when his fingers tightened on my head, he was urging me forward. "Do it," he whispered. "Please."

*Oh, yeah.* I smirked and wrapped my chilly hand around the base of him, then licked a broad stripe up the underside, holding his gaze the whole time. He shivered and inhaled a huge, stuttering breath, like his lungs had forgotten how to work. I could just imagine how the hot and cold felt together, and I wanted to give him more.

Sex was supposed to be like riding a bike... or some bullshit like that... and maybe that was so with the basic mechanics. But I'd never had sex like this before, and the logistics of blowing a very tall man against a tree in a fucking forest were the least of what made it different.

Sex had always been fun, but more like a means to an end, a race to an orgasm. I couldn't ever remember feeling an urgency like this, an ache in my own balls every time my fingers grazed Silas's. I'd never needed to give someone pleasure that reflected back just a tiny portion of the joy they'd rekindled in me. I'd never sunk to my knees with the lash of desire and gratitude and need at my back. I'd never sucked someone's dick down my throat with a noise so animalistic it startled me.

And I'd never, never been so attuned to someone's responses. I wanted to hoard his every reaction, to collect his every sigh and groan, every thrust and shudder in the corner of my mind, like a pile of lucky river rocks I could worry over later.

I was on a cliff. Surrounded by mist. Wearing jeans that were going to be fucking *ruined* by the mud and make it really obvious that this "hike" had mostly happened on my knees. My dick was hard behind the fly of my jeans, and I barely noticed. And somehow it was so damn *good*, all of it. So right, my belly flipped.

Who the hell *was* I right now?

I didn't know. I didn't care. I sucked harder.

"Ev," he moaned. He tapped my shoulder in warning, but I gripped his hip with one hand and tightened the other, jerking as I sucked, wanting him to spill down my throat. He did a second later, hot and bitter and musky-perfect, and I wanted more. I wanted to sink into this forever.

A tear tracked down my face and startled the hell out of me.

*Oh, nice, Ev. Extraordinary.*

I barely swallowed his cum before I started crying — big fat tears rolling down my face, shoulders shaking, breath hiccupping, the whole nine yards.

I was twenty pounds of fucked up in a ten-pound bag.

"Ev?" Si said, cradling my cheek in his palm. "Are you… No, obviously you're not okay. Can we talk?"

I shook my head, unwilling to look up at him.

"We should go," I whispered.

"Please don't do this," he begged. "I'm sorry. I shouldn't have let things go this far."

I shook my head. The only thing worse than talking about this would be letting him think that it was in any way his fault.

That there was *any* fault to be found in this at all.

I wiped my damp cheeks on my fingers, and my fingers on the legs of his jeans, then I pulled his underwear up and pushed myself to my feet.

"I'm not upset about this," I said firmly, staring down at my own boots. My cock was still half-hard, which was possibly more fucked up than anything. "I wanted that. I'm *glad* it happened. It's just… a lot."

"Okay," Si said. He buttoned and zipped his pants, then reached for my shoulders, probably to pull me into his embrace, but I couldn't handle it.

I turned away instead.

"I want to understand, but I don't," Si admitted. "Is this about… about Adrian?"

I sucked in a breath. Hearing his name was a shock, and not just because it was Si saying it, or because of what we'd done.

"I don't talk about him," I told Si.

"It still hurts?" he guessed, frowning. "I mean, there's no time limit on…"

"Ugh!" I covered my face with both my hands. "That's not it. Or maybe…" I sucked in a breath, tried to make sense of what made *no fucking sense*. "I do better when I don't talk about him, okay? I keep all the memories in my head, locked up safe." My voice was muffled, but whatever. I was pretty sure he wouldn't understand me even if he could hear me. I sounded insane to my own ears.

"And you keep his memory safe by keeping it to yourself?"

I nodded miserably.

"Like Frank and Myrna with this land?" His voice was teasing but soft, easy. "You don't want people trampling all over it or using it all up?"

"Go ahead. Tell me it's fucked up and superstitious." You couldn't use up a memory or dilute it. I knew there was no logic to that. "I already know."

He grabbed my wrists and pried my hands away from his face. "Careful," he said. "You're starting to sound like your grandfather now."

But then he put his finger under my chin and forced me to look up at him. "You're okay, Ev. You are. Grief isn't linear, and it doesn't *end*, it just evolves. Really fucking slowly sometimes." He bent and pressed a soft, chaste kiss to my lips and then to the top of my head.

He grabbed my hand before I could think to pull away

and held it tightly, like maybe my bullshit didn't scare him. My heart cracked a tiny bit and a few more tears leaked out.

I heard voices heading our way — chatter and laughter loud enough to mean a whole bunch of people were tramping around out here, likely searching for the missing camper. I scrubbed at my eyes furiously. *Crying? Why yes, I am, because as you can see from my jeans, which are fucking soaked with mud, I gave Silas Sloane a blow job and then lost my mind.*

"Come on," Si said. "I doubt they'll come this way, but let's head over the top of the falls anyhow. There's no trail, but it's gotta join up with the area around John Carpenter's campsite eventually."

I sniffed loudly, wiping the last of my tears on my shirt. "Local cop and art teacher found mauled by squirrels in woods…"

"Squirrels?" Si frowned. "What?"

"…after suffering from exposure…"

His expression cleared. "Afraid it's not nearly cold enough for that, babe," he said, turning me to face away from him and pushing me gently between the shoulder blades. "And not a cloud in the sky."

"…or possibly dehydration."

"Uh-huh," he grabbed my hand again, like I wasn't moving fast enough and towed me along behind him. "Your backpack has been sloshing on my back for the past mile, and we're feet from fresh water."

I sighed. "If the worst happened and you were starving, I wouldn't care if you had to eat my corpse to survive."

"Where do these thoughts come from?" Si demanded, but his eyes were dancing with laughter, like these weird tangents delighted him. "Your mind is like a labyrinth; you steer down a path and I never know if you're going to find a secret garden or a dementor."

"No shit," I said sourly. "Welcome to my life. And here's me without a wand or a Patronus."

Si grinned. "Ev, honey, if the worst happened, I'd take one of our cell phones and call for pizza. We're only a mile from Frank's place. There's still a signal out here."

"But just in case…"

"Just in case," he agreed. "I consent to this cannibalism pact." He pressed another kiss to my lips like a seal.

"I might have a tendency to be overly dramatic," I confessed a second later. I brushed the fingers of my free hand over my mouth because I could still feel Si's lips against mine, and I waited for the guilt I *knew* I should be feeling to assail me, but it didn't. "It can be a bit much."

He stopped and turned completely. "Hilarious, that's what it is. And sexy. And *frustrating*, which somehow is also sexy. I like you, Everett. Keep that in mind. Just in case."

He turned and started walking again and I scrambled to keep up. My diaphragm was having trouble working properly.

"Shouldn't be too much further," he said. The sound of the falls had receded slightly, though I could see peeks of water through the trees from the river that fed it. "Maybe just a…"

He stopped short, and so did I.

"Bells," I whispered, remembering the sound I thought I'd imagined before.

They weren't really bells, but wind chimes — enormous wooden ones that clanked satisfyingly, smaller, tinkling glass ones, and even a couple of sets of metal ones that clinked like coins — all tied to tree branches in a loose circular shape, like some kind of fairy ring.

"What is it?" I asked wonderingly.

Si shook his head. "I don't know," he said, sounding more annoyed than impressed. "I'll ask Frank and Myrna, but I don't know if they ever come up this far."

I took a step around him and reached out a hand to touch one of the hundreds of short bushes that filled the circle. Their leaves were already gone and they looked oddly skeletal, long bones topped with fully intact seed heads.

"Don't," Si said, grabbing my hand. "That's giant hogweed. It's poisonous."

"Poisonous?" I gasped, and Si shook his head, looking at me like I was adorably naive.

"Think poison ivy, not arsenic. If you touch it, it'll make your skin blister like you wouldn't believe, but it wouldn't kill you."

I put my hand in my pocket anyway.

"Dare is gonna bitch about this," he predicted. "Hogweed's invasive. The state's gonna have to come out here and remove it all."

"That's sad." I looked around at the chimes again. "Do you think they'll leave these alone? Someone went to a lot of trouble."

"Yeah," he agreed. "I wondered if they were Molly's, at first. She was super into stuff like this. But most of these look new. Metal's barely rusted." He lifted a hand to the closest set of chimes and frowned again.

"You don't like them? Mystical, kind of. Like a real-life version of relaxation songs. You've got water, and chimes, and trees. It's pretty."

"Pretty *weird*, if Frank and Myrna didn't set this up." He took out his phone and snapped a couple of pictures before sliding it away. "But as far as I can tell without a map, all this will be part of the new visitor center area anyway."

I frowned. "That's too bad. It seems wrong to change a place as natural and perfect as this one."

"This from the man who was convinced we'd be mauled by squirrels?"

"Not here. The chimes would protect us."

Si managed to frown and raise one eyebrow at the same time. The epitome of intrigue and disbelief.

I sighed. "In a lot of different cultures, wind chimes repel evil spirits and attract good ones. It's a *thing*. The chimes exist in a place between the physical and spiritual worlds."

"Where did you learn all this?" he demanded, not annoyed but fascinated. "Do you believe in it?"

"I don't *not* believe in it, I guess. And I learned because my grandmother was… you know, into this stuff. New age things."

"Not Anna," Si said. "There's no way."

"Oh my God, no. Can you imagine? Grandpa Hen would've birthed kittens. No, my dad's mom. She lived near us in Boston." I elbowed him lightly. "She's the one to blame for my superstitious nature."

One side of his mouth turned up in a smile. "Then I think I would have liked her. How about if we head back to the car, I'll let Dare know about this *place*, and then I can take you back to my house. I, uh, have something of yours."

"Something of mine?" My eyes narrowed, but he clapped a hand over my mouth before I could speak again.

"Yes, something of yours. Yes, back at my house. No, I don't have a dungeon, but keep it up and you might inspire me to build one. No, I don't have candy, little boy, but we have your water bottles, and there are still no banjos, just freaky, weird chimes. Okay?" He laughed.

I sighed, even though my heart was leaping. This guy

just totally *got* me. "Fine. If you wanna take all the fun out of the thing."

"Who gave you your *suspicious* nature?"

I laughed. "Oh, that's all me, I'm afraid."

"Just trust me," he said, tugging on my hand.

And I didn't say it out loud, but I was pretty sure I already did.

# Chapter Ten

SILAS

I THREW OPEN the door to Hoff's, and the wall of heat pouring out of the place nearly made me want to turn around and go back outside. Half an hour before kickoff, the bar was already packed so full of O'Learians I imagined there was some kind of fire code violation happening.

Or maybe a noise violation, because *holy shit* was it loud.

I looked around the bar for Ev, or for Henry, who might know where Ev was, but I didn't see either one and I was pretty unreasonably disappointed about that.

"Si! Over here!" Jamie Burke screamed from a tall table in the corner where he was standing with Frank, Shane, and Julian Ross. Jamie's face was already flushed, his dark red hair was askew, and his eyes were suspiciously bright. I wished I could blame the overheated room, but I was pretty sure the array of empty glasses on the table in front of him were the culprit.

Why did the guy keep coming back to this bar when it fucked him up so badly? Why couldn't he stay away?

"Hey, guys," I said, shucking my sweatshirt and tying it around my waist. "What's going on?"

"Heard about the memorial service your mom's putting together," Shane offered. "Sounds real nice."

"Yeah," Jamie grunted. "It's really kind of her to also include Molly. I appreciate that." He chugged more beer.

I smiled wanly. The fall was the worst time of year for my mother. From January to August, it was possible to have a conversation with her that didn't revolve around memories, but once the pumpkin-spice started flowing, it was like a switch flipped in her brain. All she could think about from September onward was Matty — how sad she was without him, how much she missed him when she lit a fire in her fireplace, what she would have liked to get him for Christmas.

It made me angry every time I talked to her — angry that she was holding on to the past so hard, she was missing the present — and I'd been avoiding her calls all week, hoping to minimize my exposure to The Weeping.

Clearly, my absence hadn't dimmed her enthusiasm.

"So… Day off, Dr. Ross?" I slapped Julian on the shoulder.

"Yep. Unless any animal emergencies occur," Julian said, tapping a black cell phone that rested on the table, next to a platter of appetizers and a half-empty pint glass. "We're just, uh, trying to relax and have fun." He glanced at Jamie, then widened his eyes at me.

"What Julian's trying to convey is that Jamie here is already on his fourth beer, won't eat the food because it all *tastes like sewage*, and won't listen to Shane or me when we try to get him to leave," Frank said.

Julian tilted his head at Frank in exasperation and Frank shrugged. "What? Am I wrong?"

Jamie rolled his eyes so hard, he had to grab the table

to keep his balance. "You guys are all ridiculous. I'm not *drunk*. I'm just not going to eat the third-rate shit that Parker serves." He picked up a chicken wing from the platter and let it drop back with a wet *thwap* that splattered hot sauce all over his blue t-shirt.

"Jamie, come *on*," Shane said, bracing a hand on the base of Jamie's neck, even though Jamie had a few inches and a couple of dozen pounds on him. "I knew this wouldn't be a good idea. Let's just leave. I'll walk you back to your place, and…"

"I'm not leaving," Jamie shot back, jerking away from Shane's hold. He pushed the brim of Shane's Jets hat down so it covered his eyes. "I'm not letting *Parker Hoffs-traeder* and the fact that Parker is an incompetent, soulless asshole who doesn't understand essential concepts like *friendship* and how much fucking *sauce* to put on a *chicken wing* prevent me from enjoying the game with my friends!" He spread his big hands wide. "This is *my* town."

Shane adjusted his hat and sighed.

Julian, Frank, and I exchanged glances, but I figured it fell to me to state the obvious. "It's Parker's town too."

Jamie shook his head and took another deep drink of his beer. "Nope. No, Si." He wiped his mouth with the back of his hand. "That's where you're wrong, actually. I mean, legally? Sure. Whatever. But he moved away to Boston. He left us all behind. You don't just get to… to *leave*, then come back like nothing happened." He spoke with the utter reasonableness of the exceptionally drunk. "You don't just get to *do* that." The pain in his voice was a palpable thing.

"Have you tried talking to him? Since he came back?" Julian suggested. "Maybe it'd be better if you, like, aired your differences, instead of you getting upset every time you walk in this place? Maybe he could tell you his reasons for coming back or… whatever?"

Jamie laughed, an ugly sound. "Now, *that* is an idea. That is a *hell* of an idea. I'll ask him how many of his Boston friends he fucked over when he moved back *here*."

Jamie looked around the bar like he wanted to ask Parker now — with his fists.

"Ah, shit," Frank said under his breath. "How good are you at patching up humans, Julian?"

"Text your brother," I told Julian, nodding at his cell. "He's on call today. Ask Constantine to come and get Jamie home."

Julian nodded and started texting.

"No fucking way! The game hasn't even…"

"Jamie," I said, as seriously as I could. "Not again. We've brought you in way too many times already this summer. You need to sort your shit and stay away from Parker until you can figure out how to get right with him. This isn't helping you, Jamie."

"Bullshit," Jamie yelled. He slammed his glass on the table, and it slid forward, rocking precariously. "But fine. You want me to leave? I'll leave!" Conversations stopped as people turned to look at us.

Shane wrapped an arm around Jamie's shoulder, tugging him toward the exit, and Jamie let him. But before Shane could push the heavy wooden door open, Jamie turned back like he wanted to say one more thing. And of course, the crowd chose that moment to part like the fucking Red Sea, leaving nothing but empty space between Jamie and Parker Hoffstraeder, his former best friend.

Parker stared at Jamie, his gray eyes stormy and completely bewildered. He ran a hand through his short, blond hair. "Jamie, I…"

For a second, I worried that Jamie was going to

attack Parker, the anger on his face burned so hot, and I was stunned into immobility because that wasn't the Jamie I knew. Jamie Burke was friendly, affable, and funny as hell.

Then again, maybe Molly and Matty's anniversary was messing with his mind.

"Looks like you win again, Parker," Jamie said bitterly. He glared at the folks nearby who'd stopped what they were doing to stare at him. "Enjoy the game." He shouldered Shane out of the way and shoved the door open, escaping into the chilly afternoon.

Parker swallowed and shook his head like he was trying to shake off Jamie's anger. He smiled hard at the people who'd likely be feasting on this drama for a week. "Who needs a refill before kickoff? There's still a few minutes left."

His words were like a starting pistol, and suddenly everyone was in motion. Even Frank and Julian headed for the bar and the buffet table, respectively. Only Parker stood motionless.

"You alright?" I asked him, laying a hand on his shoulder.

He didn't look at me. "Of course. Fine."

Right. Of course. "Parker, you've gotta stop letting him in here," I said. "Or if you do let him in, don't let him drink. You're not doing him any favors when he ends up causing a ruckus and we have to bring him down to the station to sleep it off."

"I haven't pressed charges," Parker said staunchly. He stared at the door like he was hoping Jamie might reappear. "And I won't."

"But one of these days he's gonna hurt someone, or maybe himself."

"Nah. Jamie knows how to control himself. He's pissed,

but he'll come around," Parker said. He sounded like he was trying to convince himself.

"I hope so." I clapped him on the shoulder. "So, have you seen, uh… Henry Lattimer?"

Parker's face lightened. "Henry? Why? You need some building advice for that apartment over your garage?"

I sighed. Figured Parker had heard about the apartment. Some helpful resident had probably put together a *Welcome Back to O'Leary* fact sheet with all the important recent town happenings on it.

"Or maybe it's not *Henry* you're looking for?" Parker continued. "I met Everett earlier when they came in. He's a good-looking guy." He clasped his hands behind his back and rocked on his feet, like a little kid with a secret. "*Really* good-looking."

Parker had no idea. He hadn't seen Ev on his knees staring up at him, his cheeks flushed, his gorgeous green eyes hazed with need, and his lips kiss-swollen. And if I had any say, Parker never would.

*Whoa.* My stomach rolled. *Where the hell had that come from?*

I liked Ev a lot, yes. A *very* lot. But possessiveness implied commitment, and I wasn't sure I was there yet.

*Baby steps*, I reminded myself. Tiny, infant, fetus steps.

"Yep. He's good-looking. And he's a *friend*," I said, ignoring Parker's triumphant grin. "You know better than to listen to gossip."

Parker's grin changed to something fonder. "Well, good, because I think the man could use a friend right now. Henry hopped himself over to the table where Diane and Marci were sitting, and you know how those three are when they get together. The gossip had to be flying fast enough to scare off any sane person. Last I saw, Ev was standing by the food table, stuffing his face."

I bumped Parker on the shoulder again and headed deeper into the bar.

My plan for the previous day had gone spectacularly *wrong* — I mean, as wrong as a surprise blow job could ever be. After the oral and the tears and the bizarre cluster of toxic plants and spooky wind chimes, I'd hoped we'd have a chance to just hang out and find some level of normalcy last night. I'd gone over and rescued Ev's art supplies from his car earlier in the week, when Joe Cross had mentioned it was headed for the junkyard, and I'd hoped to surprise Ev with them last night. I'd wanted to convince him I was a decent guy who wouldn't expect more than he was ready to give, and who would try to give him as much as I could in return.

I'd wanted to spend time with him, because something about the prickly, mistrustful, sensitive, gorgeous man just *did it* for me. That was the God's honest truth. He was beautiful and fascinating and mercurial. I wanted him in my bed, and after yesterday I was no longer fooling myself into thinking that was all I wanted from him.

But of course fucking O'Leary had blocked me yet again, this time in the form of a couple of teenagers shoplifting *condoms and lube* from Hardison's Drug, because irony (like trees, festivals, and gossip) was something O'Leary had in abundance.

I'd dropped Ev off with a promise to call him when I was done, but by the time I'd finished explaining to Logan Simms that the benefits of safe sex didn't quite outweigh the implications of petty larceny, it had been way too late to just show up at Henry's.

I'd spent my night staring up at the ceiling — which I could safely report had exactly the same number of bumps and cracks as it had for the past two weeks — and wondered if it made me an asshole that I couldn't help remembering every second of that blow job, up to the part with the tears.

I'd expected to find Ev standing in the corner alone, hiding out or something, but he wasn't. Instead, he stood behind the table, chatting animatedly with Ash Martin, who was probably a foot taller than Ev and a whole lot broader. Ash made some remark that got Ev laughing, his face tipping up as he smiled, and I swear to God, he was the hottest guy in the entire bar at that moment, the hottest guy in the whole damn town. The sight of him made me stop short and take a deep breath, acutely conscious that my palms were fucking sweating. I was about twenty-five years past middle school, but it didn't seem to matter.

There was no such thing as fate, just a series of choices and outcomes, but looking at Ev now felt like standing on the edge of a precipice, and I couldn't remember how I'd gotten myself into such a precarious position.

Ash excused himself with a smile and moved to the table where his brother was sitting, but Ev stood where he was, half-hidden by the cluster of football-shaped balloons that served as a centerpiece, munching on a plate of snacks and watching the table in the center of the bar, where Henry was. I could barely restrain my smile as I walked around the table and sidled up next to him.

He was so busy spying, he didn't notice my presence.

"What are we doing?" I whispered in his ear.

He jumped and the celery stick in his hand went flying, landing in the center of the table with a *plop*.

"*Silas!*" he scolded. "Really?"

I bit the inside of my lip to keep from laughing at his outrage. "Sorry!" I lied. "I didn't want to disturb your concentration."

"Right," he snorted. He picked up the celery stick and

bit into it fiercely. "And to answer your question, we are snacking. I recommend the jalapeño poppers."

I grabbed one off his plate and bit into it. "*Mmm. Agreed.* And what are we looking at while we're snacking?"

Ev rolled his eyes but transferred his plate of food to his other hand so I could reach it better.

"We're watching the mating ritual of the mature heterosexual," he said quietly. "It's fascinating."

I choked on my popper. "The what?"

He tipped his chin at the tables in the center of the bar and leaned slightly closer to me. "Behold the male preening before the female."

I glanced over and saw his grandfather sitting beside Diane Perkins, smoothing his white hair back with his hand. I chuckled. "Are you kidding?"

"It should be noted," Ev continued, "that last night, the female brought the male sustenance in the form of some insanely good brownies she'd *baked herself from scratch* and a three-cheese lasagna. But when asked to stay and partake of the meal, she said she was *just being neighborly* and didn't want to intrude since she wasn't *family.*"

I nodded. "Uh. Right, okay."

Ev turned his head to look at me. "Brownies, Si. Brownies *and* lasagna. And this is at least the fourth time she cooked for him this week."

"Well, yeah, but she *is* a cook by trade, Ev," I told him. "The diner is only a couple of doors down from the hardware store. And O'Learians tend to look out for each other. She was helping him for a couple weeks before you got here." It sounded reasonable enough to me.

Ev somehow managed to make his smile both pitying and amused all at once. "Do you not see the way she's leaning forward, just the way he is? She's mimicking his posture."

"She's drinking water and eating snacks." I grabbed another popper off the plate. "I mean, maybe she doesn't want to spill them all over herself."

Ev laughed and shook his head. "Okay, fine. What about *them*?"

He pointed at the next table, where Marci the dispatcher was sitting with my boss Mitch Turner and Lisa "The Dragon" Dorian, the librarian. Ms. Dorian was talking excitedly about something, and Mitch and Marci were shooting each other amused glances that Ms. Dorian didn't seem to catch.

"Yeah," I said. "What about them?"

"Are you being serious? Don't you see the way the blonde is brushing the hair back from her face and crossing her legs in his direction. That's a *classic* sign she's into him." He crunched a chip from his plate. "Don't they teach you people anything at policeman-school?"

I chuckled. "Yeah, they teach us not to leap to conclusions based on appearances." I jabbed him lightly with my elbow. "That's my boss, Mitch. And the woman he's chatting with is Marci."

"The one who called you about the shoplifting yesterday?"

"The same," I confirmed. "They're colleagues. Friends. That's all." I looked back at Mitch who was laughing hard at something Marci said and completely ignoring Ms. Dorian. I shook my head. "If you knew these people," I said. "You'd know that Ms. Dorian is being ridiculous, so of course they're laughing together. No more, no less."

"Huh." Ev tilted his head and smiled at me. "You're blind," he declared. "I can't decide if it's funny-strange or funny-hilarious. Can't you recognize attraction when you see it?"

"I hope so." I smiled just a little bit sharply.

He blushed and looked away. "I'm serious, though. I think you're letting what you *think* you know blind you to what's really happening. Where there's smoke, there's fire."

"Everett!" Henry yelled, waving a hand at Ev. "Everett, come here and tell Diane how your demon cat has decided she loves me!" Henry was positively grinning.

Ev sighed and passed me his plate of food. "The mature heterosexual grows tired of the courtship ritual and has decided to bait his offspring."

I let my hand brush over his hip briefly, where no one could see. "I'll talk to you later?"

He nodded.

"*Everett!*"

Ev gritted his teeth, and I watched him walk away.

I wondered if Ev could see the pride on his grandfather's face as he approached. Ev thought he was so savvy about relationships, but I was pretty sure he was clueless about how much Henry loved him.

"A-*hem.*" Dare came out of nowhere and slung an arm over my shoulder, directing me away from the buffet table to a high-top nearby, where Cal was already standing. "What's up, lover boy?"

I shrugged him off. "What?"

Cal grinned at me across the table. "I've gotta say, I wondered if Frank was exaggerating, but I see he wasn't."

"What are you talking about?" I demanded, but of course I knew.

"You and Everett, obviously," Dare said.

"You're the topic *du jour*." Cal gave me a sympathetic shrug before taking a sip of beer. "And the way you're looking at the man isn't doing much to dispel the rumors."

"Frank's been telling everyone how you and Ev were holding hands out at his place yesterday." He raised an eyebrow at me. "Didn't you once tell me that was against your religion?"

"Si told *me* last summer that he was absent the day they handed out commitment genes," Cal said, pushing a chunk of red hair back from his forehead with his fingers. "Mocked Ash and me for being in love."

"I mean, to be fair," Dare teased. "You guys *are* disgusting."

Cal shrugged, completely unconcerned. "You remember what I told you that day, Si? I said love was gonna come and whack you when you least expected it."

I huffed out a breath, but my instinctive denial got stuck somewhere between my lungs and my mouth. The best I could come up with was a lame little eye roll.

"It's not *love*, Cal," I scoffed. "He's been in town a couple of *weeks*. And most of that time he wasn't talking to me."

"I knew Ash for two minutes."

"That's the exception, not the rule."

Cal drew his phone from his pocket and read the display. He chuckled, then downed the rest of his beer in one gulp. "Well, I'm about to go rescue my *exception* from the clutches of his mother and sister-in-law. I feel a terrible headache coming on, and I won't possibly be able to stay for the game." He winked at me. "And for what it's worth, I think your guy's pretty exceptional too."

I shook my head as he walked off. "He's crazy," I told Dare. "*My guy.*" I was desperately trying to ignore the newly possessive part of me that wanted to roll around in the idea.

"Uh-huh. So what *did* happen yesterday?"

"Nothing. We hiked. We found that weird place with the chimes that I told you about yesterday."

Dare grunted. "I sent Elliot Marks out to look at it this morning. We're gonna have to remove all those weeds and destroy them. Damn things are invasive."

"Well, don't blame the messenger," I told him. "I didn't plant them, I just found them."

"While you were hiking. With Ev," he prompted.

Dare gave me the same penetrating gaze he'd given me at the restaurant yesterday, and though I tried to ignore him, once again I found myself spilling my guts.

"Fine, fine. We kissed." I glared at Dare. "You can't keep using that look on me."

"Why not, when it's so effective?" Dare challenged. He sipped his beer and watched me carefully. "And that's all that happened?"

This time, I wouldn't answer no matter how long he stared. What happened between me and Everett was... ours.

"We talked," I said. I shifted my stance so I could keep Ev, who was standing next to Hen's chair and watching the football game with a tiny frown on his forehead, in my line of vision. "Did you know he was married before?"

Dare shook his head. "No. How would I know that?"

I shrugged. "I dunno. Hen, maybe? O'Leary gossip? Mitch seemed to know a lot about him."

"If Mitch knew that, he didn't tell me," Dare said. He studied Ev also. "He doesn't wear a wedding ring. Did they break up a while ago?"

I shook my head and snagged Dare's beer. "They didn't break up. His husband died." I took a long swallow. "Sixteen months ago."

Dare whistled and his brown eyes went wide. "Shit."

"Yeah."

"Ev still messed up over it?" Dare asked. Then he waved his hand dismissively. "Forget I even asked. Of course he is. God, the poor guy."

I nodded slowly. *Of course he was.*

Shane Goode shuffled up to the table, adjusting his baseball cap, and I pushed over to make room for him, even though that meant losing sight of Ev. "Um, hey, guys. Just wanted to let you know I got Jamie home safe."

I slapped Shane's arm, which was surprisingly solid beneath his shapeless clothing. "Good man," I told him. "Jamie needs a loyal friend, for sure."

"He's gonna be okay," Shane said. "I think he's upset about… you know. Molly."

"I know, Shane."

"And maybe about Parker, too." Dare said.

Shane nodded and rapped the table lightly with his knuckles. "He never should have gone to Boston. Parker, I mean." He sighed. "Do you ever think about how everything would have been *fine* if no one left town, Si?"

I frowned. "If we stayed here like prisoners?"

"It's not a prison! It's a *home*. If Matty hadn't left, Molly wouldn't have gone with him. If they'd both just stayed here, nothing would've had to happen to them." His nostrils flared and his throat worked like he was fighting off tears. "If Parker hadn't left, Jamie wouldn't have missed his friend all these years."

"Well, yeah, but everyone has a right to find happiness as long as they're not hurting anyone, Shane."

"But that's just it! They *were* hurting people! They hurt you, and your parents, and Jamie, and *me*."

"Shane," I began, but Dare caught my eye and shook his head subtly.

Shane took a deep breath and let it out slowly. "Sorry,"

he said. "Second time in two days I've gotten all upset. I just hate thinking about the waste of it all."

"Of course," Dare said, frowning at Shane. "Anytime someone that young dies, it's a tragedy, and Molly and Matty were special."

Shane nodded once and adjusted the brim of his hat again. "Anyway. I'll keep an eye on Jamie," he said. "Just in case."

"I appreciate that," I said solemnly. "And listen, if *you* need to talk…"

"Nah." Shane shook his head. "I said all I needed to say twelve years ago. But your mom's memorial service will help, I bet."

"If you say so. I'd just as soon skip it."

Shane's eyes narrowed. "You don't mean that."

I sighed. "I don't mean I want to forget them, Shane. I could never do that. I just… want to stop remembering their deaths, that's all."

"Same difference, if you ask me," Shane insisted. He cleared his throat. "Uh, any news on the camper, Dare? I was a little late getting out to Frank's yesterday. I think I missed most of you."

Dare shrugged. "Well, Si found a whole fucking *forest* of invasive plants that are gonna be a bitch to remove. So there's that."

"Hey! I *told* you not to shoot the messenger!"

Dare scratched the back of his head. "Otherwise, though, nothing."

"That's good," Shane said. "Real good."

I raised an eyebrow at him. "Why's that good? I was hoping we'd find something, give the family some closure."

"Well, I dunno. Just that if you don't find anything, maybe he's still alive, right?" Shane offered. "While there's still hope?"

"Maybe," Dare said skeptically. "Either way, I think his folks would want to know."

Shane nodded. "Well, anyway. You let me know if you need help again. I know those woods pretty well. I can help you with your hogweed problem, too."

"I'll remember that Shane, thanks," Dare said. But when Shane walked away, Dare's eyes followed him.

"Remind me again about your brother's car accident," he said.

"What about it?"

Dare glanced at me and shook his head. "Nothing," he said. "Never mind. My memory is failing me, but it doesn't matter." He leaned both elbows on the table and turned that interrogative gaze on me again. "Let's get back to talking about Ev."

"Uh, let's *not*." I grabbed Dare's beer again, and his lips twitched in amusement as he watched me.

"He's a widower. Has he been with anyone since his husband died?"

I scowled. "How the fuck should I know? It's none of my business and sure as hell none of *yours*." But I would have bet my house he hadn't.

Dare nodded. "Fair enough. But if this is his first time with someone else, it's gonna be hard for him, I'd think. Grief crops up at strange times, even when you think you're past it. Two steps forward, one step back. Even if you're attracted enough to kiss someone."

*Even if you give them a blow job.*

"Yes, thank you, Dr. Phil. Like I just told Cal *and Parker*, since you're all a bunch of gossips, Everett and I are friends." I ran a hand through my hair in frustration.

Fuck. I'd known this. I'd *known* it. A guy who'd avoided me for weeks, then freaked out after hooking up like Ev had was clearly *not* ready to move on, no matter how much

I wanted him to be. But hearing it spelled out made my unease multiply until it felt like a thousand tiny bees pricking my chest from the inside. I'd let myself want Ev enough to overwhelm my caution, and I'd gotten so caught up that I'd found myself in a place I'd *never* wanted or expected to be. If I didn't stop this train immediately, step back from the precipice, I was going to find myself losing something I hadn't even known I wanted until Ev walked into my life.

And even now, even knowing that? I felt a tug in my gut to turn around, to look for him, because I knew the sight of him would calm me.

*Fuck*, again.

"Listen, I'm not trying to wet blanket you here." Dare's brown eyes were sincere. "God knows I *love* seeing you actually making an effort for a guy for once, and Ev seems great. I'm just saying maybe slow down and have a discussion, make sure you're on the same page."

I nodded and took another sip of Dare's beer, but my heart twisted in my chest. Sure. Talk about things. Put my shit out there and risk him saying, *Oh, sorry, Silas, you lose*. No, thanks. Besides, the answer was obvious, now that the fog of attraction and connection had dissipated. I'd meant it when I said grief wasn't linear, but if Ev couldn't bring himself to *talk* about his husband, there was no way I was more than step one in his healing process.

The rebound. The regret.

*Fuck*, a third time.

Here I was, falling for a guy for the first time ever, and if I didn't figure out a way to stop this immediately, the landing was gonna be fatal.

"I appreciate the advice, Dare, honestly. But I meant what I said earlier. There's nothing between Everett and me." I forced my lips into a grin.

Dare widened his eyes and shook his head. "Si, stop!"

"No, dude, I'm telling you," I said, raising my voice to talk over him. "Ev's a good guy, and he's hot as hell, but he was never gonna be more than a hookup. He's a *mess* for God's sake, and there are a million other guys out there who are drama-free." If only I could make myself want them. "You've gotta nip this gossip in the bud before people start getting the wrong idea. I do *casual*. I don't need a guy who's gonna sob all over me."

I rolled my eyes… and someone behind me cleared their throat.

Dare's devastated expression told me all I needed to know before I even turned around, and when I did, I wished I hadn't. Hen Lattimer stood looking at me like I was shit on his shoe, and Ev… Ev was smiling, this huge, heartbreaking, false approximation of humor. His green eyes burned like I'd just told a joke and he was determined to laugh along.

"Si's not wrong," Ev told Dare. "God, I wept all over the poor guy in the woods yesterday. Did he tell you? It was, like, the least attractive sight ever."

Dare shook his head mutely.

Ev put his hand on my back just above my shoulder blade, a fleeting touch that was barely there before it was gone but managed to take some part of me with it. He raised his voice, loud enough to carry. "But I can confirm, the gossip is completely false. There is absolutely nothing between us. Si was just being a decent guy yesterday. No surprise there, right?"

To my horror, someone shouted, "Si's the best!" And someone else laughed and demanded, "You owe me five bucks, Jack! I told you it was just a rumor!"

Ev snickered, a high, hysterical sound, and clapped his hand over his mouth like he wanted to force it back.

"Come along, Everett," Hen said, jabbing the ground with his crutch. He leaned heavily on Ev's shoulder for the first time I could recall. "I'm suddenly tired, and I need to go home."

"Yeah." Ev nodded. "Thanks for the, um… everything."

Paralyzed by my own idiocy, I stood and watched him walk out the door.

"Well," Dare said a moment later, once the door had shut behind them and the rest of the bar had gone back to watching the game. "I guess you got your wish. Gossip effectively nipped." The *dumbass* on the end of his sentence was unspoken but evident.

"Yeah," I agreed. I'd gathered my pride around me like a shield and had managed to clobber Ev over the head with it. I couldn't remember feeling so hollow since the day Matty died.

Go, me.

I'd thought I was still standing on some fucking precipice, that I could save myself by walking away. But feeling Ev's pain lance through me like it was my own, I realized it was way too late for that. I'd already fallen.

# Chapter Eleven



"THERE YOU GO. One gallon of Petal Pink room paint." I smiled down at Sera Davies as I slid the bucket of freshly mixed paint across the counter to her father. "Can't wait to hear how it turns out."

Sera smiled, showing the giant gap where her front teeth used to be. "I'm going to paint elephants on the wall when it's done," she said. "Purple ones. Because elephants *can so* be purple if I want."

John Davies rolled his eyes and rubbed his daughter's head affectionately. "That's all we hear these days at home. *Mr. Maior says elephants can be purple, Mr. Maior says imagine it first and prove it second…*"

I winced and leaned my elbows on the counter. "Uh. Sorry?"

"No way." John chuckled. "Given a choice between her painting fantastical elephants on the walls, and her watching videos all day like a zombie? I'll take the elephants every single time. I'm just hoping you do a unit on *Why vegetables are our friends!* Maybe then she'd eat some."

I laughed. "You know, that's not a half-bad idea. It's still-life, but also delicious."

"There you go!" John grabbed the gallon off the counter and lifted it in a salute. "Later, Ev."

I nodded and sent Sera a wave as she skipped off. "See you tomorrow, Sera!"

"Well, now. Aren't you Mr. Popularity?" Grandpa Hen came clomping out of the back room, leaning heavily on the cane that he'd finally consented to use only after I'd pointed out that his one-crutch routine looked like a bunch of abortive pole-vault attempts. "Was that John Davies?"

I closed my eyes and inhaled, doing Dr. Trainor's deep breathing techniques. I was *inside* the bubble, gripping tightly to my patience. All the negative forces were *outside* the bubble, and they couldn't…

"Hey! Everett!" Grandpa Hen waved his hand literally an inch from my face, and my protective bubble popped. "You hear me?"

For the first time, I wondered why the fuck I was imagining a protective *bubble*. Bubbles were, like, the least protective things in the universe. Next time, I was going to imagine myself in a panic room.

"Yes, I hear you," I said sweetly. "And yes, that was John Davies. As you know, because you've clearly been listening to my entire interaction with him from the back room."

"Hmph. Only to make sure you…"

"Do things properly," he and I finished at the same time. "Yes, I know. I'm going to go tidy the front of the store. To the best of my limited abilities."

Grandpa frowned.

I pushed back from the counter and stalked to the front area near the door where I could pretend to organize shelves of lawn bags and giant bins of rakes for a while.

The good thing about Grandpa being on that damn cane was that it was impossible for him to sneak up on me.

And yeah, you knew it had been a bad week when you felt a victorious thrill at the fact that your *elderly grandfather with the broken leg* wouldn't be able to chase you down.

I started stacking boxes of purple Halloween lights with more force than necessary.

My mood wasn't Hen's fault, of course. If anything, he'd been unexpectedly kind for the past few days. Maybe he felt bad that the *good guy* he'd wanted me to date had turned out to be an asshole. Or maybe he'd gotten cautious after I'd stomped around the apartment Monday, cooking nothing but wholegrain, meatless meals and daring him with my eyes to complain.

Hen hadn't mentioned Si's name in my presence once since Sunday, and when Diane had innocently made some remark about Si still searching for the missing camper, Hen had thumped his fist on the table and said if Silas Sloane was half the man people claimed he was, he'd have found John Carpenter by now. Diane had looked at me, and I'd shrugged, pretending not to know what had triggered my grandfather's temper.

It would have been kind of cute, if I had any capacity to recognize cuteness anymore. Instead, I was a rage demon in human form, able to see nothing but injustice. Why the hell was O'Leary so goddamn likable, anyway? Why the hell had Silas lied to me in the woods when he said I was okay? Why the hell was I letting this hurt me when I knew what *real* hurt felt like, and this was nothing compared to that?

I kicked at a display of leaf blowers, glad that John Davies was gone. *No, it's fine, parental unit! I am totally setting a good example for your children.*

I sighed and thunked my forehead against one of the

heavy wooden shelves my great-grandfather — or hell, maybe it was *his* father? Who even remembered anymore? — had built.

It wasn't logical to be so upset, I knew it. For one thing, I barely knew Si Sloane. And for another, if some tiny rebellious part of my subconscious had been interested in anything beyond attraction with Si, somebody needed to lobotomize me *right fucking now* because I knew better. I was *done* with that shit.

I was the new and improved, risk-averse Everett Maior. *I was, I was, I was.*

"Ev?"

I stood up so quickly I nearly whacked my head on the shelf above me. O'Leary, New York, the place where my dignity came to die. "Hey! Yeah?"

Ash Martin watched me with concerned eyes that probably saw way too much. "You okay?"

"Yeah, of course." It was completely normal for a grown man to rest his head on a shelf that had likely held nails and fertilizer in the not-so-recent past. "Do you need something?"

"Yeah. Well, kinda." He jammed his hand into the pocket of his jeans to grab his phone, then cleaned the screen on the front of his red plaid flannel shirt. If ever there was a man who could pull of *lumbersexual* it might be Ash Martin. "You see this?"

He thrust the phone out and I took it, scanning the image on the screen. It was a canvas backdrop, like the kind mall photographers used, painted with a dizzying array of autumn *things*. Acorns and leaves, pumpkins and cornucopia, all plopped down with lots of enthusiasm and zero design.

"Yeah." I looked back up at him. "What about it?"

"What do I need to make one?"

I frowned. "Do you… really need one?" Did anyone really need one?

"Well, the Pumpkin Festival is coming. I don't know if anyone's mentioned it to you?"

I remembered my first conversation with Silas. Why did *everything* fucking remind me of Silas?

"Yeah," I said shortly. "I've heard about it. There are pie-eating contests?"

"Yeah." He ran a hand through his dark hair and looked more harried than I'd ever seen him. "And baking contests. And pumpkin-growing competitions, and flower arrangement… competitions. I don't really know how that works," he confided, "but my mom used to be really into it. And uh, there are cider donuts and hay rides and costume contests."

"Wow. That's… a lot."

"You have no idea. And we have loads of town celebrations here — Cal says if something stands still for ten minutes, they'll celebrate it — Pumpkin Festival might be the biggest." He paused. "That one or the Light Parade at the end of December." He glanced at my face and laughed out loud. "Oh my God, your expression right now!"

I could only imagine it was some cross between fascination and horror. "There's a *Light Parade*?"

He smiled. "It's nondenominational."

"Of course it is."

"*Anyway*, they take pictures of the winners to put on the town website…"

"There's a town website?" I rubbed my forehead with the back of my hand. "That's so… twenty-first century."

"I know, right?" Ash grinned like I was joking. I wasn't sure I had been. "But it turns out they've been storing the backdrops in the church basement, and it flooded over the summer, so I need to find new ones."

"You, personally?"

Ash flushed slightly. "My mother and sister-in-law are on the planning committee. I've been told that Karen *cannot be upset* right now in her delicate condition."

I rolled my eyes. "I see."

"Yeah. So I figured since you're the art teacher, you'd know what I need? I'm guessing I need some rolls of paper stuff, some stencils. Paint, obviously," he counted off on his fingers. "Oh, brushes for the paint would be good. Um…"

I ran a hand over my mouth. Ash looked so lost, poor guy. I was pretty sure I would deeply regret what I was going to say next, but what was a little more regret?

"I can paint you something," I told him. "I think." I looked down at the picture again. "I mean maybe not exactly this."

"Oh, for real? I hate to ask, but…"

"You didn't ask, I offered." I handed him back his phone. "You need canvas, really, not paper. And it would probably take me half the time." Or less. This kind of painting, like the kind I did with the kids at school, took almost no effort whatsoever.

"Cal and I will owe you big. We'll pay you in cupcakes." He grinned. "Anytime you like."

I snickered. "Now, *that* is what I love to hear. Throw in some coffee and I'm in."

"Done!" Ash said, heading for the door. He pointed at me. "Okay, planning meeting tonight at Goode's, 6 PM. Cal and I will save a seat for ya."

"Wait, I have to go to a planning meeting?" I shook my head, panicked. "No, no, no. *Paint a background*, you said."

"Yeah, but uh… people are gonna ask me who's doing the work, and they're probably going to have opinions." Ash's smile turned sheepish.

The regret found me more swiftly than I'd anticipated.

"It'll be better this way. I promise! They'll all talk to you at the meeting, and they won't accost you on the street. Plus, there'll be free food."

I let out an undignified whimper, and Ash chuckled.

"Just think of the baked goods, Ev."

———

SADLY, promised baked goods could only get a person so far.

"I really think it would be adorable if we put *puppies* on the backdrop." Ash's mom stood next to her chair, wringing her hands together in a manner that reminded me exactly of my own mother. "Puppies playing in leaves, maybe?"

"Thanks for your input, Margo," Paul Fine said. He ran a hand through his thinning gray hair, and his blue eyes were patient. As the head of the town council, he was attempting to run tonight's meeting, which was a little like herding cats... blindfolded.

"Some of us are allergic to dogs, *Margo*," Ms. Dorian said, peering over the top of her glasses from the other side of the room. After this meeting, I could understand why Si called the librarian Dragon Dorian. The woman smelled like stale coffee and hadn't shut up in forty-five minutes, mostly because she kept talking over everyone else.

I propped my elbow on the dining counter and rested my cheek in my hand. It amused me that the town's largest dining establishment had completely closed down *at dinner-time* for this planning session and that it almost didn't matter because so much of O'Leary was packed into the room already.

"You do know that the dogs won't be real, right, Lisa?" a woman seated in one of the booths said dryly. "I'm sure

Everett is a talented artist, but even *he* can't make dogs so real they trigger your allergies." I decided I loved this woman on the spot, and I turned my head to smile at her.

She was brunette and slim, with kind eyes and a conservative yellow twinset. But unlike a couple of the other ladies in the room, I got the feeling she wore the twinset because she liked it, not because she thought she should.

I enjoyed that.

"Who's that?" I murmured to my sidekick, who'd insisted on perching next to me with his cane laid on the counter like a sword.

"You don't know?"

I turned and gave him a look that said, *If I knew, would I ask?*

"Carol Sloane," Grandpa said. "Silas's mama."

*Huh.* Well, that was interesting. Looking at her again, I could see the resemblance. The same coloring, the same smile, the same eyes. It was sad how well I could recognize those things. I remembered the things Si had said about his mother grieving for his brother, and wondered if maybe that put-together twinset was a kind of armor.

"I think we're wasting Ev's time," Cal said, throwing me an apologetic glance. "I mean, we don't need to reinvent the wheel just because the old ones were ruined. And Ev is doing us a favor. Just recreate the old one."

"I say we take this opportunity to get something new. Something that's really reflective of the town," one of the other councilwomen said.

*Reflective of O'Leary?* I imagined presenting them with a collage of jerkface hot guys, delicious baked goods, and my grandfather's damn cane. I had to cough to cover my laugh.

My grandfather shifted beside me, and Paul's eyes lit up. "Yes, Henry?"

"I think maybe you just gotta trust the artist. Let him do his thing."

I spun in my chair and raised an eyebrow, sure I'd misheard.

Grandpa Hen shrugged. "No one goes over to your place and tells you and Quinn how to run your theater, Paul. Nobody's telling Julian how to doctor his cats and whatsits. Nobody's telling Diane how to make the best pie in all of O'Leary." Grandpa took this opportunity to shoot a dirty look at Shane Goode, the recipe thief. "'Specially after she gets her title back at this year's festival."

"Henry!" Diane protested from the back of the room. She blushed to the roots of her red hair, but she couldn't hide her smile.

"I think Hen's right," Julian said. He gave me a friendly grin. "Ev's the artist, so let him figure it out."

"You're saying you trust me to do this?" I asked my grandfather. "Me? The man who can't be trusted to sell Jamie a handsaw without you watching over my shoulder?"

He raised one eyebrow right back at me, like I was being particularly stupid. "Saws are my business, Everett. To my everlasting disappointment, they're not yours. You picked art, and you're good at it." He shrugged. "So, go be good at it."

I turned back around, but I didn't pay much attention to the conversation after that.

His words stung a little. *To his everlasting disappointment.* But the sting gave them the ring of truth. And he thought I was a good artist? How would he even know?

"Well, I'm convinced," Paul said. "Everett, do whatever you like and knock our socks off!"

I forced a smile and nodded. "I'll do my best."

"Alright!" Paul clapped his hands. "Thirty-minute recess! Jamie and Shane have the food out, and I'm famished!"

"Hen!" Jamie Burke came over as soon as the crowd had made a dash for the food tables. O'Learians took their buffets seriously. "How are you?"

"Well as can be," Hen said, nodding. "How about you?"

Jamie shrugged and his red hair fell over his forehead. "Good. Good." He glanced at me.

"Jamie, have you met my grandson, Everett?" Hen said wryly. "Everett, this is Jamie Burke."

"Not officially. Nice to meet you," I said, shaking his hand.

"Same." Jamie grinned. "You hungry?"

I glanced over at the throng of people crowding the food. "Not that hungry. But I'd love a soda."

Jamie's eyes brightened in a way that was either O'Learian over-friendliness or possibly some kind of romantic interest, an idea that only made me feel unbearably *weary.* "Come on, I'll take you out back."

I glanced at Grandpa Hen, who shrugged like it was all the same with him whether I stayed or went. *Typical.* I jumped down off my stool.

"So how are you liking O'Leary?" Jamie asked as he led me through the crowd.

"Oh. Uh." I blinked. "It's fine."

"Wow. Unqualified endorsement, huh? I can't wait to see the backdrop you paint."

I laughed. "Yeah. Me neither. Considering I have no supplies and haven't painted anything outside of the classroom in a long while. Puppies playing in leaves would probably be better than asking me to come up with something representative of the town."

He hesitated, almost shyly. "You know, if you need any help with…"

"Jamie?" Carol Sloane popped out of the crowd, all sunshine-yellow.

"Oh, hey, Ms. Sloane. Do you know Everett?"

"Hi," I said, giving her my best smile. "Nice to meet you."

"And you." She looked me up and down impassively. "I hear you know my son."

"Uh." Si had not been wrong about the rumor mill in this town. More than one person had casually-but-not-casually brought up Si or hiking in conversation, and when Grandpa wasn't there to kill the topic dead, I'd done my best to smile through it. "I do. A little bit." *Enough to know he has complicated feelings about you.*

She nodded. "Has he invited you to the memorial service?"

I looked at Jamie for a clue, but he was looking at me expectantly, just like she was. "No, he hasn't mentioned it at all."

She frowned. "Oh. It's a few weeks away, but I thought he would have invited all his friends."

My stomach churned. "We're more like acquaintances than friends," I told her. "We're not close." Not really even friends at all.

She looked strangely disappointed.

"Well, I'd like it if you'd come," she said. "It's a little get-together to remember his brother, Mathias." She put a hand on Jamie's arm. "And Molly, of course. Three weeks from Sunday. I'll get you the details once we iron them out."

I nodded. "I'll definitely try to be there." There was no way in *hell* I would be there.

She smiled, almost like she understood what I wasn't

saying. "You know, I wish Silas would bring more friends by the house." Her gaze, deep blue and a little sad, met mine. "The quiet days are the worst this time of year. Can't help but notice what's not there."

Jamie squeezed her hand.

I gave her a ghost of a smile and hesitated. I had absolutely no standing to say anything on Si's behalf, *especially* now, but… "You know, maybe instead of, um, noticing what's not there, you could do some of the things Mathias liked to do? Like, uh… I heard he liked hiking? Or art?"

She tilted her head and narrowed her eyes, studying me, and I thought, *Here comes the part where she squashes me like a bug.* But instead, she said, "I think that's a really inspired idea, Ev." She smiled and frowned at the same time, the same look Silas had given me more than once, like I'd pleased and confused her all at once.

"Thanks."

The bell over the front door chimed, and a blast of refreshingly chilly air blew in. Carolyn's expression cleared. "Oh, look! Silas is here!" She raised her arm and waved to get his attention. "Silas!"

No, but really though. *All the baked goods in the world were not enough to justify my presence here.*

I turned my head and saw Silas walk in along with Daniel Michaelson, the man we'd met in the woods a few days before. Daniel looked like he would rather be literally anywhere else, and I felt a total kinship with the man.

Silas looked every bit as good as he ever had, which was to say twice as good as any mortal had a right to look. It was lowering that even though I was pissed at him, so pissed I could imagine walking over, throwing him against the wall, and smacking his smiling face, I was equally turned on just by his presence. I wanted very badly to push him up against the wall for an entirely different purpose.

To my shock, Si clapped Daniel on the back and pointed in our direction, leading him over. I hadn't thought Si liked Daniel.

"Hey, Mom," Si said, bending down to give his mother a kiss on the cheek. "Jamie. *Ev.*"

I lifted my chin to acknowledge Si's greeting, but said nothing.

It was ridiculous how badly I wanted to smile at him, to pretend that I wasn't mortified and hurt and rejected. The connection between us was still there, at least on my side. Electric currents zinged between us, and I was hyper-aware of every move he made, even though I really didn't want to be.

I gave Daniel my friendliest smile. "Good to see you again."

"Uh. Yeah. Si, um, saw me at the grocery store and, uh… said I should come." He shuffled his feet awkwardly and only made fleeting eye contact with me. I could feel the discomfort coming off him in waves, far different than he'd seemed when we met him out in the woods.

"He was buying a frozen dinner, so I told him he could come here for free food and leave right away." Silas shrugged. "That's what I'm here for."

Carolyn laughed. "That's what most people are here for. Help yourself, Daniel."

"Oh. Uh. Thank you, ma'am."

"Shit! *She-Ra!*" someone yelled. "Get back here!"

I turned just in time to see a tiny ball of fluff launch itself at Daniel's leg and climb him like a tree.

"What the hell is that?" Jamie demanded, taking a step back, but Daniel laughed and caught the creature in his big hands.

"It's a cat," Julian Ross said. "A kitten, actually. She's been sleeping in my pocket."

"You carry kittens in your pocket?" I said. Daphne would barely tolerate the cat carrier, let alone the indignity of a small, dark cave.

"Not generally, just this one." Julian blushed. "She likes Daniel."

"She smells the woods on me," Daniel said, smiling down at the floof in his hands.

"She smells your dog on you," Julian countered. "She-Ra has a crush on Honoria, Daniel's dog."

"Well, that's just great, and I hope they're really, *really* happy together, but get her out of my restaurant," Jamie said, exasperated. "There's like, a billion health code violations happening right now!"

Julian bit his lip. "Sorry, Jamie." He tried to take the cat from Daniel, but she protested. Vocally.

It was so amusing, my eyes lifted involuntarily to Silas's face, and I found him watching me.

I looked away.

"It's fine. I'll take her outside." Daniel seemed relieved to go.

"I'll go with you," Julian said, and he didn't seem reluctant either. Wasn't *that* interesting?

*Oh, my God*, I thought, recognizing that I was speculating about two perfectly innocent people. *I've become an O'Learian. I* am *the problem.*

"So, Silas, I was telling Everett about the memorial service," Carolyn said into the silence after Julian and Daniel departed. "I invited him to come."

Si stiffened like he'd been struck, and *wow*, that was my cue to leave.

I coughed. "Jamie? Could we get that drink?" I motioned toward my throat and gasped, "*Parched.*"

"Sure," Jamie said easily enough, putting a hand on my back. "Come this way."

He led me through the busy kitchen, where he got me a can of soda, then out the back door into the cold night. The air smelled like wood smoke and it was dark enough that I could see the stars, the only light coming from the door Jamie had left propped open.

He leaned against the building and watched me drink.

"Better?" he asked, concerned.

"Yeah. Thanks."

He nodded, then tilted his head speculatively. "So… you and Si, huh?"

I clutched the can more tightly in my hand. "Pardon?"

He raised an eyebrow and grinned.

"The gossip in this place is unreal," I said, shaking my head. "There's no *me and Si*. We literally said two words to each other in there." Si had said one word, if you wanted to be technical, and I hadn't said *any*.

"Uh, Everett? I realize that we just met, okay? But I'm gonna say this as your very newest, very best friend: you didn't see the look Si gave me when I put my hand on your back." Jamie laughed like this was hilarious. "Good thing my red hair makes me impervious to flame."

"Bullshit."

"Nope. I'm gay. Si knows it, and I was going to ask you out earlier, which I'm guessing he realized and *did not like*."

"You're imagining things. Seeing what you want to see. You know," I said, stepping further into the alley as I warmed up to my rant, "confirmation bias is a fucking epidemic in this town. You all make assumptions about people and events based on… *I don't even know what*. Some shit that happened a decade ago? A pie recipe that got stolen? The way your kid's birth announcement is gonna be listed in the newspaper? The fact that two people have never been together, so obviously they never *will* be together? You assume that things are always going to be the way they are because that's the way they've always been, but people change. They grow and they love and they grieve and they… they heal." I swallowed. "Some people do."

Jamie blinked. "Of course they do, Ev."

I stabbed a finger toward him. "You should evaluate things based on facts, not… history and assumption."

"You're not wrong," he agreed easily.

I inhaled, realizing how ridiculous I must have sounded. "I'm not insane, either."

"Should I evaluate that based on facts or history and assumption?" he teased.

I glared at him as best I could through the darkness, and he laughed. "Nah, I'm kidding. I know you're not."

I leaned on the building next to Jamie. It was companionable. Not remotely as nice as being with Si, though, which really sucked.

And as I stared up at the sky, I realized I couldn't really blame Si for saying the things he'd said. It was no more or less than the truth, as much as it hurt. Two weeks of total avoidance, followed by a round of messy, unscripted, unprotected, slightly hysterical oral sex, capped off with a bout of inexplicable tears, wasn't really the best way to make a good impression.

I was a giant human wrecking ball, swinging from hot to cold and back again. I wouldn't volunteer to take on this level of crazy, either, especially if I were a hot, single, commitment-cautious guy like Silas.

"My husband died sixteen months ago. His name was Adrian," I found myself saying.

"That I did *not* know," Jamie said, all humor gone from his voice. "I'm sorry."

I waved a hand at this and Jamie chuckled softly.

"Yeah, I know. Feels like one of those meaningless

things you hear over and over. The words don't take away any of what you're feeling. But it's still true, and now I get why people say it."

"Because it's a socially acceptable platitude?"

"Because it means *connection*. Losing people, it's like the great equalizer." He folded his arms over his chest and looked up at the sky. "You, me, Si. Hell, even Henry. He lost the love of his life when your grandmother died."

I turned my head to peer at him. Selfishly enough, I'd never considered that.

"Saying you're sorry is like shorthand," he mused. "Like saying, 'I've been there too, and I know it sucks, but you're not the only person who's been in this awful place. You're not alone.'" He turned his head, and I could just make out the curve of his smile in the light. "So, when I say I'm sorry about your husband, Ev, that's what I'm saying."

Because I was made of nothing but anger and salt-water these days, tears pricked the back of my eyes. "Thanks." I huffed out something that was half-chuckle and half-sob. "I'm sorry about your sister, too."

He nodded, accepting this. "So, what happened with you and Si?"

"Not a damn thing." Not a damn thing I wanted to discuss, anyway.

"You don't wanna talk about it?"

"Not even a little."

"Fine." He grinned. "Just, if there *was* anything that happened, maybe you could try to be patient with Si? After Matty died, he kinda dived into being Officer Sloane — calm, competent, Mr. No-Emotions, No-Drama. And anytime he feels threatened, he reacts by retreating into that persona even more. The more emotion he feels, the less he shows."

I huffed out a laugh. "Yeah, that's not the issue here." Si was showing plenty of emotion. "But you're a pretty smart guy, Jamie. Thank you."

"Oh, fuck yeah. I'm, like, the Socrates of O'Leary." He chuckled. "Except, you know, when I get drunk off my ass and humiliate myself in front of my former best friend at his bar on the regular."

"What's that about?" I demanded.

"Eh. That's a story for another day." Jamie sighed. "You should come to the memorial for Matty and Molly, whatever Carolyn ends up doing. I'd like you to be there. As a friend."

"I'll think about it." But I already knew I would never intrude on something like that.

"Ready to go back inside?"

I let my head fall back against the cold wall. "Do we have to?"

"Depends. How many pumpkin portraits would you like them to sign you up to paint while you're out here?"

I groaned and pushed off the wall. "Fine, let's go."

"Want me to put my arm around you and make Si jealous?"

I laughed out loud. It was cleansing. "You are barking up the wrong tree, *friend*. I've got a little too much baggage for Si. And I…" I took a deep breath. "Adrian's death hit me hard. I'm not out looking for a relationship right now."

"I get it. Probably not good for me to antagonize the police officer when I'm on the fast track to being a habitual offender, anyway." He dipped his hands in his pockets and stood aside so I could walk in before him.

"You know, if you want to talk about that…"

Jamie shook his head and repeated my words from earlier. "Not even a little."

I snickered as I followed him into the restaurant.

Si was deep in conversation with his mom when we went back inside, and yes, I noticed. But I noticed the way his eyes cut to me, and then to Jamie.

Silas didn't *want* me, but he was attracted enough to care that maybe Jamie and I had been getting friendly in the alley. Figured. But I felt calmer after talking to Jamie; more centered, less angry

I walked back to the stool next to my grandfather.

"Everything alright?" he asked.

"As ever. How long do you think we need to stick around?"

"We can't duck out before dessert, Everett!" Grandpa Hen was aghast. "That would be rude."

I sighed. "Right." I pulled my cracked cell phone from my pocket so I could play a game.

"Ev?" Si's voice in my ear made me shiver, but I gripped my phone tighter.

"Get going, Silas," Hen said in a low voice. "Ev doesn't need to talk to you."

I smiled slightly. It was nice to be on this side of my grandfather's temper for once.

"It's fine," I said. "What did you need, Si?" I didn't turn around.

"I need to talk. Please. Just five minutes. Here or wherever."

For an apology, no doubt. Silas hadn't meant for me to overhear him talking about me. Probably thought he'd tarnished his halo a little. Mostly because he *had*.

"I'm sorry," he said when I didn't respond. And that *did* make me turn around. Was he really going to do this here? "I was a total asshole, and I just…"

I widened my eyes in disbelief. There were at least three people who were avidly listening while pretending not to listen, and one — my grandfather — who wasn't giving us even the pretense of privacy, but Si didn't seem to notice or care.

"Silas, now's not the time," I cautioned.

He rubbed the back of his neck. "When would be a better one?"

I opened my mouth to answer when the door to the diner slammed open so hard it hit the wall. Every conversation stopped and we all turned to see Karen Mitchener-Martin walk in, wide-eyed and wind-blown, with one hand braced on her baby bump.

"I was just with Mitch and Darius Turner down at the station," she announced with a quaver in her voice for maximum dramatic effect. "Elliot Marks, one of Dare's men, is *missing* just like the camper! There's a *murderer* in this town!"

# Chapter Twelve

EVERETT

"Mr. Maior?"

I glanced up from cleaning paintbrushes in the child-sized sink at the back of my classroom and found Janice Turner watching me, her brown eyes amused and mildly annoyed, like she'd been saying my name for a while and I hadn't responded.

Not a huge surprise, since I'd been pretty distracted since the meeting two days ago.

"Principal Turner," I said, clearing my throat. I turned back around and switched the water off, drying my hands on a paper towel. "Sorry. This is my, uh, unofficial, end-of-week meditation hour."

Cleaning brushes was one of those mindless tasks that I found really calming. There was something about watching the color swirl down the drain, rinsing until the water ran clean, and knowing that there was a specific, measurable point when it would be finished, unlike so many of the things that filled my life. I tended to get really into it, to zone out and ignore my surroundings, which was why I saved it for the end of the day on Friday.

A smile ghosted across the woman's lips. Her eyes roamed the classroom, surveying the little displays of artwork I'd set up, while I stood awkwardly crumpling and un-crumpling my paper towel. Ms. Turner was the sort of person who seemed born to be a teacher — friendly, authoritative, and just a tiny bit intimidating. She was maybe forty years old but looked closer to thirty, and though she'd instructed me to call her Janice numerous times, I just *couldn't*. Not even in my head.

"You've had a busy year already," she remarked.

I nodded. The woman didn't know the half of it. I felt like I'd lived three lives since coming to O'Leary. Hell, I'd lived two of them just this week, especially after Karen had dropped her little bomb at the meeting the other night.

"I remember thinking, when I spoke to you on the phone last month, that you weren't particularly excited about the idea of teaching this year, especially younger students." She shot me a look I couldn't read and walked toward the bulletin board I'd lined with pictures of leaf rubbings my second graders had done. "I was glad you'd said this would only be a year-long commitment." She traced a finger down the line of a leaf.

I stood a little straighter and hid my clenched fists behind my back. It wasn't like the classroom was my private space, obviously, and none of the projects lining the walls were my own, but I still felt protective of them. The kids who'd worked on them — the insanely talented ones, the ones who insisted on drawing cats with two legs, and everyone in between — had worked hard. If she wanted to judge my lack of teaching ability, I'd be really pissed if she picked on the kids' work in order to make a point.

"But I was wrong, Everett. And I hope you've changed your mind about teaching," she continued, turning on her heel to give me a bright smile. "Because if you leave, I will never hear the end of it." She scooted herself onto the edge of a short desk and braced her hands behind her.

"Wait, what?"

"The kids don't stop talking about how *cool* you are, the parents are crowing that the art display at Lilac Day will be *leveling up* this year, you bought the teachers' affection with pastries from Fanaille…"

"That was only one time."

"We're a bunch of pastry whores, Ev. It doesn't take much."

I threw the paper towel in the trash and leaned against the edge of my desk. My stomach fluttered with leftover anxiety and acute relief. "I figured you were coming in here to fire me or something."

She laughed out loud. "Please. The parents would fire *me* first."

"No, they wouldn't."

"Maybe not, but only because no one else would take the job." She winked. "So, tell me. Are you enjoying the kids?" She looked pointedly around the empty classroom, and stage-whispered, "You can speak freely. This is a judgment-free zone."

I laughed. "No, I do. I really like it." I was surprised how much. I'd assumed I was coming here to teach a bunch of backwoods philistines and instead, I was the one getting schooled. "I appreciate you pulling strings and helping me figure out how to qualify for the transitional teaching certificate. I never would have figured it out on my own."

"You're very welcome. And I really hope you'll consider finishing your certificate and staying on, even after the year is over."

I hesitated. Staying in O'Leary? Even semi-permanently? The idea didn't fill me with panic the way it might have even a few weeks before, which clearly showed that the town's cult-programming was both subtle and effective. But a permanent thing, when in just two weeks I'd already managed to become an emotional wreck in my personal life? I wasn't sure that was a good idea at all.

Then again, maybe it was a small victory that I kind of *had* a personal life again.

Maybe.

"Don't give me a decision now," Principal Turner said. "You have months before you need to decide. Just, you know… meditate on it." She winked toward the sink in the back of the room.

"I will," I promised.

She jumped off the desk. "Alrighty then. I'm going to get ready for dismissal. Make sure the fourth and fifth graders lived through their assembly and no one died of boredom."

"Which assembly was that?" I asked. "Oh, please don't tell me it was the reproduction talk."

She laughed. "No, that one comes later in the year and you'll know when it happens. Mara usually has us over to her house afterward for a debrief… and alcohol. Lots of alcohol."

"I'll look forward to it," I told her. And I thought maybe I sort of *would*. "And it was nothing about this issue with… missing people?"

Principal Turner rolled her eyes. "God, no. But I forgot! You were at the meeting the other day, weren't you?" I nodded and she shook her head slowly. "I have never *seen* my brothers as livid as they were when they heard what Karen had done. Dare and Mitch were both ready to spit. And I heard Silas was…"

"Irate?" I suggested. "Oh, yeah." I hadn't known he was capable of anger like that.

After he'd mostly quieted the crowd in the diner enough for them to hear him speak, he'd reminded all of us that there was no evidence of a crime concerning the camper, and if there was a public safety concern, Mitch would be the one to tell us. "The worst thing we can do right now is stir up more rumors. Everyone needs to sit tight and let us do our jobs," he'd insisted.

It had almost seemed to work, in the moment. But for the past two days, the only thing anyone was talking about at Fanaille, or in the staff room, or at the hardware store, was what had happened to John Carpenter and Elliot Marks, the missing camper and the missing ranger.

She sighed. "Dare's taking it really hard. Elliot Marks has worked with him for *years*. The guy called in sick Monday, then Dare didn't hear from him at all Tuesday. Went to check up on him Wednesday, and Elliot's landlady said he hadn't been back since Sunday night." Her mouth twisted. "Now Dare's thinking if only he'd followed up sooner."

I shook my head. "That's crazy."

"Yep. But guilt usually is." She shrugged. "Anyway, we definitely won't be talking to the kids about *any* of that. Today's assembly was just a drug resistance talk."

"Huh." I rubbed at my chin, noticing the stubble that was already back after just a few hours. "Drugs? I wouldn't have thought that would be a problem here," I told her. "I mean, O'Leary's so isolated, and everyone seems so...*wholesome*."

She looked at me pityingly. "Ev, honey, just because there's no decent Thai restaurant for miles doesn't mean we get a pass on crime. And it's not just the newcomers to town, either, no matter what *Karen Mitchener-Martin* says. Sometimes the very fact that we're so tight-knit makes it harder to spot."

"I can see that," I agreed. "I was just telling…um, *someone*… recently that when you've known a person their whole life, you might tend to be a little blind."

"That's for sure. Anyway, you get back to your meditation. Staff meeting Wednesday?"

"I'll be there," I said as she walked out and I returned to the sink and the brushes. My meditative mood was gone, though. All I could think about now was the idea of staying, listing all the logical reasons why a permanent place in O'Leary would probably drive me insane, and trying to push down all the reasons why my gut said insanity was tempting.

"Ev?" Si said, hesitant and cautious.

Now that was a voice that would never have to say my name more than once to get my attention. My stomach flipped as I turned my head.

"Hey. What are you doing here?"

"I was at the school for the drug presentation. But, uh… if you mean here in this room? I dunno. I just wanted to see you, mostly."

Damn if that didn't warm my shriveled, angry little heart.

Silas looked *tired*. Don't get me wrong, he also looked every bit as good as he always did. His tight black uniform pants bulged around thick thighs, his red O'Leary PD polo shirt pulled tight across his shoulders and displayed the forearms I'd drooled over like an idiot, and his wide black belt held a variety of implements, like handcuffs and a badge, that should not have been sexy, but *were*. His eyes were dull, though, and his shoulders slumped. I wanted to give him a hug.

I turned back to the sink. "How's it going?"

Silas and I hadn't spoken at all since his attempt at apologizing the other night had gotten so thoroughly derailed by Karen's interruption, and I'd been in this weird state of suspended animation ever since. I was still hurt by what he'd said last Sunday, and *yeah*, a half-apology didn't change that. But seeing him like this, worn and worried, melted away a good part of my anger.

Okay, fine, almost all of my anger. I was mostly just *sad*.

"It's been busy," he sighed, and by the scrape of the metal chair on the linoleum floor, it sounded like he'd sat down. "Exhausting."

"Any word on the missing people?"

"None." He exhaled, a sound of frustration, and the words started pouring out of him. "Of course, that means jack shit. You can't prove a negative. I mean, these guys could be in Syracuse eating ice cream right now. Or one could be in Nepal and the other at the bottom of a ravine."

I shut off the water and turned around, drying the brushes with a towel. "But you don't think that, do you?"

"A smart guy recently told me that where there's smoke there's fire," Si said with a whisper of a smile. "My gut says they're connected. But I'll be damned if we know what's happened to them, or what the connection is."

"Besides the woods, obviously." I lifted a brow when his blue eyes met mine. "I mean, they'd both been in the woods. A ranger and a hiker."

"Yeah." He rubbed a hand over his forehead. "But if that's the connection, I'm connected too. So are you, Daniel, Dare, Grace, Carmen, Mitch, Frank, Julian, Shane, Jamie, and my own father," he counted on his fingers. "And dozens more we can't even know about. Plus, both of the missing men had been in Goode's Diner and Fanaille and Hardison's Drug store in the last two weeks, and they drive the same kind of car."

"Wow," I said. "You *have* been busy."

He smiled at my surprise. "Yeah. Just a little. The thing is, these men are completely dissimilar. One is a complete novice hiker. Shiny new boots and backpack, didn't know how to light a fire or read a trail map. The other is an experienced ranger who's been trained to handle all kinds of terrain. One disappeared from the campground, and the other was last seen at his apartment in Camden on Sunday night."

Si leaned back in the kid-sized chair, his legs stretched out ridiculously long in front of him and his hands laced together on his stomach. My fingers itched to paint him this way, even though I hadn't had the urge to paint all week.

Si's face was tilted up to the fluorescent lights on the ceiling, his forehead creased like he couldn't calm his mind, even here, and as mixed up as my emotions about him were, I wished he could find a way to forget his troubles, even temporarily.

*God.* I was such an idiot.

It was like watching the half-naked cheerleader in some old-school horror flick skipping out into the dark to investigate a wounded kitten, all obvious sympathy and zero sense of self-preservation, when you just *knew* she was gonna end up skewered by the pointy end of someone's hook-hand.

Except in this case, *I* was the cheerleader. Tra la la.

But I couldn't ignore someone who was so clearly in distress and pretending not to be. And Jamie's words from the other night drifted across my brain, about how Si retreated into his calm persona when he was upset, pretended he didn't need help when he did.

"You want a pumpkin bar?" I offered, dumping my brushes on the counter and moving to my desk. "I got a couple this morning and didn't eat them. Or an apple, if you'd rather."

"I'll take the pumpkin bar. Thanks," he said, taking the white paper bag from my hand when I offered it.

I nodded and propped myself against the desk, like watching him eat was my new favorite entertainment.

The hook was coming. I could feel it.

"With everything going on, Dare hasn't had a chance to touch the giant weed-circle or the chimes. Might end up waiting until next spring at this rate, sometime before they start construction on the new visitor's center," Si said around a big bite of Cal's latest fall treat. He paused and looked at the rest of the frosted square in his hand. "Holy shit this is good."

I smiled. "Is it? It looked good."

"You didn't try it?"

I shook my head. "Wasn't hungry." If I was being truthful, my appetite had been shit for days.

"Here. Have a bite." He held the bar out casually enough, but then his eyes fixed on my mouth and he swallowed.

And suddenly, it was like the past six days had never happened. It was Saturday again, and I'd just dropped to my knees in the woods. I hadn't overheard him talking to Dare, I hadn't spent nearly a week with my stomach in knots of confused hurt. His eyes were locked on me, flashing with heat, and I leaned forward to take a bite right from his hand.

His breath hitched, his pupils dilated.

I wanted to kiss him so badly.

My pulse sped and I cursed myself for being an idiot, for falling for his charm once again. The push-pull of feelings between us was like an electromagnetic force, and I couldn't imagine he didn't feel it too on some level, even if he was choosing to ignore it. Even if pretending it didn't exist was the smart, simple thing to do.

*You are such an idiot, Everett.*

"Did you hear what I said before?" Si said. "They didn't move the chimes. I… I thought you'd be glad about that."

"What? Oh. Yeah, no, I am," I lied. "The weeds can go, but I liked the chimes."

An awkward silence fell, maybe the first one I could remember between us. I wanted him to come closer to me, oddly. I hadn't realized just how badly I needed a hug until I had his arms in my field of vision.

The trouble with opening myself up to Silas was that I couldn't control the outcome. I couldn't say yes to the belly flips and the easy attraction, the comfort and laughter, and shut off the part that would worry and ache and get so pissed off I wanted to scream. I couldn't shut off the part that was really crushed my freak-out had ruined things for us, and wanted that look in his eyes to mean maybe they weren't ruined *permanently*.

It was scary as hell.

"So, how's Hen?" Si asked easily, not recognizing that I was in the middle of a transformative moment just then. "Did I miss any more clandestine Romeo and Juliet scenes?"

I took a deep breath and glanced up.

"Silas, what are we doing here?"

He licked a crumb of pumpkin bar off his lip and swallowed, watching me warily. "Talking?"

"Not good enough." I looked around at my little classroom, decked out in leaf prints and primary colors. It was an unlikely scene for life-altering revelations and a really inappropriate scene for this showdown.

But I was starting to realize that nothing ever happened very neatly, at least not for me. And that was okay.

"What is it that you want from me?" I demanded. "What is it you want for us?"

He swallowed again, and his eyes flared.

"The other day in the woods was…" I glanced at the open classroom door and the totally not-private hall beyond. "It was great. And I know I totally spoiled the moment afterward…"

"You didn't."

I shook my head. "You know I heard what you said to Dare. And I thought maybe you wanted to apologize just to be a nice guy. So we could be friends. If that's what you want, tell me."

Silas braced his hands on his knees and stood, walking toward me in slow motion while our eyes locked. It was hot as fuck. "I-If you forgive me, I'll apologize," I stuttered.

He smiled, this slow, warm glow stealing over his face. "In that case, I forgive you."

"What?"

He lifted his hand to my jaw, and I froze. "God. You're so fucking cute, even when you're not trying to be cute," he mused, stroking his thumb over my cheek. "Okay, listen up, Everett Maior, because I was all prepared to do this Wednesday, and I got upstaged. Ready?"

"Maybe?"

"I am an asshole. And worse than that, I'm a coward. Okay?"

"I guess?" I could feel my heart beat in every part of my body, nervous and excited at once. Surely that couldn't be healthy?

"*You* didn't ruin a damn thing. I ruined it. Because *I'mfallingforyou.*" He huffed out a relieved breath, like he'd just completed a Herculean task.

"Wait… what?"

"I'm falling for you," he repeated, and it was no less unbelievable, even when he enunciated. "And it scared me out of my mind, so I said a lot of stupid and patently untrue things. Like that I wasn't into you."

I frowned in confusion. "Nope. Still don't understand. You're commitment-cautious." *Just like I'm risk-averse.*

"Yeah. I am. But then this incredibly hot, overly suspicious smart-ass moved to town and apparently I couldn't resist."

"Me?"

He smiled and his eyes crinkled at the corners. "No, the other incredibly hot, overly suspicious smart-ass." He put a hand at my waist and pulled me into him. "Yes. You. And if you didn't realize it, you're the only person in town who hasn't."

"But… but you said…"

His fingertips traced the curve of my eyebrow. "You're the only thing I've been able to see or think about for weeks." He pushed his fingers back through the hair above my ear and cradled my head with his strong hand. "I thought maybe if I denied it, I could stop it. But the truth is, I was in free fall the moment we met… and I just keep falling."

His blue eyes shining down at me looked a little scared and a lot turned on, which was pretty much exactly how I was feeling, too.

My poor little not-so-risk-averse heart stuttered in my chest.

"Please forgive me for what you overheard the other day, because that was bullshit. It was me being afraid of this. Of you. Of how you make me feel."

*Ugh.* That scream you heard was me losing my grip on

the last vestiges of my anger and letting myself get lured out of my hard, protective shell.

*Hook-Hand claims another victim.*

# Chapter Thirteen

SILAS

MY STOMACH CHURNED as I waited for Ev to say something. Anything. God, I really, really hated this stuff. I couldn't remember the last time I'd felt so vulnerable, and vulnerable was not remotely comfortable.

What I'd said to him was the absolute truth: I was already too into him to turn back, and I'd realized it about ten seconds after my weak-ass bullshit had caused him to flee the bar.

I'd drowned my sorrows in three more beers with Dare, then let him take me home and pour me into bed. I vaguely remembered begging him to get me Reggie's number, and him laughing in my face and telling me Reggie's number was the last thing I needed.

Turned out he was right. The next day, I'd woken up nauseous, and not from the beer but from the memory of the expression on Everett's face as he'd walked out. That hadn't been the face of a guy who didn't give a shit about me, plain and simple.

And I was a punk-ass weakling who'd hurt a good man because I was afraid I was falling alone.

Maybe Ev was right and I needed to change the way I looked at things, because sometimes lately, it seemed like I put two and two together and got five and a half.

Ev licked his lips and my whole body swayed toward him, just as it always had from literally the first minute we'd met.

I didn't believe in fate or destiny, but there was something about this connection between us that could maybe change my mind. Every time one of us stepped back, something pulled us together tighter.

"So, let's just say I was convinced to forgive you," Ev whispered. He lifted his hands to my wrists where they rested against his waist and neck. "What would that mean?" He swallowed. "For us."

"Whatever you need it to mean," I answered promptly. I'd thought of this, too. "I get that you're here temporarily, and don't know if you're ready for a… a relationship, or a friendship, or something in between, but I'll try to go along with whatever you want."

"So if I said I wanted to step back? To just be friends?"

Goddamn it. I'd snuck that in there, hoping he wouldn't notice.

"Then I guess that's what we'll be," I said. I brushed my thumb over his cheek, just memorizing the feeling of it. "We can hang out. Maybe, um… hike and stuff." I tried for a normal smile. "Watch football, since you seemed so intrigued by it the other day."

Ev smiled. "Wow."

"Wow?"

"That's adorable. You, pretending to make an effort. I'd rate it a B. You're very sweet, but there's a distinct lack of enthusiasm."

"Are you seriously giving me shit for this?" I asked.

His green eyes danced. "I'm just thinking it's a good thing I don't just want friendship from you." He lifted himself on his tiptoes and his mouth was so very close to mine. "I want to go slow because… well, last time I jumped too fast, and I guess I wasn't ready."

"Right. Yeah, totally." Relief flooded my system, filling up all the dark places where my doubts had taken root. "As slow as you want. Just… just as long as I know you're in this with me. That you feel this too."

Ev smiled. "Yeah, I'm with you."

"Good." I forced myself to release him, to take a step back so I wouldn't crowd him. Slow, he'd said, and this time I was determined to make sure it happened that way. "So maybe we could get dinner sometime?"

Ev chewed on his lip and studied my face thoughtfully. "What are you doing right now?"

"Uh. Nothing, really." I looked down at my uniform and then at Ev's button-down shirt and khaki pants. "What did you have in mind?"

"Well, I thought maybe we could just hang out. Do something relaxing. You look like you need it."

"Wanna go for a hike?"

His eyes widened. "Uh, no way. Listen, you can say what you like about the disappearances not being connected to the woods, but I don't think I'll be spending much time there until John Carpenter and Elliot Marks are found."

"So where should we go then?"

He smiled, soft and mischievous. "I have an idea," he said.

———

IT TURNED out Everett's idea involved hanging out at the fenced-in playground right behind the school, complete with a jungle gym, swing set, and merry-go-round. The place was deserted, with every kid eager to flee school for the weekend. The school parking lot was virtually empty, too, since the teachers had also cleared out. It was as private a spot as you could get this close to town, but still...

"Are you kidding me?" I demanded as he sat his ass on a swing and threw me a smile.

"What, are you too cool for playgrounds?"

"Babe, I was too cool for playgrounds back when I was the right age to play on playgrounds." I ran a hand over the sturdy wood of the play set and jiggled the frame to test for stability before gingerly sitting my bulk down on one of the swings next to him.

"Well, you're hanging with *me* now, *babe*," he teased. "And I've never been cool."

I laughed and inhaled a deep lungful of the warm autumn air. It smelled like fresh cut grass and reminded me of years spent playing football over at the high school, or kicking a soccer ball with Matty in our backyard.

"So, listen. I have a really important question for you," Ev said somberly. "And, uh... as much as I like you, your answer to this could really impact the future of this relationship. Are you ready?"

"I guess."

I'd heard from my mom that she'd invited Everett to the memorial thing she insisted on planning for Matty's anniversary, so I figured it could be about that.

Or maybe he wanted some level of exclusivity in our relationship, which I was sure I could handle. It felt like a long time since I'd thought of anyone but him anyway.

I steeled myself. "Ask."

He leaned his head on the chain of the swing and watched me steadily. "If you had to pick three people to be on your team for the zombie apocalypse, who would you pick?"

The breath whooshed out of my lungs. "What?"

"Which three people…"

"I heard you! I mean… that's your important question?" I narrowed my eyes. "Are you insane?"

"Are you saying that the zombie apocalypse *isn't* important? Because, honestly, Si, I was hoping you were smarter than that." He shook his head sadly.

I blinked in disbelief, and he smiled, bright and wide and *challenging*, all that light and life just inches from me, warming me through.

I scratched the back of my head. "Well, Bruce Campbell, the guy who played Ash in *Evil Dead*, obviously."

Ev snorted rudely. "*Too* obvious."

"Obvious for a *reason*. God. You want a job done, you hire an expert."

"Uh-huh. Not impressed," he said airily. He pumped his legs to make himself swing higher. "Who else?"

I thought for another minute. "Do they have to be real?"

"Like Ash from *Evil Dead* is real?"

I grinned at his sass and let myself swing slightly. "Fine. Lancelot."

"From the Knights of the Round Table? Why?"

"In case the bullets run out, obviously. He's good with a sword."

Ev made a gagging noise. "That's gruesome!" he complained.

"Because zombies *aren't* gruesome?" I retorted, turning his earlier tone on him.

His laughter rang through the air. "Okay, and number three?"

"That's tough. But I'm gonna say… Dwight Schrute from *The Office*. Because he's a farmer." I tilted my head and smiled innocently. "So I'll have food, just in case it takes Ash a minute to kill everyone."

"He farms *beets*!" he said. "I'd rather let the zombies get me."

"Beets are delicious. And anyway, who would you pick? Since clearly you've given this considerable thought and done all kinds of research." I leaned back, making my swing go higher to match his.

"I haven't, actually, I just made it up right now," he said, his eyes on mine as he swung faster. "But clearly the only correct answers are Alexander the Great, Dracula, and McSteamy from *Grey's Anatomy*."

I laughed out loud. "Those are the correct answers?"

"Alexander the Great for, you know, strategy. Dracula because they can't kill him if he's already undead…"

"And McSteamy to patch up your ouchies?"

"Uh… Yes. *Yes*, Silas, let's say that I picked the iconic hot doctor for purely practical medical reasons."

"Oh, I see how it is. *Oh, Hot Doctor McSteamy! The world could end tonight!*" I simpered, fluttering my eyelashes. "*I don't wanna die un-fucked!*"

He giggled, a light, free sound as he swung higher and higher. "No shit! I'm no idiot. But listen, good luck to you and Dwight. I'm sure you'll make the most of whatever time you have, also." He cocked his head. "I wonder if he's a top or a bottom."

"That's… not… *ugh*." I shuddered, and he laughed.

"Lancelot might be gentler," Ev said, deadpan. "If you're into that kind of thing."

My mind stuttered, wondering if gentle was something Ev was into… or not.

"There's only one way to settle a deep, intellectual debate like this one," I told him once my brain was back online. I swung myself higher, and the chains above my head creaked.

"You mean…?"

I nodded. "Playground rules."

He looked at the flat, open space in front of us and then back to me.

"Whoever jumps the furthest wins? *Jesus*," he muttered. "You do remember that I just bruised the shit out of my knee a couple of weeks ago?" But he, too, started swinging higher.

"Oh, shoot, I forgot." I grinned at him evilly. "Does that mean I win?"

He laughed, breathless. "No fucking way. You're stronger but I'm lighter. Even odds."

"Okay, count of three, then, lightweight."

He pumped his feet, frantically gaining height as I counted and then finally, at *three*, we both let go and flew…

And fell.

I landed on my hands and knees, with Ev sprawled inelegantly on his front a few feet away — in a nearly dead-even tie, not that either of us cared.

The whole situation was so absurd — Officer Silas Sloane, thirty-eight years old, trying to win a zombie debate by playground rules — that I flopped over on my back, stared up at the blue, blue sky and laughed so hard I cried. I couldn't remember the last time I laughed that hard or that long, just completely giving myself over to it… unless maybe it was the night we met, a few weeks before.

We lay on the grass sniffling and chuckling a few minutes later, watching the clouds roll by and the tops of the trees become gilded by the sinking sun. The whole world glowed.

"The golden hour," Ev said softly, and I knew he meant the light and the atmosphere, but…

This time was exactly what I'd needed and not known I needed. This interlude where I could just relax and remember why I loved this town and the peace that could be found here.

I couldn't have achieved this on my own. I'd needed Ev to bring me here. I reached a hand across the cool grass and let my pinkie brush his. "Thank you."

"For what? Beating your ass at playground rules? *Pfft.* Anytime."

I chuckled. "Okay, you didn't win. It was a tie. At *best*." I took a breath as he giggled. "I meant for bringing me here. For being exactly what I needed. If the zombie apocalypse comes tonight, this was a cool way to spend my last day."

He rolled onto his elbow facing me and edged a tiny bit closer. "Silas?"

"Yeah?"

"*Oh, Silas… The world could end tonight…*"

I shifted my head to watch him warily.

"I really don't want to go home right now," he said. And then he leaned toward me slowly, so slowly that I could see the golden light play off his beautiful green eyes and memorize every single flicker of emotion I read there. Caution and hope and affection and want.

His lips met mine for a second before he pulled back to watch me, like *he* wasn't sure how *I* was going to react. It would have been comical if I'd been capable of laughing in that moment.

"Come back to my house," I blurted, but we both knew that I was offering more. Offering everything.

Hell, he could have any damn thing he wanted, all he had to do was ask.

But all he said was, "Okay." And then he stood up and reached down a hand for me.

I let him help me to my feet, then wrapped my arm around his waist and led him to my truck, which was parked on the side of the road by the school.

We walked slowly, and I helped him in slowly, just as I had that night a few weeks back. I drove us back to my place slowly, and drove slowly down the driveway to park right in front of the garage. I wanted to give him every opportunity to think, to rethink, to test all of his suspicions and superstitions and come to a decision.

Because once I got close to him again, I didn't think I'd be able to go slowly at all.

"Come on." I nodded at the garage. "I have something to show you."

I climbed down and unlocked the garage door, then rolled it up to reveal the mostly disassembled pieces of what had been my grandfather's pride and joy.

"What is it?" Ev said, stepping forward to run his hand over the primer-coated quarter panel. "A sports car?"

"Mmm hmm. A 1984 Porsche 944. It used to be orange. My grandmother used to call it my grandfather's midlife-crisis-mobile."

He smiled. "And you're restoring it?"

"Kinda," I acknowledged. "I haven't touched it in a while. I like knowing it's here. But, uh, here's what I wanted to show you."

I nodded at the box in the shadowy back corner.

He looked from the box to me, then back again, and frowned. "Are those... mine?"

"Your art supplies, yeah. I drove over to Rushton and

grabbed them out of your car last week before it got junked, just in case you wanted them."

"This is what you were going to show me Saturday night?"

I nodded. "Before I got called out."

He closed his eyes and shook his head, but a small smile played over his lips like he was pleased and surprised. "Are you likely to get called out tonight?"

I shrugged. "I don't think so, but I never know. It could happen."

"Well, I really, really hope that doesn't happen, Silas." He stood and stalked toward me. "I want you."

"Are you sure?" I couldn't help but ask. "Be sure, Everett."

"Positive."

That was all I needed to hear. I grabbed his hips and hauled him against me, loving the way the breath huffed out of his lungs at the contact. He smelled like green grass and sunshine, and I savored it.

Ev surged forward so his lips pressed against mine, but I pushed him back just slightly.

"We don't have to rush anything, Ev."

"We don't have to go too slow, either," he whispered. He trailed his hands down over my chest, finding my nipples through the soft cotton. "It's okay, I promise."

There were still so many things I wanted to talk to him about, shit that I wanted to get sorted in my mind. Like, we still hadn't exactly talked about why he'd cried after the first time we'd done anything physical, and I wanted to be sure he was really okay.

And... what exactly did he want from me, besides *not-friendship*? The irony of being on the other side of the coin, wondering if the guy I was into wanted something besides a friendly hookup was pretty fucking un-funny.

It felt so good and so right to have Ev beside me, but the ghost of that vulnerability I'd been feeling earlier… hell, that I'd been feeling since Saturday, if I was being honest… still clogged the back of my mind.

He grinned up at me and shook his head like he could sense my hesitation. "I can practically hear you thinking. It feels like a weird kind of role reversal. I thought I was the suspicious overthinker. There are no squirrels here to eat us, Silas."

I huffed out a laugh.

"What was it you were saying last weekend? Not everything needs to be a struggle? Don't make things harder than they need to be?"

He was right. After a week of worrying that I'd fucked things up beyond repair, he was in my arms again and he wanted me. Why the hell was I hesitating?

I laughed and ran my hands down over the curve of his ass, squeezing his cheeks and pulling him against me again. "Why don't you tell me how *hard* they *need to be*, Everett?"

He moaned.

"Why don't you tell me everything you'd like to have happen right now," I continued, whispering in his ear. "Just to make sure we're on the same page."

"T-tell you?" he stuttered, rubbing himself against me. He was getting hard already, and *fuck, yeah* that turned me on. I felt my own cock respond with a happy throb.

"Exactly," I replied, tracing the seam of his ass through his khakis. "You're the artist. Paint me a picture."

"Don't stop doing that," he breathed, clutching my shoulders.

"Then start talking."

He licked his lips. "T-tell you one of my fantasies? About you?"

"Is there more than one?" I rucked up his shirt in the

back, slowly pulling it from his pants, eager to get my hands on his skin.

It occurred to me that I hadn't really ever touched him, not anywhere you wouldn't touch a casual friend, and I needed to rectify this immediately.

His cheeks became ruddy and his eyes dilated.

"There are several. I think about, um… blow jobs." He punctuated the word with a tiny thrust of his hips, like he couldn't help himself from seeking friction.

"And?"

"Uh… You coming into the hardware store, all pissed off like you were the other night at the meeting, with your blue eyes blazing and your jaw clenched." He lifted one hand from my shoulder to trace my jaw, and his eyes met mine. "And you take it out on me by fucking me over the counter."

"Jesus." I ran both palms over the smooth, hot skin of his back, but it wasn't enough to feel it. I wanted to see it, to taste it, to *mark* it.

"But my favorite one is about… your truck." His breath stuttered and my hands stopped roaming.

I looked over Ev's shoulder, through the open door of the garage, to the driveway where my truck sat innocently reflecting the yellow-orange glow of the setting sun. "What *about* my truck?" I growled.

"The first night we met you…You made that stupid comment. Do you remember?"

I shook my head. "Something dumb about…"

"About strapping me down… in the bed of your truck. *Yeah.*" He swallowed. "I've never done anything like that before, but… it kinda got me thinking."

I looked down at his fever-bright eyes and the flush that had spread down his neck to the open collar of his shirt. *Fuck* I loved that. Loved that he was turning himself on even as he turned me on. All of the available blood in my body rushed south.

I pushed him away from me abruptly, almost violently. "Get inside, Ev," I said, pointing a finger at the little red door that led from the driveway into the kitchen. "And I'm warning you right now, unless you'd like to make that fantasy a reality, *right now* and *in front of my neighbors*, do not stop at the truck. Do not look at the truck. Try as hard as you can not to even *think* about the truck. Understand?"

He nodded, eyes wide.

"Move!"

He scurried out the door with me hot on his heels, but he hesitated as we passed the driver's side door, and he let his fingers trail over the sideview mirror.

"Everett," I growled.

"It's like not thinking about *elephants*," he wailed. "You tell me not to think about the truck, and all I can think of are all the ways you can bend me over it!"

I picked him up around the waist, total battering-ram style with zero finesse, ignoring the little *eep* noise he made, and ran him up to the door. I unlocked the single lock in what had to be record time, and had him with his belly pressed against the inside of the door in five seconds flat.

"Jesus! Your neighbors are scandalized!"

"I seriously hope Mrs. Daley was looking out the window right then," I growled. "The poor woman needs some excitement in her life."

And I really didn't want to talk about Mrs. Daley.

I moved my mouth to the side of his neck and licked a stripe up the side at the same moment that my hand found the button of his waistband.

"Tell me more about being strapped down," I instructed.

"I don't... I..." He shook his head like he was trying to

clear it, like he was too excited for words. *Perfect.* "You tied my hands behind my back and pushed me down and I kept struggling."

I snorted as I flicked his button open. "What a strange fantasy. You, argumentative?"

He shot me a glare over his shoulder that melted into a slack-jawed moan as I rubbed my hand down the front of his underwear. The side of his head thunked against the door as he gave himself over to it.

"You were struggling uselessly," I prompted. "And…"

"And you… put me over your shoulder and tied me down in the bed of the truck with my arms spread wide."

*Fuck.*

"And then what?" I demanded, stroking him through the cotton while I wedged my own erection against the curve of his ass. *Too fast, too fast,* I kept thinking, but with him talking this way I didn't, *couldn't*, care.

"I-I don't know," he whispered.

I pulled him off the door and spun him around to face me. I could just make out his eyes in the fading light. "Bull-shit. Tell me."

He shook his head, bit his lip. "I don't know."

"Everett…"

"I came before I got to that part," he admitted in a quiet voice, looking somewhere over my shoulder. "I've never played that way before. I don't know what would happen next. I don't know how it ends."

God, this man. He made me *want* things.

"I have an idea," I said, giving him the same soft, mischievous smile he'd given me earlier, in his classroom. "Come on."

I led him down the hall to my bedroom, bypassing the tiny living room with its stone fireplace, the dining area, and the bathroom. If I got my way, there would be plenty of time to give him a tour later. I flipped on the light switch as we entered and shut the door behind us, locking us in this little space closed off from everything.

He stepped around me, looking around at the iron bed frame, the plain wooden dresser and end tables, the comfortable quilt. "This is not what I would have pictured," he said quietly. "But I really like it."

Not nearly as much as I liked having him here. I couldn't remember the last time I'd brought a man home. Years, maybe. And I was glad of that. Glad, because it made Ev special.

"Take your shirt off," I told him, pushing back all the other stupidly *real* shit that threatened to spill out of my mouth. "You want to go fast? Do it now."

He blinked once, slowly, and his mouth curved into a smile.

"I don't know why your bossiness is doing it for me right now," he said suspiciously. "When you ask me to do that, like the beginning of some bad porn…"

"Everett? I wasn't asking."

His smile fled, his eyes flared, and his fingers moved to unbutton his shirt very, very slowly.

"Pants too," I said, and this time he didn't argue, just kicked off his shoes and socks, undressing until he stood there, nearly naked and completely delectable.

His stomach was flat and lightly muscled, with three little beauty marks scattered just above the waistband of his boxers, like some tiny constellation guiding me home. I reached out a single finger and traced them, watching his cock jump behind the red cotton that restrained it.

My poor cock, which hadn't been remotely satisfied by last week's blowjob after weeks and weeks of drought, was so hard it was damp, and I prayed for the patience to hold out long enough to finish this.

"Let me see if I remember the circumstances," I said, adjusting myself as I walked behind him. I took off my belt and left it on the dresser, kicked my shoes into the corner, and pulled off my shirt and pants until I was nearly as undressed as he was. "You were trying to handle something you couldn't handle. I was afraid you would get hurt."

He huffed out a half-laugh that was nearly giddy. "I'm hurting right now."

"We can't have that," I said. "Get on the bed."

I waited until he'd laid himself facedown on my bed, like a starfish — a sight I knew I'd relive every time I walked in this room for the foreseeable future — before kneeling on the bed to straddle him and pushing his hands into the bed on either side.

"Was this what you were imagining?" I curled his hands into the edge of the mattress.

"Y-yeah…" He swallowed. "This is better."

"Everett, you'd better hold on. If you move those hands I'm going to be mad."

He shivered again, like this was part of the fantasy, too, or maybe even better, and I swear to God, I felt like a king.

I had never played this way with anyone. I'd never felt so… focused and so free with anyone. What the fuck was it about this guy that had changed everything I wanted from one heartbeat to the next?

I sat back on my heels and ran a hand down the red cotton of his boxer briefs, tracing his crease.

"*Ohmygod*," he breathed, grinding himself into my mattress, which was so hot I could barely stand it. "Hurry, hurry, hurry."

But instead, I slowed down, taking my time palming and squeezing the muscles of his truly delectable ass, snapping the waistband hard when he whimpered at me to speed up. I pulled them down oh-so-slowly, unwrapping him like a present, thrilling with every inch of skin that was revealed. In this moment, he was mine.

He turned his head on the pillow, his cheeks hot and temples damp, one hot, angry eye meeting mine.

"Are you just about done?" he demanded. "Because I'm dying here."

"Not quite," I said.

He huffed out a breath and it was so adorable I had to lean forward to brush a kiss over his lips.

He shifted beneath me, giving up his grip on the mattress entirely and turning his torso over to kiss me better.

"Was this the fantasy?" I asked.

Ev shook his head. "Fuck the fantasy. In the fantasy I wasn't kissing you, and I really, really want to kiss you." He looked surprised by his own admission, but I was pretty damn happy.

I lifted my hips so he could turn over fully, and when I leaned back down again, our cocks rubbed against one another, separated by only the thin layer of my boxers. *Fuck.* I couldn't remember anything feeling so good *ever.* And then he ran his hand down my back, pushing my underwear down to my thighs so he could grip my ass in both hands. He pulled me more firmly against him while he lifted his hips to rub mine.

"Just like this," he whispered. "Better than the fantasy, Silas. Kiss me."

So I did. Tiny laughing kisses and long drugging ones, tiny nips at his jaw and my ear punctuated by Everett's sighs and my groans. I rocked against him like a teenager with no skill at all, just joyful and wide-eyed and alive to the sensation. And when his breathing hitched and he said, "Holy shit. I… I'm *close,*" like he couldn't believe it, I swear to God, it felt like the first time I'd ever done this; stunning and artless and natural and beautiful.

It was a novel experience to think that this was the first time with Ev. In the past, I'd never considered that it was the first, because I hadn't cared whether there would be a follow-up. Ev was my first *first*.

I wanted to laugh, but it came out closer to a sob, and I let more of my weight fall on him and rocked myself against him more firmly. I let my hand coast down his side to grab both our cocks, messy with precum, and shuttled my fist over them, jacking us together. I could feel my orgasm building at the base of my spine, unstoppable as a freight train, and I moved my hand faster still, needing him to come first.

"My God. *Silas!*" he yelled, and then he came, his release spilling on his stomach about five seconds before I did.

With my underwear still tangled around my damn legs.

I buried my face in the crook between his neck and shoulder and chuckled.

"Okay. That was," he panted. "That was… some very *good* porn."

I laughed harder and reached down to smack the side of his ass. I felt his grin against my cheek.

Then I rolled off to the side, taking him and the mess we'd made along with me. He lay with his head on my chest for a long minute, staring out the window as the sky turned pink and then purple-gray. But as far as I was concerned, it was still the golden hour. Heavy and fated and a tiny bit magical.

If you believed in that stuff.

"If you'd told me on the night we met that this would happen, I wouldn't have believed you," Ev said finally. The sky had darkened so completely I couldn't see his eyes. "I didn't know I could feel this way again."

"What way?" I asked, and I wondered if he was going to say something crazy, something ridiculous, something impossibly fast, something I'd never wanted to hear from anyone else. My stomach flipped with something that wasn't quite fear.

"I feel… *happy*," Ev said, leaning up to kiss me.

And I told myself that was good enough.

# Chapter Fourteen

SILAS

"You need another drink?" I yelled from the kitchen. "Popcorn's nearly done."

"Nah," Ev said from his spot on my navy blue sofa. "I'm good."

I opened the refrigerator and heard the channel change in the living room. "I swear to God, if you're putting on that stupid show again…" I yelled, but I didn't finish the threat. I never did. Mostly because I liked arguing with Ev almost as much as I hated the shows he liked to watch.

"Uh, how about a little respect? This was the best-rated drama on television."

"Like ten years ago!" I said, rescuing the popcorn from the microwave as it dinged.

"Making it a classic, old man."

"Making it *outdated*, whippersnapper." I dumped the popcorn in a bowl and sprinkled it liberally with salt then carried it out to the living room, where Ev was sprawled on two-thirds of the sofa under a blanket. I handed him the bowl and sat on what had become *my* spot, with my feet propped on the little coffee table in front of me. "Not that it was ever that accurate to begin with."

"That guy is cute."

"*That guy* is at a crime scene without gloves," I sighed. Ev elbowed me in the stomach. He hated when I interrupted his viewing with comments about realism.

Which was why I did it.

"Okay, but seriously though. It's daytime on that show, right? They just walked through the sunshine to get inside? Explain to me why they're in the *dark*, using *flashlights.*"

"Because that's how real police work is done, Officer Sloane," Ev said. "With dark-lights and fluorescent spray. Pay attention. Learn something."

I pushed my lips together to hide my smile, but I couldn't quite do it, and when he saw me smile, he smiled too.

"And that's why they never turn the lights on in the lab, either?"

"They're concerned for the environment! Some people take this stuff seriously." He pointedly looked at the doorway kitchen, where I'd left the light on.

I rolled my eyes. "The victim guy is trapped in a cave…"

"Underwater." He shrugged. "I've seen this one before."

"Right. And meanwhile, the cops find his girlfriend at work, tending bar? If you can't call in sick because your boyfriend is trapped in a cave…"

"An underwater cave," Ev supplied.

"Uh-huh. If that's not a good excuse to not smile at customers all night, what is?"

"Maybe she doesn't like her boyfriend all that much," Ev mused. "Maybe he's an annoying person. Maybe he interrupts her when she's trying to watch television."

I grabbed the throw pillow from beside me and bopped Ev on the head. "If you were trapped in a cave, I'd be out looking for you. I think that's, like, a baseline for boyfriend behavior."

Ev went tense and I mentally rewound my comment to see what had set him off. *Oh.* The B-word. More perilous around here than dropping an f-bomb in front of Dragon Dorian back in the day.

Ev selected a piece of popcorn from the bowl and crunched it methodically, watching me like he was waiting for me to say something more, but I kept my mouth firmly shut. I'd learned, over the past three weeks of being *not-just-friends* with Everett Maior that it didn't do to push him to define exactly what we were, or to come any closer to suggesting we were boyfriends than I'd already done. It didn't do to ask him why the box of paint supplies was still sitting in my garage, untouched, or why he'd never stay the night. Otherwise, he'd…

"I should probably get going," Ev said, throwing the blanket back like he'd heard all the things I hadn't said. He set the popcorn bowl on the table and felt beneath it for his shoes.

"It's still early," I reminded him.

"But you wore me out before dinner." He wiggled his eyebrows. "And I have school tomorrow and you have work." He kneeled on the carpet so he could wedge more of his arm under the table. "Speaking of which, anything new?"

I shook my head. "Believe me, if I found anything on John Carpenter or Elliot, I'd have told you," I said glumly. "You know, you really don't have to go."

Ev found one shoe, dug it out, and looked fixedly at the laces as he untied them. "I really do, though," he said. "Remember, I have a grandfather who expects me home by *a decent hour*." He rolled his eyes. "I swear he's taught Daphne how to meow in a really guilt-inducing way, too."

I said nothing. There wasn't much *to* say. This had been our routine for the past three weeks — three weeks in which I'd learned every inch of Everett's delectable skin and all the best possible ways to make him come with my mouth and hands, three weeks in which we'd christened my shower and couch and bed and kitchen table (and on one delightful occasion, the front seat of my truck), three weeks in which we'd talked around the idea of anal sex but I hadn't pushed the issue because I was too busy watching Everett systematically wall off any deeper connection between us, brick by careful brick.

I thought I finally understood why Jamie kept going back to Parker's bar, though. Why he kept slamming himself against a brick wall, and couldn't manage to stay away, even when he knew it was going to fuck him up relentlessly.

My phone dinged on the side table, and I reached over to grab it, then sighed as I read the display.

"Called out?" Ev asked, sliding his shoe on.

"No. My mom's worried she'll have to cancel the memorial hike for Matty's anniversary next Sunday."

Ev looked up from tying his shoe to blink at me. "Why don't you sound happier? You haven't exactly been looking forward to this."

I leaned my head back against the sofa cushion. "Because she's canceling it on account of people in town being afraid to go in the woods since Elliot and John are still missing."

Ev winced. "That's not your fault," he said.

"I know it isn't!" I said, exasperated. "But that doesn't mean I don't feel like there's something else I should be doing. I'm sitting here with you and maybe I could be… I don't know, out looking for someone."

Ev stopped digging under the sofa for his second shoe and plopped next to me. "You've followed every lead, Silas. You've done everything you can."

"And it's not good enough." I scrubbed my face with my hands. "Nothing is ever enough."

"What does that mean?

I shook my head. "Nothing. I'm just… frustrated."

"About the case?" He was cautious.

"About a lot of fucking things." I was getting tired of caution. "I don't get why she needs to have a memorial for Matty in the first place, but I sure as fuck don't understand why it has to be on *that* particular day. Are we celebrating his life? Or celebrating his *death*?"

Ev sat quietly for a second. "I know it's exhausting, but she's trying. She reminds me a lot of my mother — constant wailing and hand-wringing. Just agreeing to make it a hike instead of some graveside thing was a concession…"

I pushed to my feet and stared down at him. "I'm sure it felt like a concession to her. It doesn't feel like a concession to me. I want to be patient with her, but is it wrong to wish that she could learn to be just a little happier about what she has right now, rather than focusing on what she's missing?"

Yeah, caution and I weren't even in the same *room* right now.

I wanted my fucking boyfriend to say that he was my boyfriend. I wanted us to sleep together all night and wake up in the same bed. I wanted us to be *together*, so maybe I didn't feel like he had one foot out the door all the time and was taking two steps away for every one we took forward.

I wanted to be the bakery treat. I didn't want to be the potato.

I ran a hand through my hair and sighed. That was literally the stupidest thing I'd ever thought about myself, and I owed Reggie What's-his-name a huge fucking apology for ever thinking it about him.

I fucking *hated* that I'd become an insecure, whiny fuck.

Maybe I should have foreseen it from the beginning, though. I'd known we weren't in the same place. I'd just sort of imagined that we would start where we were and move forward together slowly. I hadn't anticipated that we'd be detouring backward first.

"Grief is like a security blanket sometimes," Everett said, staring at his own hands. "It's hard to throw it off all at once. Maybe give her time."

I huffed out a breath and stretched my neck from side to side. "How long?" I asked.

We both knew I wasn't talking about my mother.

"Is it so terrible?" he asked.

I tried to find the words to tell him without sounding like an idiot. I wasn't sure I could. I rubbed the back of my neck.

"Sometimes. It's really, really hard to compete with someone who's dead, Everett. There's no way to win. I'm always going to be second best."

Second best to my parents, second best to Ev's husband.

Ev peered up at me, stunned. "You… you really feel that, don't you?" Ev said.

I shrugged. "I mostly try not to think about it at all."

Ev frowned. "This is why you ignore your mother?"

"I don't *ignore* her."

"I mean, you don't visit her either."

I turned to glare at him. "How the fuck did this conversation become a debate on my treatment of my mother?"

Ev shook his head. "It's not. It's *not*. I just sometimes don't understand how you and I look at the same facts and come up with two completely different interpretations."

"Right, and mine are all wrong?" I was defensive and I couldn't stop it.

"In this case?" Ev stood too and stepped forward until he was right in front of me, one shoe on and one shoe off. "You're dead wrong, Silas."

He grabbed my jaw in his smooth, cool hands and forced me to look at him.

"Silas Sloane, you are *no one's* second choice. You're a second chance."

I wanted to believe it. God, I did. So, I closed my eyes and let him kiss me, let him tow me to the sofa and attempt to prove his words to me.

But when he drove out of my driveway a few hours later, I knew they weren't true, even if I wanted them to be. I just wasn't sure what I wanted to do about it.

# Chapter Fifteen

### EVERETT

"Daphne?" I walked up and down the hall of Grandpa's apartment for the third time, shaking the box of cat treats and making kissy noises. "Daph, come out and eat!" The sound of fresh treats was usually a siren song to the little beast, but of course not *today*, because today I was in a hurry.

"Daphne, you are such a shithead," I muttered under my breath as I crossed back into the kitchen and set the box on the counter.

"*Language*, Everett," Grandpa Hen called from the living room, and I rolled my eyes. His hearing was more acute than most men half his age, unless his doctor was delivering some warning about taking it easy on his recently un-casted leg, in which case Henry was conveniently deaf.

"You ready to go?" I asked, dusting off my khaki pants and rolling up the sleeves of my jacket as I entered the living room. "I told Silas we'd grab a table if we got to the diner before… *Seriously?*"

Grandpa was rocking in his favorite recliner with

Daphne sprawled on his lap like a giant blanket, the white of her fur a perfect match to the hair on his face and his head. They both looked up when I walked in, and it was a tossup as to who looked more smug.

I folded my arms over my chest and gave them both a dirty look.

Daphne gave me the feline equivalent of an eye roll, then lay back down like she couldn't *even* with my drama, as the kids at school said. Grandpa shrugged and stroked a hand along her back.

"I thought she was a demon cat," I challenged. "A tripping hazard? A menace?"

"Hush, Everett," Grandpa admonished, holding Daphne protectively. "You'll hurt her feelings."

I gave him a slow blink. "Is this… reality?"

He hmphed. "Daphne and I have come to an understanding," he said. "She has discerning taste just like I do, and neither of us likes our routines to be upset. Isn't that right, sweet girl?" he cooed.

Daphne purred, right on cue.

"And just how did this unholy alliance form?" I demanded.

"Well, you haven't been around very much the past few weeks," he said. "Someone's abandoned us, haven't they, Daphne? Someone got cozy with Silas and left us to our own devices, hmm?"

"Oh, please," I sighed. "I'm still here working at the store almost every afternoon. I still sleep in my bed every night."

"And why is that?"

"Why is what?"

"Why is it," he repeated with ill-concealed impatience, scratching at Daphne's ears, "that you spend part of almost every evening with Silas, but you come back here and sleep in your own bed?"

I stared at him as a thousand thoughts flew across my head, but what I said was, "Because you need me. Daphne needs me. I live here."

Grandpa Hen eyed me skeptically. "I got my cast off last week. I'm lighter on my feet than you are these days. Daphne only needs someone to feed her and listen to her troubles, which she's got." He pointed to himself. "And even when you're *here*, you ain't really all the way here."

I huffed and planted my hands on my hips. That was *ludicrous*.

"So I'm gonna ask you again, Ev. What are you doing with that boy?"

If he'd asked it in a judgmental way, or a teasing way, or even in a gossipy way, I would have been enraged. But instead, he asked it kindly, gently, with that tenderness that was still so new, coming from him, I didn't know how to defend against it.

"I don't know," I said instead. It sounded bleak because it was.

"He in love with you?"

"It's been a *month*, Grandpa." I ran a hand through my hair and paced the narrow room.

"That s'posed to answer my question?"

"No. I… I don't think he loves me." But that wasn't quite true, and my heart picked up speed at the question. There were times when Si looked at me and I thought I saw something in his eyes, or when he asked me a question that sounded like he was asking something else. I'd ignored it. Or tried to.

"You love him?" Grandpa asked, just like I'd known he would, and at this my heart skittered in my chest like a pebble thrown across a lake, shallow and uneven.

"No," I whispered. "It's not like that. It's just… we're just…"

"Friends with benefits?" he said sagely.

"Where the heck did you hear that phrase?"

He rolled his eyes. "We have internet here, Ev. As you know."

*Ev.* It occurred to me belatedly that I'd never heard him call me by my nickname. Were we friends now, just like him and Daphne?

"I have a story I wanna tell you," he said, sitting back comfortably.

"Grandpa, we really need to go." I pointed lamely at the door that led downstairs.

"Then stop interrupting, so it can be a *fast* story," he retorted. "And sit down. You're making me nervous."

I threw my head back and huffed a sigh at the ceiling, then flopped on the sofa.

"Your Grandma Anna and I," he began.

"Oh, Grandpa, please. I do not want to hear how your relationship with Grandma Anna has anything to do with me and Silas."

He hmphed. "It doesn't have a goddamn thing to do with that, far as I know. I dropped a rock on her head when I was six and she was seven, she cried, and I kissed her so she wouldn't tattle on me." He smirked. "You're a little old to be throwing rocks, Everett."

I snorted. "Sorry. Tell me your story."

"Well, like I was saying, I can't remember a time when I was ever without her. Good or bad. I knew her way back when she was in pigtails, and she knew me when I was a brash young idiot who spoke before he thought…"

"Way back then?" I echoed, raising one eyebrow, and to my surprise, he laughed.

"That hasn't changed, I'll grant you." His smile turned a little melancholy. "I loved her so long, I can't even tell you when it started, Everett. She wasn't just the love of my life, she *was* my life. Everything good in it, anyway. Gave me two daughters I'm proud of, made me a beautiful home, smiled at me every day in that way she had that made the day sunny even when it damn well wasn't. You know?"

I thought of Silas, God help me, and I knew exactly what Grandpa meant. And then I felt a pang of guilt so acute I actually clutched my stomach because it should have been Adrian's face I saw. It *should*.

I was so fucked.

I'd thought I could do this thing with Silas without having it tear me up inside, but it turned out I couldn't. The last three weeks had been the most incredible of my life, but that didn't negate the fact that I owed Adrian my loyalty. And the deeper things with Silas got, the guiltier I felt that I was forgetting him. Letting someone take his place.

I wasn't giving Silas what he needed.

I wasn't giving Adrian what he deserved.

And I was being split in two.

"When my Anna died, I was broken, Everett. God, I missed her so bad. Most of my life kept right on going — the shop, the bills, hunting in the fall and tending her roses in the spring, but there was no sunshine in it anymore for me."

I nodded. I knew exactly what he meant. *Exactly*. I had vivid memories of being surrounded by a hundred Milky Way wrappers last Halloween, sick to my stomach and feeling like life would never be fun again.

And it hadn't been, really. Until Si.

"Then one day, I was pruning those damn plants, and

my knees ached something *fierce*… not that there's anything wrong with my knees," he assured me quickly.

"Right. Of course not."

"And all of a sudden, I could hear your grandmother's voice in my ear, like she was standing right beside me. *Henry*, she said, *I love you, and I always will.*"

I bit my lip and frowned, remembering how I'd once wanted Adrian to haunt me. It felt like I hadn't thought that in a long time.

"And then she said, *But you're a damn fool, tending these roses when you never gave a shit about roses in your life.*"

I shook my head, sure I'd misheard. "What?"

Grandpa smiled softly. "She was a practical woman, my Anna. And somehow, I'd gotten so caught up in sentimentality, I'd forgotten that. She wouldn't want me kneeling down and worshipping those rose bushes for the rest of my days. She'd have laughed herself silly to see me. I didn't have to love what she loved in order to love her, and I didn't have to keep living the life we'd lived together once she was gone." He hesitated. "That's partly why, after I broke my leg, I asked your mom to send you to me. I thought maybe you were stuck in a rut after losing your husband, same as I was after losing your grandmother."

"You asked Mom to send me?" I narrowed my eyes. "But I thought…"

"That I didn't care about you? I don't know where you get your fool ideas, Ev. It's true that your grandma was more the kind, caring one of the two of us, but I've loved you since the day you were born."

"But you've never approved of me," I said, too shocked to keep my mouth shut. "It was always Ev being too high-strung, or Ev being too artistic. You didn't approve of me being gay."

"Artists have a terrible lot in life," he sighed. "No stability. No money. No pension, even when someone's as talented as you are. And I don't give a shit who you love, Everett, but being gay's a hard row to hoe, too. Gotta fight at every turn." Grandpa shook his head. "Maybe I shoulda wished the *world* were different, not you. But if I ever tried to change you, it wasn't because I didn't love you. It was because I loved you too much."

"How have you seen my art?"

"Told you I have the internet," he said reasonably. "Your mom sends me pictures."

I gaped at him. "You didn't come to my wedding," I protested.

He hesitated, looking down at his hands as they settled on Daphne's head. "I don't know what you'd've wanted me there for anyway. Not like I knew any of your city friends or anything. Not like you'd ever brought Adrian to visit me."

"Because I thought you wouldn't want me to."

"Well, then you thought wrong, son. I'd've been proud to be introduced to the man you loved."

I pressed the heels of my hands against my eyes as tears threatened. I hadn't cried as much in my entire nearly thirty years of life as I had in the past two months.

Grandpa cleared his throat and carried on as if we hadn't just had a moment.

"Anyway, after that business with the rose bushes, I decided to put the house on the market and move here to town. And you know what? You grandmother moved with me." His lip quirked, like he was remembering. "I make coffee in that tiny kitchen back there and think of her. And I hear her voice when I'm adding numbers downstairs. Sometimes I hear her in my ear when I'm talking to you, telling me to be patient and that people don't always know what's going on in my head when I say things." He smiled.

"Clearly," I muttered. I'd been so wrong. As wrong as Silas ever was, and I wanted to tell him so.

"But the point is, Everett, I loved her. And she's inside me. I can't ever forget her or stop loving her. It's carved deep in my bones, and they'll find it when I die: Henry Lattimer loves Anna Lattimer. Forever and ever. No matter where I go, or what I do, or who else I love."

I sniffled and blew out a breath. "That's really beautiful," I said. "Thank you for telling me that."

He scoffed. "Don't be a dummy. I don't say things just to hear myself talk, Ev. You think about what I said."

I frowned and nodded. "I will." But honestly, I was still stuck back on him loving me, approving of me.

Grandpa grunted and grabbed his cane from the side table. "Time to get up, Highness," he told the cat. "We've got breakfast plans." Daphne yawned prettily and stretched like she understood.

"Adrian used to call her that," I said. "*Highness.*" I smiled. "He was the one who rescued her, you know."

"I didn't know that," Grandpa said. He looked at me and nodded. "You should tell me more about him. Sometime."

I nodded and I meant it. The tight knot of Adrian inside me was loosening, I could feel it, but it felt strangely like by letting go of the stranglehold on my memories, I was giving them new life. Maybe I didn't have to be the only one who remembered him anymore.

Grandpa pushed himself to his feet with the cane, then regarded it for a moment, like he wasn't sure whether he should take it with him or not.

"I think canes are badass," I remarked, like I hadn't noticed his dilemma. "A good weapon, in a pinch."

He grunted again, but leaned on the cane as he crossed the room to the stairs.

"My hair tidy?" he asked, pausing at the top.

"Yeah, great. Why?"

"You never know who you might see when you're out and about, Everett. Always want to look your best."

"Uh-huh. Diane Perkins working at Goode's today?" I asked.

"Diane works most every Saturday," he answered blandly, beginning a cautious descent. "Best cook they have."

"You ever gonna tell me what's going on with you two?"

He snorted. "'Bout when you tell me what's going on with you and Silas."

"I already told you… I don't know."

"Well, I don't know what's doing with me and Diane, either." He hesitated. "You wanna know the truth, Everett?"

"No, lie to me."

He ignored me. "Truth is, I was fixing to… to court her. To *date* her, as the kids say."

*As the kids say.* I shook my head as I followed slowly down the stairs behind him. "What went wrong?"

"I broke… I mean, *bruised*… my fool leg."

"So what?"

"So the poor woman ended up taking care of me, that's what." He shook his head and paused with his hand on the railing to look up at me. "Don't wanna be a burden on anyone. And that's just what I told her when I told her to stop coming around to see me."

"You told her that?"

He sighed. "You may not have noticed, but the woman's a good bit younger than I am. Fourteen years."

"I noticed."

"Don't want her tied down to me, taking care of me forever."

"But you care about her, don't you? And she cares about you, otherwise she wouldn't have kept bringing you dinner all the time and blushing whenever you say something nice about her."

He clomped down to the bottom step and opened the door. "Yep. Goes to show, you haven't cornered the market on idiocy, Everett."

"What's that supposed to mean?"

He turned around once he reached the sidewalk and lifted a hand to my shoulder. His green eyes were serious as they met mine. "It means when a good person loves you, Everett, you don't turn your back on it. You don't let your pride or your *fear* hold you back."

"That's not what's happening with me and Silas." It wasn't. It wasn't fear or pride that held me back, it was… it was *loyalty*. A totally different thing.

"Of course not." Grandpa Hen sighed. "Well, one thing's for sure, you're a Lattimer through and through." He clapped me on the shoulder and turned toward the diner. "No one can ever say we did anything the easy way."

I frowned and followed him as he opened the glass door of the restaurant.

The diner was packed this morning, its bacon-and-coffee-deliciousness spilling out onto the street along with the noise of two dozen O'Learians chattering away.

I recognized most of them already, oddly enough, and I lifted my hand to return wave after wave as my students and their parents, and O'Leary Hardware patrons, and people I recognized from the Pumpkin Festival meeting a few weeks back, all greeted me by name.

I was starting to think I enjoyed the aggressive O'Leary friendliness.

"Hey!" Silas said, standing up as Grandpa Hen approached. Si and Dare had gotten a table in the center of the diner, right between Frank and Myrna Lucano's table and the table where Jamie Burke, Julian Ross, and Julian's brother Constantine were sitting.

I greeted Dare as Grandpa shook Si's hand. Hen's annoyance with Silas had disappeared about an hour after I'd come home from Silas's house the first night. *"Good to see you smiling, Everett,"* was all he'd said, but the next time Si's name had come up in conversation, he'd smiled and nodded.

After Grandpa sat, Si turned to me. His blue eyes were so warm when they met mine, and I could see by the way he looked at my lips that he wanted to kiss me hello.

I stuck out my hand and watched the light in his eyes dim just a little as he shook it and sat back down.

*Fuck.* Every interaction with Si was fraught with emotional landmines and I didn't know how to navigate my way through them without blowing something up. I knew how Silas felt about commitment, especially about parading it around O'Leary. It *meant* something that he wanted to kiss me, even just a peck on the lips in the middle of a crowded diner, and I wasn't sure if I could handle that. It wasn't fair to let Silas proclaim something when I couldn't follow through.

And yeah, it also wasn't fair to keep leading Si on in private, if that's what I was doing. But he'd said we could take things slow, and I… I just didn't want to give him up.

"Morning, Ev, Henry," Diane said. She pulled a pen from behind her ear and her order pad from the little apron at her waist. "What'll it be this morning?"

"Pancakes, please," I said. "Bacon and coffee, too."

She nodded. "Sure thing, honey. Henry, what'll it be?"

He looked startled. "You never ask, you usually just bring me something you know I'll like."

She lifted one eyebrow. "Maybe today you could just *tell me*, rather than me trying to figure it out."

Dare coughed. "Omelet special sounded good, Henry," he offered.

"What? No! I don't want the omelet special," Hen said obstinately. "I want what I usually have."

"I can't remember," Diane said, tilting her head. "If you want something, tell me."

His moustache quivered. "Fine, then. Pancakes and bacon, same as Everett," he said a moment later. "Please."

Diane lifted her chin and walked off.

"What the devil got into her?" Hen asked the table.

"She seemed fine to me," Si said brusquely. "Sometimes it gets frustrating trying to figure out what people want."

I could practically hear him grinding his teeth, and I sighed internally.

"Morning, Everett! Hen, how are you feeling?" Shane said strolling over to our table to clap Grandpa on the back after dropping off food for Myrna and Frank.

"'Bout as well as a person can when other folks are upset at them for no reason," Grandpa complained.

Shane frowned in confusion. "Well, I know something that'll cheer you up. Karen Mitchener- Martin, Angela Ross, and Ms. Dorian were in here earlier, and they said there's been a break in Elliot Marks's disappearance. You don't have to be afraid anymore."

"What?" Si and Dare demanded in unison. The conversations around us grew quiet.

I winced. Just hearing Karen's name was enough to

make me itchy these days. The woman hadn't stopped speculating and accusing people since the day Elliot Marks went missing, and more than once I'd heard Maura at Fanaille say she couldn't wait until Karen had her baby, so she'd be too busy to interfere in other folks' lives.

"Well, Ms. Dorian said there was a camera outside a store near Elliot's apartment building," Shane said, eyeing Si warily. I couldn't really blame him. "Showed a tall, blond guy walking in, and that's the suspect. She said it was obviously that new guy, Daniel Whatever."

I stared at him. "Are you *sure?*"

Shane shrugged.

Julian leaned over from the next table. "Excuse me. Did you say they're accusing Daniel Michaelson of being involved in the disappearance?"

"No." Si shook his head vigorously.

"Nobody's accusing anyone of anything," Dare said, holding up his hands. "Karen Mitchener-Martin's spreading rumors. Again."

"I heard he lives in the woods because he's not right in the head," an older man I'd never met yelled from one of the booths.

"I heard he came here because he got into trouble with the law and he was on the run," Myrna Lucano said, frowning. "But he seems real sweet."

"I think that's a load of horseshit." An older woman with graying blonde hair stood up from one of the tables in the back. She was sturdy and ruddy-complected, with deep-set laugh lines around her eyes. "Daniel Michaelson helped me work on one of my sculptures the other day. He's a good man."

"Christ alive, Rena Cobb, don't you tell me that he was modeling for you!" Kelley Dwyer, one of my student's parents said, sounding horrified.

"Modeling for me? 'Course not. He's helping me with the pride flag sculpture in the front yard."

Silas blinked, momentarily distracted. "Did you say… it's a pride flag?"

"Sure," she said easily. "Rainbow-colored stripes, like trees growing up from the ground. What else would it be?"

Si looked at me and shook his head in disbelief.

"Nothing," he said, at the same time Jay Turner, one of Grandpa Hen's cronies, yelled, "They thought it was a buncha dicks, Rena."

Rena tilted her head to the side, then nodded. "I mean, I can see why you'd think that. If you'd never seen a dick before."

Her words surprised a laugh out of me that made Grandpa scowl in my direction.

"Listen to me, everyone," Julian Ross said, standing up from his breakfast. He was cute, in a small, dark-haired, *youthful* sort of way. "Daniel Michaelson didn't have anything to do with this."

"We know, Julian," Jamie said. "It's alright."

"I wanna know how he knows that!" someone yelled.

"Yeah, how do you know that, Doc Ross?" Kelley asked.

Julian's face burned. "I know, because…I know because… Daniel was with me the night Elliot Marks went missing."

"What?" His brother Constantine stared up at him in disbelief. "With *you*?"

"Yeah," Julian said. "We're, um… together."

"Since when?" Constantine demanded. "I didn't even know he was gay!"

"Maybe because it's none of your business," Julian retorted.

"Damn," Constantine said. "Mom is going to *freak out*."

Julian's face burned hotter. "I'm… I've gotta go," he stuttered, throwing money down on the table.

"Julian!" Silas called. "Daniel's not in trouble!"

But Julian either didn't hear him or didn't care. He was already out the door, with Constantine jogging after him.

"Well, that was damn entertaining," Grandpa Hen told Shane. "What've you got planned for an encore?"

Shane scowled out the door at Julian, looking almost petulant. "Why'd he have to go and do that?" Shane said.

"Do what?" Jamie asked. "Speak up? I noticed the way Julian and Daniel were looking at each other at the meeting the other night."

"Same here," I said. "They had chemistry. I'm not surprised they're together, and if he cares about the man, it just makes sense that he spoke up."

"Does it?" Si said, so low that only I could hear.

*God.* I felt my heart tear a little bit more.

"I just wanted everyone to stop worrying," Shane said, frowning. The poor guy looked lost and young, although I knew he had to be around thirty since he and Molly had dated.

"I know, Shane," Silas said. "I appreciate that. But it'd be best if you didn't spread any more of Karen's stories, alright? It just works people into a panic."

Shane frowned and nodded. "Sorry, Si."

"Well, we have some news," Frank said, leaning over to Silas. He laid his hand on Myrna's and squeezed, looking at her affectionately. "We decided you were right, Silas. We're giving up the fight against the eminent domain case. We're going to stop fighting and focus on finding peace instead."

"What?" I said. "Really?" I couldn't lie, I was a little sad to hear it, for their sakes.

"Really," Myrna said. She hesitated, then shrugged.

"No sense trying to keep a secret in this town. I found out last week I have cancer. Nothing too serious, hopefully. I'll be around to keep this one on his toes for a good while longer." She winked at Frank. "But it was enough of a scare for us to realize what's important."

"Family," Frank said, his white curls bobbing. "Friends. Each other."

Myrna nodded. "Enjoying the land, whoever owns it. And the time we have together."

"But no! No, that was Molly's place," Shane said. His face crumpled. "Up by the falls. I go up there to think about it." He looked to Jamie like he needed assistance. "Molly would be so upset if she knew they were gonna tear down all those trees!"

"I know, Shane. I know. She loved it up there." Jamie stood and braced a hand on his shoulder. "They're not destroying anything. It's just changing hands, is all."

Frank and Myrna exchanged a look. "It'll be alright, Shane. Nothing's going to happen until next spring. There'll be time to get accustomed to the idea."

"Silas," Shane said. "Silas, your brother liked it up there almost as much as Molly. You remember? They were out there all the damn time. All the time, even when they were supposed to be studying. Sometimes even when she was supposed to be with me. You remember?"

Si's face was locked in grief and sympathy. "Yeah, Shane. I remember. But…" He broke off helplessly.

I stretched my hand across the table and laid my hand over Silas's, much the way Frank had with Myrna's, and gave it a comforting squeeze. Si shot me a grateful look. He twisted his hand beneath mine and laced our fingers together.

"Wait." Shane's eyes widened in surprise. He straightened and sniffed, like he'd been shocked out of his distress. "Are you two… together?"

I took a deep breath. "Yeah," I said softly. *Mostly. Sort of.* My stomach churned, but Silas's smile made it all worthwhile.

"But I thought you were married, Ev," Shane said, frowning in confusion.

The simple words were like the lash of a whip across my sensitive heart and I flinched mentally and physically. I detangled my fingers from Si's and folded my hands beneath the table.

"Widowered," I said softly. "He died."

"Oh." Shane shrugged. "Isn't that the same thing?"

"No," Grandpa Hen said sharply. "No, young man, it's damn well not. And you know better."

"Sorry, Henry," Shane said. "I don't mean to offend you. It's just… Molly and I never got the chance to get married, but I can't imagine loving anyone but her for the rest of my life." He sounded proud and so unbearably young, even though he had to be a few years older than me. "If it's real love, it lasts forever, and you never give up on it. Right?"

"You don't have to give up on it to love someone else, Shane." Hen's jaw set. "Some folks have the capacity to love more than one person in their lifetime. Some folks think loving someone else is the best way to honor the ones we've lost. In fact…"

He leaned on his cane and stood up from the table, his eyes fixed on Diane, who was across the room refilling coffee from a carafe.

"Diane?" Grandpa Hen called.

Diane spun and frowned. "Yes?"

"I've been too proud to ask you what I should have

asked you a long time ago," Hen said. "Can I take you out to dinner tonight?"

Diane's jaw dropped and her face turned as red as her hair. "Well, I… I mean…" She swallowed. "Yes, Henry. I think I'd like that very much."

Grandpa beamed and glanced down at me, as if to say, *And that is how it's done, Ev.*

# Chapter Sixteen

SILAS

"So…" Ev said, buckling his seat belt as I pulled my truck out of the parking space in front of the hardware store. "Are we going to talk about what happened at brunch today?"

I shifted my eyes right and assessed him briefly before sliding the truck into Drive and turning down the street toward my house just a few blocks away.

Ev looked like he might vomit, which was pretty much how he'd looked ever since Shane had ventured into serious What The Fuck territory at the diner earlier today.

Part of me wanted to scoop Ev up and comfort him, to tell him I hadn't realized Shane was capable of being so ignorant and hurtful. The other part of me, the petty part I liked to pretend wasn't there, was angrily *satisfied*. I was scraped raw and aching from the way Ev had retreated from me, from *us*. I wanted him to feel that way too.

"Do we have things to talk about?" I asked.

Ev sighed, like *I* was the one being difficult or something.

"Silas, I'm sorry I pulled away from you. It wasn't

intentional. I was just shocked by what Shane said, and I didn't have time to process it."

"That means your instinct was to pull away."

He sighed again and put his hand over mine where it rested on the gear shift. "You're reading this whole thing wrong. It was the last straw in a long, emotional morning. It wasn't me pulling away from you, it was me retreating back into myself, like a human turtle. But it had nothing to do with us and it wasn't meant to hurt you."

I said nothing. Of course it wasn't meant to hurt me. That didn't mean it hadn't. And I wasn't dumb enough to believe Ev didn't know the difference. He was deflecting. Just like he had for the past three fucking weeks.

"Okay, then," I said. "Tell me about it."

"About what?"

"About your long, emotional morning. Help me understand."

He slid his hand away from mine, retreating again, but I caught it and held it on top of the console.

"Grandpa Hen was telling me stories about my grandmother," he said. "About losing her. And about how he cared about me and has never hated me for being gay." He picked at imaginary lint on his pants with his free hand. "It was a lot to take in."

"I wondered about that," I said. "The way he looked at you sometimes, I could see that he cared." I paused and looked at his profile again. "So, how are you feeling about it?"

He turned his head and peered at me, green eyes suspicious and *not* in a cute way. "Is this a therapy session now? Are we doing therapy?"

"No! *Jesus*. I'm just asking what your emotional state is right now after your long, emotional morning. It's a *question*, Everett."

"Fine. I'm fine. Emotional state is *one hundred percent fine*."

"That's great," I said, dropping his hand so I could turn onto my street. "Thanks so much for initiating this talk. It's been enlightening."

"What do you want me to say, Silas?" Ev threw up his hands in frustration. "I don't know what to do here. You're the one who said we could take things slow, and now you're upset that I'm not exhibiting enough PDA when we're eating breakfast."

"You know what I want you to say?" I demanded as I pulled into my driveway and turned the car off. "I want you to tell me something *real*, Ev. You and I met six weeks ago tomorrow." He looked surprised, and I nodded. "Right? Seems like it should be more, doesn't it?"

Seemed like it should take longer for a person's life to be turned inside out and upside down. But apparently not, because here I was, with my fucking guts spilling all over the truck.

I turned in my seat to face him, my eyes narrowed.

"The night we met, we had something special. The way you laughed, the way you smiled, the way you just… *got* me. I have never in my life felt the connection I felt with you. We were together for an hour, and you were all I could think about the next morning. Hell, you were all I could think about *every* morning after that."

"Silas…"

"And then you pulled away. And I get it. I *do* get it. Grief isn't linear. I said it, I meant it. And I fucked up, because I got scared when I felt myself falling for you, and I worried you weren't feeling that way. I said a whole bunch of stupid shit that I regret, and I think you know just how much I regret it."

He nodded once, a short bob of his head, but the rest of him was frozen still.

"But then we got together and I thought… I thought *this is it*. You know? That if we were *connected* from the first minute, surely it would just *grow*, right? That everything would get better and deeper as we spent more time together, and I would like you even more, the more I got to know you, and some things about you would drive me crazy, but in a good way. And it has! All of that has been true. *For me.* But for you…" I shook my head. "It's the opposite."

"That's not true. I care about you Silas. So damn much."

"But?" I added, voicing the unspoken end of his statement. "But?"

Ev sucked in a harsh breath and turned to face me, his eyes bright with anger. "You say you get that grief's not linear. You say you understand why I have hang-ups. But then you push and you push and you *push*."

"Because you're pulling away!" I ran a hand through my hair and tried to calm myself. I hadn't intended to have this conversation now, or maybe *ever*, if I could avoid it, and I was really afraid I was fucking it up. "You are one of the strongest people I know, Everett Maior. Showing up in this town with nothing but your cat, to take care of a man you thought hated you, limping along the fucking highway in the dark, scared out of your mind that you'd seen a ghost in the road, but still *moving*. Not giving up." I shook my head, willing him to understand. "It wasn't destiny that put you there, Ev. It was choice. *Your* choice. Your choice not to stay back in Boston, your choice not to sit in your car and wait for someone else to come along and fix things. You were brave, and you were strong, and you kept walking."

He shook his head. "This is all… pointless. What does this have to do with *anything* that happened today?"

I ran a hand over my mouth and let my head fall back on the seat. "If you really don't know, then maybe I've been wrong about a connection between us from the beginning."

"What exactly do you want me to do, Silas? Hmm? How does a person prove they're trying?" He cast his eyes to the roof of the truck.

"By talking to me! Like, okay, here's an example." I took a deep breath. "Tell me about Adrian."

His mouth fell open. "What? How the *hell* would that help?"

"Because you don't talk about him," I whispered, reaching across the console to touch his cheek. He was burning hot. "Because he's important to you, a part of you, and I want to know that part. And I don't *want* to have to push, Everett. I wish you wanted to share."

Everett held my gaze for a long minute. "Fine," he said. "What do you want to know?"

I smiled, just a little. "Adrian was a finance guy, right?"

Ev nodded.

"How'd you meet?"

"At a party." His voice was low, hesitant. "There was nothing dramatic. No instant connection. He was a friend of a friend. We, uh, knew each other for a while before we felt a spark. He encouraged me a lot with this art show I was putting together and then we just… started dating." He shrugged. "It was more like a peaceful river. Less like a crashing waterfall." His mouth twisted up in a wry smile.

"How did you know you were in love with him?"

"Really?" He made a noise of discomfort. "God, I don't know. He was good at things I wasn't good at, I guess. We smoothed each other out." He huffed. "Why would you want to know this? Doesn't it make you feel weird or jealous or something?"

"Should it?" I asked, honestly curious. Because hearing this stuff didn't make me feel bad in the slightest. It was when he *refused* to share that I wanted to smash something. "Dude, I don't know. I've never had a… boyfriend or whatever before. Am I supposed to be jealous of every person you ever dated or ever loved?" I opened my eyes in horror. "Wait, are *you* supposed to be jealous of every guy *I* ever dated? Like, go around giving them all the evil eye?"

He laughed once, and some of the tension left him. "I can see myself being jealous. But your men are safe from me. I mean, there have been so many, I'd have to, like, quit my job and devote myself to it, which would be bad since Janice Turner mentioned *again* this week how badly she wants me to keep it."

I grinned, absurdly excited that he'd admitted that he could be jealous. "I think she likes you because you keep bringing food to the staff meetings. She's like Daphne — feed her a couple times and she'll be your friend for life."

He slapped my arm lightly. "Are you calling my cat *easy*?"

"Easier than *you*," I said. I reached for the door handle and pushed it open. "Let's go in."

Ev climbed down from his side and met me in front of the car, sliding his hand into mine.

"Does this mean the conversation part of the afternoon is over?" Ev teased. "Can we please go on to the fun part?"

"And which part is that?" I asked, as if I didn't know.

"You know, that first night, you told me your game was *smooth*," he reminded me as we clomped up the porch stairs to the kitchen door, our arms around each other's waists.

"Are you saying I haven't proved how smooth my game is already?"

"I'm just saying you can always try to prove it again." He gave me a brilliant smile. "Don't rest on your laurels, Si."

I chuckled and pulled him against me. I wrapped my arms around his waist, letting the warmth and ease of being with him replace some of my doubts and fears, at least temporarily.

"I'll try not to," I promised. I pushed open the door and led him into the kitchen.

"Oh, hey, you got more apples!" he said, spying my fruit bowl on the counter. He backed me against the door frame. "Want me to bake an apple crisp for dessert?"

I coasted my hands down his back and over the curve of his ass. "I thought I was showing you my *game*," I teased. "You'd rather have baked goods?" Honest to God, I didn't care. I liked the easy domesticity almost as much as I liked the sex.

Yeah, *I* said that. Silas Sloane, the formerly commitment-cautious.

"I mean, I'd rather have both," Ev said. His gaze heated as he lifted on his tiptoes to brush a kiss over my lips, letting every part of him rub against every part of me. "I could make this first and then let it bake, and we could have *sustenance* when we were done. For round two."

I snorted. "Fine. I can be patient."

Ev's smile dimmed slightly. "Yeah. I know you can."

He grabbed a bowl down from the shelf above the sink and that tiny action tightened my chest. I liked that he knew his way around my kitchen as well as I did, that he felt at home here.

And I fucking hated this *tension* still between us, like we were both trying to avoid touching a bruise.

"So it turns out you were right about Rena Cobb," I

offered. "And the rest of us are seeing phalluses where none exist."

"Because I'm always right."

I rolled my eyes. "God, this will make you insufferable forever, won't it? Ten years from now, it'll be, 'Remember how you were wrong about Rena Cobb's penis sculptures?'"

Ev giggled. "You and the whole rest of the damn town. That's one that *deserves* to live in the O'Leary memory banks forever and ever. The time you all took some perfectly innocent cylinders and imagined it was a *field of cocks*."

"I'll say you were right if you promise me you'll never say *field of cocks* again."

He grinned.

"You know," I said, hefting myself onto the counter as he grabbed a knife and cutting board. "I've been thinking about what to do with that apartment over the garage. I always imagined I'd fix the place up and make it a rental unit. I'm not too far from the center of O'Leary and it might bring in some money. But now I'm thinking maybe the loss of privacy isn't worth it."

He glanced over at me. "What do you mean?"

"Just having someone around all the time." I shrugged. "I mean, what if I want to kiss you out in the backyard or have sex first thing in the morning with the curtains open?"

"Well, I mean, you can't make decisions based on *that*," he said reasonably, turning the apple in his fingers as he cut off a long, spiral peel.

"Based on what? Wanting to have sex with you without giving a potential tenant an eyeful?" I leered at him. "Do you have some exhibitionist kink I don't know about?"

"I mean, based on me and you," he began. He paused.

"I mean, me and you having sex in every room or whatever."

My stomach dipped and my smile died. "That's not what you were going to say."

He lifted the hand holding the knife and rubbed the back of his hand against his forehead. "Please, can we not do this again? Can't we just… enjoy the afternoon? Please, Si?" His voice was pleading, a little panicky.

I shook my head slowly and felt about six times my age. "No, Ev. I don't think we can."

He slammed the knife and the apple down on the counter. "What happened to everything not being a battle? What happened to letting things go, Si? What happened to *slow*?" His eyes were dry, but there were tears in his voice, and it almost made me hesitate.

But this had gone on too long. Three weeks too long. Things needed to be said if we were going to move past this or… not. And I was accusing Ev of holding back and not talking to me about important shit, but here I was, doing the same thing.

Choices, Silas, I reminded myself. Choose to move forward or you'll have no one but yourself to blame for being miserable.

"Maybe this *is* my fault," I told him, looking at the dark stone tile a foot below my feet. "Maybe… maybe I'm changing the rules here. I've never done commitment before. I don't know how you're supposed to define the parameters of it. But when I talk about you bitching at me in ten years, I mean, I want you to do that over breakfast, right here in this kitchen. And when I want your opinion on whether to rent out the apartment, I'm asking you as a boyfriend, and someone who might have a stake in the matter. I'm asking because maybe you want to turn that into an art studio, and you should be able to do that because… because this is your home. With me. If you want it to be."

I chanced a glance up at him, and the sadness on his face made me want to cry, myself.

"I'm guessing… you don't want it to be." I sucked in my lips and nodded. "Looks like we were dealing with different definitions of *not-just-friendship*, huh?"

He stared at me, wide-eyed and horrified. "You don't know what you're saying," he whispered. "Commitment isn't something *you* do. You don't even know what it is. You're Mr. Commitment-Cautious. You… you've never had a relationship in your *life*. You have half a car sitting in your damn garage because you can't even commit to fixing it."

I scowled. "That's bullshit, Ev. I haven't fixed that car because it doesn't need to be fixed. I like having it there, I like having it in pieces. It never needs to be finished because the work is the point."

"You were mad that I pulled away from you in the restaurant today."

"Not mad. Hurt."

"Because it risked your reputation," he insisted shakily. "You don't want to be committed to something unless it's a sure thing. *That's* what's wrong here. You think you're ready for a commitment, b-but you don't want to be tied to anything that causes gossip. You want something risk-free, and there is no such thing."

I jumped off the counter. "That's not true. You know it's not!"

But he'd tuned me out completely, arms folded over his chest like he wanted to protect himself.

"What I know is that I have *been* in love before. I have *been* committed before. And if you truly are committed to someone, you take care of them. You don't… you don't push them to do things they're not ready to do just because *you* are feeling insecure."

"I haven't pushed…" That was a lie. I'd totally pushed. I was pushing right now. I sliced my hand through the air. "I just want to know we're on the same page. That we're moving toward something."

"How can I move toward anything, Silas? How is that fair?" Ev shouted. His face was mottled red, and his eyes were shining with tears. "Tell me, how is it fair that I get to move on and he doesn't? It's selfish, that's what it is."

He stopped short and sucked in a deep breath, eyeing me warily like he was frightened by his admission. And holy shit, I was too.

This was the crux of the problem, right here. Not that he didn't care about me, but that he *did*. And it was *killing* him that he did.

"Why is it selfish to want to be happy?" I said softly, my heart breaking for him *and* for myself. "Ev, why is it a betrayal to remember that he *made* you happy and to want to feel that again? If it was me, I'd be proud to have that as my legacy. And the real betrayal would be you thinking that happiness had to end just because my life did."

Ev shook his head, tears streaming down his cheeks, but I pushed on because I didn't know how to turn back. "If love is an eternal thing, Ev? Then he loves you still. And he wants you to be happy. Your grief is a monument to his death, just like my mom and her endless fucking memorials. Your *happiness* is a monument to his love."

"You're wrong. That's not…" He broke off with a harsh sob that I felt resounding in my own chest. "You don't *know* what it's like to love someone, Silas. You don't know what it's like to lose them."

I was pretty sure he was wrong about that.

I was pretty sure I was going through that very thing, right then and there.

"I love you, Everett Maior," I told him. "And yeah, that scares me. It scares me that everyone in town will know it, and they'll be pairing our names together until the end of time, because I don't want to be endlessly reminded of someone who didn't love me back. Unlike you and fucking *Shane Goode,* I don't want my life to be a shrine to lost love."

His eyes widened, his chest heaved, his hands clenched on air, like he was fighting some kind of monster, some demon in his head that no one could see but him. And for one second, I almost believed he was going to beat it. That he was going to take one single step toward me — just one, and I would have met him the rest of the way, I swear it — but instead, as I watched, his eyes shuttered and he finished that brick wall he'd been building between us.

He pushed past me to the kitchen door and threw it open.

"You say you love me? That you want to be committed to me? Well, love isn't a stick you beat your beloved over the head with, Silas. It's not a thing you can push or manipulate or threaten."

And not a thing I could stop, either, I realized, as I watched the man I loved walk out the door.

# Chapter Seventeen

SILAS

I PULLED into a parking space in front of Fanaille and got out of my truck, just as a gust of wind sent a bunch of brown and orange leaves scattering across the sidewalk. It was fucking *chilly* out here this early in the morning, with the sun barely cresting the trees down at the end of Waterford Street and glinting off the lace-curtained window of the bakery.

Cal and Ash were inside, joking and laughing as they moved in tandem, two souls with one purpose. I'd seen them like that a million times over the past half-year or more, and I'd shaken my head each and every time. I'd never understood that kind of closeness, never wanted it. Now that I'd had just a taste of it, though, I craved it more than my next breath.

It was ridiculous that it took a disaster to make you realize how grateful you should have been before the disaster struck. And that was what the fight with Ev had been — a complete, unmitigated clusterfuck of a disaster.

After Ev had walked off the day before, I'd spent way too many melancholy hours roaming my damn house, where every room already had an Ev-shaped memory imprinted on it, even after just three weeks. I couldn't go to the diner or Hoff's without being asked about Ev, I didn't want to drive past the playground or the school because they'd make me think of him, I couldn't be in my kitchen or smell a fucking apple without replaying our fight. I was a prisoner in my damn life if he wasn't in it.

Finally, I'd fled to the damn garage to work on the car — because I fucking *could too* commit to something — when I finally realized, a little too late, the subtext of what Ev had really been saying all along.

Jesus Christ. If I was scared to love him when he couldn't love me back, if I was missing him after *three hours* without him, what the hell would it be like to lose someone after years together? After marriage and promising forever?

Everett was *scared*. And the very fact that he was so scared meant he was in love, or was close enough to love to scare the shit out of him. But instead of holding onto him with two hands, instead of going with my first instinct and wrapping him up in my arms to comfort and reassure him, I'd let him walk out the door.

Alone.

Again.

But this was the last damn time.

I loved Everett Maior. I loved every minute I spent with him, even when he was teasing me relentlessly, every suspicious and superstitious thought that danced through the man's head, even when he made me crazy. And maybe it was too soon to be thinking that way, but... the way I looked at it, I had a lifetime of commitment stored up and only one man I wanted to use it on.

I pulled open the door to the bakery and stepped inside the cinnamon-sugar haven.

"Officer Sloane!" Cal called, turning from Ash to greet me with a smile still bright on his face. "How's it going?"

"Pretty good. You?"

"Very good. He's just about convinced me we want a dog," he said, hooking a thumb at his boyfriend. "But not until the spring."

"Cal and I are planning a…" Ash began before pausing dramatically.

I raised my eyebrows. "A date night? A party? Oh, God, a *family*?"

Cal laughed out loud. "Yeah, slow down there, Sloane. No families right now."

Ash folded his enormous arms across his chest. "Yeah, Caelan needs to make an honest man of me first."

Cal's lips twitched. "Okay, your heteronormative ideas of how families are made *aside*… Don't rush me, Ashley. I have plans."

Ash grinned at him — totally sappy, totally in love, totally content to wait for whatever Cal wanted.

*Ugh.* I needed Everett so badly my gut clenched.

"What Ash meant to say is we're planning a *vacation*," Cal said. "We're going down to Florida to visit my grandmother sometime this spring, and we'll wait to get a puppy after that."

"Florida?" I said. "That's cool."

"He *claims* it's to visit his grandmother," Ash teased, "but it's totally because Ethan Scott called to tell him he'd won a trip to Disney World, and Cal realized I'd never been, so he wants to take me."

"Ethan!" Ethan Scott had been a friend of Cal's back in high school, more than a few years younger than me. We'd never been close, but I'd run into him when he'd come home for a visit over the summer. "How's Boston?"

Cal shrugged. "Not so great now that Parker's moved

back to O'Leary. They moved east together, and now that Parker's back here… I got the impression Ethan was lonely."

I could understand that all too well.

"So where's Everett this morning?" Cal asked, giving me a knowing grin.

"At this hour? Asleep in his bed, hopefully. I'm planning to grab some pastries and go wake him up. Whatever kind is his favorite this week."

"That would be pumpkin muffins with cream cheese frosting," Ash said.

"And the largest black coffee," Cal added.

"Now that's a hell of a way to wake up," Ash said. "What did he do to deserve that?"

Cal swatted Ash in the stomach as he passed on his way to the bakery case. "Ashley!"

"Hey! Not like *that*," Ash said. "Mind out of the gutter, *Caelan*. I just meant is he feeling okay?"

"Actually," I hesitated, but then I figured if anyone would get relationship stuff it was these two. "I fucked up yesterday. Bigtime."

"How big?" Ash asked, eyes wide, as he put a to-go cup of coffee on the counter next to the box of muffins Cal had prepared.

"Uh, huge?"

"How huge?" Cal folded his arms over his chest.

"Like, *I called him six times last night and texted him fourteen times, but he didn't answer* huge. Like, *let me bribe you with your favorite pastries to even hear my apology* huge."

Ash winced, and Cal pursed his lips. "Better let me throw in some cupcakes, too," he said, opening the box again.

I chuckled. "Thanks."

Cal's phone rang, and he and Ash swapped places so Ash could ring me out while Cal answered it.

"You don't seem too worried," Ash said, a smile quirking one side of his mouth. "For someone who messed up that badly."

I shook my head. "I'm weirdly… not. I dunno. I came to a whole bunch of realizations after I, you know, fucked up. And one of them was that Everett is it for me. He's scared and it'll maybe take a long while before he feels the way I feel, but…" I shrugged.

"There's something really freeing when you figure out what you can live with and what you can't live without," Ash said, nodding. "I get it."

"Hey!" Cal said, frowning. "That was Myrna. She's looking for Frank. Have you seen him, Si?"

I shook my head. "I haven't been anyplace but here."

"Myrna said their daughter Regan came up for the weekend with her dog, since Myrna's starting treatment next week. Frank promised them a big breakfast today. But when they woke up this morning, Frank and Banjo were both gone. Myrna and Regan don't know if he took the dog out for a walk early or what, but he's been gone since at least four, when Myrna got up."

"Four?" I pulled my phone out of my pocket to check the time. "It's nearly nine."

Cal nodded, concern in his eyes. "I mean, it's possible that he just got sidetracked or lost track of time."

"Not with Regan home," I countered, frowning. "Wonder if he fell down or something? He's getting older."

"Don't let him hear you say that," Ash joked, though he was clearly concerned, too. "If you want someone to help look for him, I'm game." He looked at Cal. "You'll be fine?"

"Yeah," Cal said. "O'Leary's waking up slow this

morning anyway. And if they get impatient, I'll tell them to sit the fuck down and wait." He smiled grimly.

"That's the customer service O'Learians have come to expect," Ash said, kissing Cal on the mouth. "Be back."

"I'm going to run these to Ev," I said, taking the pastries. I needed to see him just for a second, to press a quick kiss to his lips and tell him I would be back later, to let him know that he could talk and this time I would really listen. "And then I'll call Mitch…"

But my phone was already ringing. "Hey, I was just going to call you," I told Mitch. "I heard about Frank, and…"

"Myrna called me," Mitch interrupted. "Constantine and I are already out at the campground. Regan Lucano's dog came back, Si, but there's no sign of Frank. And…" He hesitated, then continued in a low voice, like he didn't want to be overheard, "We found blood traces. Up in the campground where John Carpenter was staying."

My own blood ran cold. "Could be animal?"

"Could be," Mitch agreed. But neither of us believed it.

"I'll be there in ten," I promised. "Ash Martin's coming with me."

"Good."

"I'll drive," I told Ash. "Meet me at the truck."

"Yeah. Lemme grab boots and a coat," Ash said, heading into the backroom, which led up to their apartment.

"Be back," I told Cal.

I rushed across the street and rang the doorbell repeatedly, the warmth of the coffee cup searing my hand.

"Keep your shirt on!" I heard Henry yell, followed by a clomping sound that I knew was his cane on the stairs. "I'm coming."

He threw open the door a second later. "Silas?" Henry was still in his pajamas, his white hair sticking up around his head.

"Morning, Henry. Sorry to barge in. I just need to see Ev really quickly. I got called out, and I…"

"Silas," Hen said, eyes wide. "Ev isn't here. He stayed with you last night."

"No, he came back here," I told him. "We had a fight. A really *stupid* fight, and…"

But Henry was already shaking his head. "I took Diane out to dinner last night, Si. And when I came home, the place was deserted. Far as I know, he hasn't been home since he left here with you yesterday afternoon."

"But then… Henry, if he's not here, where the hell is he?"

# Chapter Eighteen

EVERETT

THE COLD WAS the first thing I noticed; frigid dampness beneath my cheek and bare feet that should not have been there. The wind howled through my window, and it sounded like somebody crying.

In that amorphous, half-awake state when reality and dream-reality were impossible to distinguish, I thought this was the most fucked-up dream I'd ever had. I tried to roll over in bed, to find the blanket I'd kicked off, but I encountered only…mud. There was a loud *crack* on the other side of the room that didn't sound at all like Daphne.

I came to in a moment of panic, thinking *Where am I?* followed quickly and illogically by *Where is Silas?* I tried to sit up, but I couldn't. My left arm was trapped beneath me, prickly numb like it was asleep, and my head emitted tiny little lightning-shocks of pain when I tried to open my eyes, draw a deep breath, or move in any way.

I was going to throw up.

*What the actual fuck?*

I forced one eye to open, even though the action made pinwheels burst across my brain, but it was nearly as dark with my eye open as it had been with it closed. The air smelled like pine and decay and I heard… the ocean? Or maybe just the wind rushing through leaves.

Either way, I was *outside*, I realized. It was fucking cold, I was dressed in nothing but a thin button-down and jeans, my shoes were not on my feet, and *I was outside*, when I couldn't remember how the fuck I'd gotten here.

I tried to move again, but I realized I was immobile for a reason. My right arm was tied at the wrist to something above my head. If I moved my fingers just slightly, I could touch the fucking rope.

I was tied down. With *rope*.

Sweet baby Jesus, I *had* ended up in a *Criminal Minds* episode. And oh my God, if there was a real serial killer on the loose, Karen Mitchener-Martin would *literally* never shut up about being right.

The moaning noise I'd mistaken for crying came again and I forced my cheek a bare half-inch off the ground, just enough so I could get both eyes open and turn my eyes *up*. I could barely discern the indigo-blue of the sky through the inkier darkness of the trees, but it was enough to realize that it was late, so late it might nearly be morning.

Something moved on the ground not far from me and I turned my gaze down. There was a lump of blackness there, like a large dog or maybe a person covered in blankets, and I froze in place, shutting my eyes just in case the person or thing had better vision than I did.

*Don't let them see you move.* This fact had been drilled into me by a hundred hours spent watching police procedurals, because the really depraved shit always happened after the killer saw that you were awake. And that thought made me think of how Silas would laugh his ass off when I told him that my shitty police shows actually were good for something after all…

If I got to tell him.

*Fuck.*

I cudgeled my memory, trying to recall how the *hell* I had gotten here, but my brain was sluggish at best. I'd been at the diner with Silas. I remembered that. Then we'd gone home and… God, I remembered the fight in Si's kitchen with total clarity. The terrible, selfish things I'd said, the devastated look on his face. I remembered walking out the door and barely making it down the street before I'd wanted to turn around and apologize, to beg him to hold me and give me another chance.

But what had happened after that?

Where was I? And where was Silas?

I heard footsteps and whispers. Someone was walking around out here, talking to someone else. And I wondered for a second if it was Silas coming to get me. I remembered him saying he wouldn't stop searching for me, if I were ever trapped and… *God.*

*Okay.* Okay, brain, we are going to think of productive things now. Getting free. Getting home. Getting to Silas.

I squinted my eyes open again and saw a figure the size and shape of a human walking back and forth. The sky had lightened enough, or my vision had cleared enough, to make out that I was in a clearing, with trees all around me.

The lump on the ground moaned again, and the walking and whispering stopped for a second. The human walked closer, hesitant and slow, and suddenly turned on a flashlight, illuminating the lump.

"You just… you just *stay quiet*, Frank. You hear me?" the person threatened, kicking the lump on the ground. "You stay right where you are or… or I'm gonna have to do something bad."

The voice sounded familiar, so familiar. Like it was

someone I'd spoken to before, recently, but I couldn't place it. Why wouldn't my brain work?

"W-what's happening?" Frank whispered from the ground. "Where am I? W-why are you doing this?"

"No talking!" the person instructed, kicking Frank again, and Frank cried out sharply. "No talking! I need to think. I can't… I can't *think*."

The man turned on his heel and walked away a short distance. It seemed like he was tapping himself on the head as he muttered to himself once more. "It wasn't supposed to happen again. It wasn't my fault, with the other ones. The camper. The ranger. She understood that. But I promised no more and now look what I had to do. I'm going to have to kill you, too, and she's gonna be *so* mad."

"I don't understand," Frank whined softly. His voice broke. "Shane, please. I can help you…"

Oh, *God*. Oh, dear God. The crazy man was *Shane*?

I gasped, just a soft little inhale I prayed he didn't hear, but a second later the glare of the flashlight was turned on *me*, and I squeezed my eyes closed to protect myself from the light.

"Oh, no," Shane moaned. "You weren't supposed to wake up. Neither of you was supposed to wake up. This would be so much easier if you stayed asleep."

Except I hadn't been asleep. I remembered now. Shane had seen me walking home. He'd pulled over to offer me a ride. I'd said no, but he'd insisted.

*Don't worry, Ev*, he'd said, once I was sitting in his little red car. *It'll all be alright.* He'd offered me a napkin and a bottle of water.

And I'd been so grateful for his comfort, for the kindness of this virtual stranger, I'd decided that O'Leary was the best place in the world.

*Take me back to Silas's house?* I'd asked, after taking a deep drink, and he'd smiled and said he would.

And then… nothing. My mind fuzzed out, like an old-school television with no reception.

"Shane, what's happening?" I asked, even though I was really confident I did *not* want to know.

"I'm sorry, Ev. I liked you. I mean, I do like you. I do."

I could barely keep my eyes open, my head was throbbing so badly. "I like you, too, Shane," I lied.

"But I thought you understood how it *was*. How *love* was. You're married."

"I was," I whispered. "I was. His name was Adrian."

"And you love him so much," Shane said eagerly. "You love him more than anything in the whole wide world."

I frowned. There was no way Shane could know that, since I'd barely spoken Adrian's name. "I love him a lot," I agreed. "I took care of him until he died."

"But then how could you cheat on him with Silas?"

"I didn't," I whispered.

"That was *wrong*, Ev," Shane insisted.

And… okay, here's the thing. I'm not exactly *proud* to say that it took a fucking psychopath repeating my bullshit back to me to recognize it for the total lie it was, but… yeah, that's pretty much what happened.

Because when Shane said, "That was wrong," in his over-eager, crazypants voice, I could hear how ridiculous it sounded. How weak and stupid. All I could think was, "No. It's the rightest thing *ever*. It was destined, and ordained, and meant to be. It's exactly the way it should be."

Yesterday, I'd accused Silas of using love as something to beat me over the head with, when in truth, that's what *I* had done. Every time things with Silas were wonderful, I'd conjured an image of Adrian, forced myself to remember how painful it was to lose him and how much I owed to him, like if I could somehow hold myself back from loving Silas, I'd be able to protect myself.

What a terrible thing that was. Terrible for me, terrible for Silas, and maybe most terrible for *Adrian*, who deserved to be remembered for the funny, kind, supportive, fussy, proud, candy-loving man he had been.

At the end of a life, did it matter if anyone remembered the way you smiled or exactly the way you'd parted your hair? Did it matter if they used your stocking hangers at Christmas, or planted the flowers you liked? Or was it more important to live in a way that honored the way they'd loved you and the way they'd changed you? Because those were things I would never, never be able to forget, not until the day I died. No matter who else I loved.

Just like Grandpa Hen had said, damn it.

"People can't just change their minds," Shane explained, almost kindly. "Not about things like this."

"I haven't changed my mind about anything," I told him with perfect honesty. "I loved Adrian when he was alive, and I love him still. Grief is eternal, just like… just like this land. It changes a little, but the essential parts stay the same."

Shane shook his head and his flashlight swung wide, reflecting off Frank again. The man had somehow managed to push himself to sit up, but his hands were tied in front of him. But Frank's eyes widened as he watched Shane.

"No," Shane said more vehemently. "That's where you're wrong. Love doesn't change. If you love someone, you have to stay in love forever. Molly didn't understand that, either." He shook his head sadly.

"I thought… I thought Molly *did* love you," I said. "That's what everyone says."

"She did," Shane said proudly. "She did. We loved each other for *years*. But she listened to the wrong people, and they steered her wrong. Told her she could leave town, leave *me* and everyone else who cared about her."

"She was going to school," I reminded him. "And it was a terrible accident that took her, Shane, but that doesn't mean she didn't love you. She didn't have a choice. When Adrian died…"

Shane cut me off by waving his hand through the air, and as his arm passed through the beam of the flashlight, there was a dull, metallic gleam.

I thought I understood why Frank's eyes had gone wide. Shane had a fucking *gun*.

I tried to roll over again, but the hand beneath me wouldn't cooperate. I shifted my weight and tried to move my fingers, but the pain that sang up my arm made me bite my lip and stay still.

"That's not what happened," Shane sighed. He squatted down near my feet like he was about to deliver a friendly, paternal lecture. You know, with a gun.

"Listen, Ev, here's the thing you have to understand. Molly was confused, okay? It wasn't her fault."

I frowned, but nodded along like I was totally listening, because the guy with the gun was always right. I'd learned that from television, too.

"You know, I was the first one to show her this place, back when we started dating? She'd never been to the falls before." He smiled, like he was reliving the memory. "First time we ever kissed was up here."

"It's a pretty place." I fought to keep the fear and pain from my voice.

"It is. And I didn't mind when she shared it with Matty, not much. They were just friends. People have a lot of friends, but they only *love* one person. You know?"

Oh my God. Shane was talking like he was eight, like the whole world was composed of simple, black-and-white truths.

"Sure," I whispered. "Hey, Shane, something's not right with my arm."

"Hmm? Oh. I'm pretty sure you broke it when I dropped you." He shrugged apologetically.

"You… dropped me?"

"Yep. Had to carry you up here last night all alone, you know? I'm stronger than people think." He grinned.

"Yeah. Wow," I breathed. "Do you think maybe you could help me turn over? I… I really think it might be broken."

Shane tilted his head to the side, like I was a child. "Ev. You know I can't do that. You'll try to run away, and I can't have that."

I swallowed.

Shane was literally crazy. The cold reality of that was beginning to really seep into me. He was literally crazy, and he had a gun, and he wouldn't let me get away.

I fought the rising tide of panic that threatened to swamp me. I *would* get away, because I owed Silas an apology and I needed to tell him I loved him. This would not end with us in a fight. No fucking way.

"So what happened?" I asked. *Keep him talking.* Lesson three of police procedurals. Let him do his villain monologue.

"She said some hurtful things." Shane shook his head. "Said she wasn't sure she wanted us to be committed when she went off to school. Said she wanted to *take a break*." He snickered. "I mean, come on, right?"

I swallowed and nodded. "Crazy," I breathed. I was definitely talking about *him*.

"I just wanted to stop her, you know? To show her I was serious about not letting her leave."

Frank made a strangled sound. "Oh, God, Shane. What did you do?"

"I didn't do anything!" Shane surged to his feet, brandishing the gun at Frank. "It wasn't *me*. It was Molly. Molly and Matty. They were going back to school, and I wanted to stop her. So I took my car out on the Camden road to meet her, and I… tried to get them to stop. That was all. Just to *stop*."

A chill shivered down my spine that had nothing to do with the relentless chill in the air, or the cold, damp earth on my feet. "What happened?" I asked, distracting him.

"Matty didn't know how to drive!" Shane clasped both hands to his head, pressing the side of the gun against his own temple. "I pulled up alongside them and he ran off the fucking *road* and into a tree." He sobbed. "That's *not* what I meant to happen."

"Of course not. You loved her," I agreed. I bent my legs slightly, trying to lever myself over. Every millimeter of movement ricocheted up my arm.

"I do love her," he agreed. "I got her out of the car, but it was too late." He sniffed. "She was dead."

"Oh, Shane," Frank said, and honest to God, I just wished he would *hush*, because every word out of his mouth just made Shane swing that fucking gun around again.

"It was an *accident*," Shane screamed.

Frank nodded vigorously. "No, of course. Yes. An accident."

Shane panted for a moment, then swallowed audibly. "But it was okay, Frank. It was okay, because you know what I figured out?"

Frank shook his head.

"It was better this way," Shane whispered. "This way, she would always be mine and *no one else's*."

It was such a warped version of what I'd thought about Adrian just a couple of months ago that I once again fought the need to vomit.

"I made a place for her," Shane said. "In the woods. The place *you* found."

He swung the gun toward me, and I cowered. I did.

"It was beautiful, Shane," I said. "A beautiful tribute. With the chimes." And the invasive, poisonous weeds.

"Molly loved chimes," Shane said, his mouth quirking in a smile. "I buy some for her every birthday."

A shrine to lost love. Fuck. Silas had been right, but neither of us had understood just how far Shane had gone.

"That's nice," Frank offered.

Shane swung in his direction again. "It *would* have been nice, *Frank*. Until *you* gave up the land!"

"I didn't give it up," Frank protested. "Honestly! I fought and fought, Shane, you know that!"

"And now?"

Frank was silent.

Shane nodded. "You've just decided to let them have Molly's place." He stepped away. "This is the *problem*," he said. "Things need to not *change*. We need to keep them the way they were. I need to put things right."

"W-what does that mean?" Frank asked.

*Jesus, God, Frank. Shut up!*

"That means I have to take you to the falls, just like I did with John Carpenter," Shane said sadly. His lips twisted. "I wish I didn't have to, Frank, but you're *responsible* for this."

"I… But I… But Myrna!" Frank babbled, near tears.

Shane shook his head, and something nearby buzzed. He frowned and dug his phone out of his pocket.

"Shit," he said. "Shit." He looked at Frank. "They know you're missing! They're sending out a party to look for you."

I closed my eyes and sighed. Of course Shane was on the list of people they'd call when they needed a search party. Shane knew everyone. Everyone thought they knew him.

"We've gotta go," Shane said. "Stand up."

I knew I wasn't supposed to go with him. He was taking us to the place where he planned to kill us, after all. But what the hell was I supposed to do? Would it be better to just have him shoot me here?

"I can't," I reminded him. "I'm tied down."

"Ah, shit," he said. "Frank, untie Ev."

"My head," Frank complained. "I can't hardly…"

"It'll be worse than your head when I kill you right here," Shane countered. "Do it!"

Frank crawled over to me, his hands still bound in front of him.

"I-I can't get the knot," Frank said, his voice quavering. "I need a knife."

"Jesus Christ, I'm not giving you a *knife*," Shane yelled. "Untie him or I'll shoot you right here!"

"Shane, think for a second," I soothed. "Just think. If you shoot us here, they'll find you. You know they will. They'll trace the gun and know it was you."

Shane frowned, like he hadn't considered this.

"Who'll take care of Molly's place if you get caught?"

"You're trying to trick me."

"I wouldn't!" I so would. "I just know how it feels to lose someone, remember? Toss Frank a pocketknife, if you have one, and he'll give it back as soon as he cuts me loose."

Shane frowned, but I held his gaze. The sky was lighter

now — pink and gold, like sunrise was coming — and I could see him clearly, read the indecision on his face.

"Course I have a pocketknife," he said. He tossed it at Frank. "No funny business."

I shook my head solemnly. "No way." And then I added, just to keep him distracted, "What happened with John Carpenter? Did he disturb Molly's place?"

"Yeah," Shane admitted. "I go there to talk to her a lot. I was telling her I forgave her, and I was sorry it had to happen like that, and next thing I knew, he was right there. Listening."

I shuddered. Poor John Carpenter.

"And then Elliot Marks?" I prompted.

"Same thing," he said. "I had to go back and make sure Carpenter hadn't left anything behind for you guys to find and Elliot saw me there. He tried to pretend it was fine, but I could see he was suspicious." Shane shook his head. "He had to go."

Fuck. Seeing how paranoid Shane was, it was likely Elliot hadn't been suspicious at all.

"It was easy," Shane mused. "No one in town suspected a thing."

"That's for sure," I agreed. And as much as I hated the way O'Leary never allowed people to change, for better or worse, I thought it was probably to their credit that they'd never think one of their own capable of something like this.

I really hoped they stayed that way after someone figured out what Shane had done.

Because they would. I believed that truly. Whether I got out of this or not, whether he was mad at me or not, Silas wouldn't rest until he'd caught the person responsible.

Silas didn't give up. And I swore right then and there, I would never give up on him.

Frank cut through the rope behind me and straightened. "It's done," he said.

"Toss me the knife."

Frank hesitated for a second, then threw it high and wide so it sailed off into the woods behind Shane. "Sorry!" Frank said. "Sorry! My aim is terrible!"

Shane fumed, and his jaw worked. For a second, I thought he was going to kill Frank then and there. But instead, he jerked his gun to the side. "Move. Ev first."

We headed out — me fucking *barefoot*, not that it mattered at this point where my shoes were — and I tried to think of a way out of this, but my panicked brain refused to comply. I could jump to the side, duck behind a tree. I might be able to run far and fast enough to get away at first. But then Shane would shoot Frank and come after me… and I knew for a fact that I wasn't nearly good enough at orienteering to elude him for more than ten seconds.

"I killed him the day you came to town," Shane said from behind me. "John Carpenter, I mean. I'd left my car parked down one of the paths off the Camden road, and by the time I'd cleaned up, it was full dark. I thought you were gonna hit me with your car." He chuckled.

I stumbled to a stop. "Wait. That was *you*? Out on the road."

"Almost hit me," Shane repeated. "Wouldn't that have been something?"

I turned in place, stunned. I'd thought he was Adrian. I'd thought he was some kind of ghost or sign from above…

I almost wished I had hit him.

"Walk on," he said sharply, nudging Frank in the back with the gun.

Frank stumbled forward a step, crashing into me. I

nearly blacked out from the pain and sank to my knees. He pressed something into my hand that I caught when I went down.

*The knife?*

Frank knelt to help me up, his eyes widened significantly. For the first time, I could see how badly his head was bleeding, like he'd been coshed over the head, and his face was a grayish white that didn't bode well for him being able to survive the walk, let alone whatever Shane had in store.

"Whoa! You okay there, Ev?" Frank asked loudly, helping me to my feet. "Go for Shane," he whispered in my ear. "I can hardly see straight."

Go for Shane? I wasn't exactly sure how this was going to work at all — funny how they never showed *this* shit on police shows. Maybe Silas was right about them after all — but I knew we had to try something or else I would die here, and Silas and I deserved far, far better than that.

"My arm," I yelled, cradling my broken arm to my chest with my good one. "Shane, please help me! The bone is sticking out and everything!"

Shane took a half-step closer, peering down at my arm like he couldn't help himself, and I knew that was the best shot I would get. Risk aversion had a time and a place, but this was not it.

I palmed the knife I'd been holding in my good hand and stabbed at the hand that held Shane's gun. He screamed as the blade glanced off his skin and the gun went tumbling to the ground. Frank dropped to his knees to grab it at the same time Shane did, the two of them scrambling across the fern-and-leaf-covered forest floor.

Fuck.

The knife was still in my hand, and I didn't hesitate,

not even for a second. I jammed the knife into the back of Shane's shoulder and twisted it as hard as I could.

He screamed and fell, and I fell with him, all out of balance and clutching my poor arm, which might never work properly again. I hit the ground hard, the knife still stuck in Shane's back.

Shane lunged for me, grabbing my bad arm with his good arm and *yanking*, which was more effective than pretty much anything else he could have done. I cried out in agony and lay on my back staring up at the treetops and the pinkening sky.

It was *not* going to end like this. I rolled to the side as Shane brought his good hand down toward my face…

And a gunshot ricocheted around the forest.

I pushed to my feet and found Frank, kneeling in the wet leaves and panting, both hands gripping Shane's gun, staring at Shane's lifeless body. He'd shot him directly in the chest.

"Jesus," I breathed, stunned. "You… Frank… you…"

"I swear I saw two of him," Frank wailed. "I'm just glad I hit the right one." He slid to the side and landed on his ass.

I snorted. Then chuckled. Then buried my head in my good hand and *cried*.

"Come on, Everett," Frank said. "Stand up and let's…"

"Frank? Everett?" someone called.

"Here!" Frank yelled.

I sniffled and pushed myself to my feet.

Silas pushing through the brush a second later was like a dream of water after too long a time in the desert. I couldn't believe he was real at first. But he was staring at me, love shining in those blue eyes I wanted to see every single day for the rest of my life, and his arms were outstretched like he wasn't sure if he should come to me or not.

I ran at him, clutching my broken arm to my chest because I swear to God in that minute Silas was more important. Like air. Like gravity. Like hope. And he caught me, the way he always had.

The way he always would.

"Fuck," he said. "I love you. I love you so damn much. And I don't give a shit if you don't love me back yet, because you *will*, Ev. You've changed my mind about destiny, because you and I are meant to be together."

I sobbed, of course I did, but not because I was sad. For the first time in a long time, I realized that I didn't *have* to be. I could love Adrian and Silas. I could be brave enough to do that.

"You're wrong," I told Silas, not sure he could even understand me because I was a hot mess of tears and pain and love. "I love you. I do. I have for a while now. And you were right all along. It's not destiny, it's choice. And Silas Sloane? I choose *you*. I choose us."

# Chapter Nineteen

## EVERETT

"Shit," I muttered as the pan in my hand started burning through the embroidered *My Grandfather Is Always Right* tea towel I was using as a pot holder, halfway between the house and the garage.

Upon reflection, it might have been a good idea to let the apple cake cool for a minute before running off to impress my boyfriend with it. We'd spent a long few weeks waiting for my banged-up arm to heal, and now that it mostly had, the last thing we needed was to be down another limb, because I had *plans*. Plans that involved getting my very cautious boyfriend to make love to me, possibly over the hood of a car or up against a wall. I wouldn't be picky about that part.

Multicolored leaves scattered across the yard like confetti in celebration of my plan.

"Morning, Everett!" Mrs. Daley called from across the street, where she was stringing fake cobwebs and fairy lights along the top of her picket fence. "Going to the Pumpkin Fest tomorrow?"

"I'll be there!" I said. As the last weekend in October

drew nearer, Pumpkin Fest had become a freakin' religion around here. I was pretty sure if I'd said I wasn't going, Mrs. Daley would have run across the street to convert me to the Way of the Pumpkin.

I had somehow been talked into judging a jack-o-lantern carving contest, since I hadn't been able to participate this year, and God help me, I was really looking forward to it. Not to mention…

"Silas entering the pie-eating contest?" she asked.

"He's going to *win*," I boasted. "I've been feeding him sweets every day for two weeks as training." I lifted the cake in demonstration and she chuckled.

"I dunno. Strong competition this year," she said. "Buncha new people."

"Eh. We aren't afraid of competition," I told her. "Bring it on."

She chuckled and swiped a hand at me.

Hearing the words come out of my own mouth made me smirk internally. I could practically hear past-Ev groaning. I hadn't just *drunk* the O'Leary Kool-Aid, I'd dived head-first into a vat of the stuff and was happily splashing around.

O'Leary was my home now, and I was pretty sure it always would be. Choice or destiny, this place was stuck with me. And Silas Sloane was stuck with me too.

I pulled open the side door and paused at the bottom of the stairs leading up to the attic. The sounds of Silas singing along to some Scottish folk music drifted down, and I set the cake on the step so I could lean against the wall and listen. Folk music was a good sign, I'd learned. It meant my man was mellow and calm. Heavier stuff was for when he was annoyed by a case and went out to bang around on the Porsche in the garage, a job that would never be finished because its true purpose was to be a work in progress. Life was messy like that. And it was a fucking privilege that, after all my running and risk-aversion, I got to be here to share that messy life with Silas.

I'd promised Adrian my love and loyalty on the day we got married. I'd said *for as long as we both shall live,* and I'd truly meant for *as long as either one of us lived.* I'd firmly believed that some day when our hair was white and one of us kicked off, whoever got left behind would carry the torch for both of us until death claimed him too.

It sounded so pristine and perfect, right? But the problem was, life wasn't like that.

Life was change and mess and chaos, blurry lines and bleeding colors, and I'd known that once, but I'd allowed fear to make me forget. I'd pretended that following rules and insulating myself with grief would prevent me from ever losing anything again, but instead, it would have kept me from ever really *having* anything. The very act of risking something was what made life beautiful, and precious, and worth fighting for. And in risking my heart on Silas, I'd gotten *everything.*

Including a man who was right now spending his Saturday morning converting the attic into a studio space for me.

I grabbed my cake and walked up the stairs, smiling as Silas came into view on the other side of the landing. He was painting a wall, singing along to the song on the speakers, while white paint splatters fell on the blue drop cloth and the front of his jeans. The muscles of his forearms shifted and bunched as he went about his work, and his dark hair shone in the sunlight that filtered through the open window. Silas's voice was deep and just a little scratchy, the air smelled a little like paint fumes and a lot like apple cake, and a feeling of *rightness* just swamped me.

I'd never felt anything like it before, but I knew that I was exactly where I was meant to be.

"Hey, handsome," I said as I took the last two stairs.

Si turned, grinned, and immediately dropped his roller into the tray of paint on the floor. "Hey, yourself."

I set the cake and the tea towel, which had been a gift from Grandpa Hen, naturally, on one of the butcher-block counters Silas had installed in the back corner of the room. My art supplies were already spread across most of the surface, since I'd used the space to work on the backdrop for the festival.

The silly little project I'd envisioned had actually taken way longer than I'd expected. It had also come out better than I'd hoped, and I really hoped the rest of O'Leary felt the same. Instead of puppies and leaves and pumpkins, I'd painted the Camden road — the road that led us all into O'Leary — decked out in a splendor of orange and yellow and red. It wound in a serpentine ribbon from one corner to the other, nearly doubling back on itself again, before finally moving forward.

Because yeah, I was all about the symbolism.

They say sometimes you have to lose something to realize what you had in the first place. For the particularly hard-headed among us, sometimes you had to lose something, and then very nearly lose it *again*, in order to get the message the universe was handing out.

Grandpa was right. Lattimers never did things easy.

"I like it," Silas said, nodding at the long piece of canvas. He wrapped his arms around my waist from behind, pulling me close, and I melted against him. "A-plus for effort, Mr. Maior."

"Hmm." I turned my head and pretended to appraise the work Silas had done on the wall. "You've done a pretty good job too. I think you've earned your merit badge."

He snorted. "My advanced scouting badge?"

"Mmm hmm." He pressed his chuckle into the skin of my neck, and I shivered in response.

"And is that my prize?" he asked, nodding at the cake.

"Nope. That is fuel." I took a fork from my back pocket and put it on the counter next to the cake. "I've got your prize right here." I turned and wrapped my arms around his neck, drawing him down for my kiss.

He tasted like Morning Silas — coffee and toothpaste and *heat* — and I sighed happily as I let myself get taken over by it. I loved the slow, delicious slide, and the way his hand came up to toy with the curls at the back of my head. I loved the way that he didn't hold anything back anymore, and neither did I.

He pulled away after a second, and I swear I could practically *hear* the thoughts rolling through his head as he pressed a half-dozen brief kisses to my lips. *No sex with Ev in the living room. No sex with Ev in the kitchen. No sex with Ev at all unless I'm sucking him off while he's surrounded by a hundred pillows, just in case he breathes wrong and hurts his arm.*

Literally.

Silas had become a one-hit wonder for the past three weeks, and while it was adorably sweet, it was also completely unnecessary. Short of bench pressing a hay bale at the festival tomorrow, I wasn't sure how I was going to prove to him that I was not only ready for more, I was eager.

*So eager.*

*Dying.*

"Silas? Would you do something for me?" I asked.

"Of course."

I grinned. Total acceptance, no hesitation, whether I wanted a kidney or to borrow his truck. Was it any wonder I loved this man?

"You might not like the idea at first," I warned him. "But I'm willing to be very, very persuasive."

"Then I promise to be very, very willing to be persuaded." He combed his fingers through the hair above my ears. "Does this have anything to do with separating your grandfather and his familiar? Because you know I'm happy to have Daphne here, but Henry will be sad to say goodbye."

I shook my head. "I already talked to him about it yesterday. I'm going to let Daph stay with him. She likes it there." I smirked. "Besides, Grandpa Hen says it'll be easier for us to start a family without a cat underfoot."

Si's eyes widened. "The family talk? Already?"

I laughed. "Welcome to O'Leary."

"Right. I guess that'll never change," Silas sighed.

"None of the essentials around here do." And that was okay, because what we had was pretty awesome.

O'Leary had been shocked to learn about Shane, especially the families of the people he'd hurt. Silas's parents were devastated, Jamie Burke had smashed up a table and chairs at Hoff's, and Shane's own uncle — a guy I'd never met because he was apparently more of a hermit than Daniel Michaelson — had moved back into town in some kind of penance. But the gossip had been by and large the respectful kind, the *how can we help?* kind, the *what signs did we miss?* kind. And instead of becoming hardened and suspicious, everyone had more or less come together even stronger than before to support one another.

Even Karen Mitchener-Martin, who'd kept her I-told-you-so's to a minimum.

"So if it's not about Daphne… is it about my mother?"

"No!" I shook my head. Although the fact of the matter was, Carolyn Sloane and I had bonded just a little bit in the wake of my abduction, and she'd learned some lessons too, about how grief taken to extremes could end up causing more pain. She liked me, and she liked me and Si together. "No, this is definitely not about your *mother*!"

"Because my mom asked us to go over there tomorrow for dinner, and I…"

"Silas! This is not about my cat, and this is not about your mother!" I said, shaking his shoulders slightly with my *two* very healthy hands.

Silas arched an eyebrow, his blue eyes hot on me. "What's it about, then?"

"I have needs," I told him, bracing a hand on his chest.

He shook his head and took a step backward. "So do I Ev, but…"

"I've been patient," I told him.

"Have you?" He wrinkled his nose. "Because patience would imply that you hadn't mentioned it ten times a day, every single…"

I clapped a hand over his mouth, muffling him.

"Needs," I insisted. His laughter vibrated against my hand. "Which must be filled."

I pushed him back across the space toward an ancient sofa covered by a drop cloth and then gave him one final push, so he was sitting down. "I am *fine*," I vowed. "Never in the whole history of the world has a man been finer than me."

Those wicked blue eyes danced up at me. "Well, that's for damn sure," Silas said softly, and I felt myself blush.

He took my hand and turned it over, like he was inspecting my arm for soundness. Besides being a shade paler than the rest of my skin, thanks to the cast I'd just gotten off, it looked exactly the same as ever to me, but Silas frowned like he was seeing inside the skin, to the hairline fracture that had now healed… to what had very nearly happened out in the woods with Shane Goode.

He drew me forward an inch until I stood between his legs, and his eyes locked on mine. "Do you have any idea how important you are to me?" he asked, pressing a kiss to my palm.

I nodded. I did know. It was there in everything he said and did, in the way he pushed and the way he waited, in the way he'd never given up on me even when I'd made it nearly impossible to keep the faith.

"I'm guessing it's about as important as you are to me," I said. I planted one knee on the sofa beside him and swung the other over to straddle him. I took his face in my hands and bent my head to kiss the tiny scar near his mouth. "Trust me, Silas. I am *okay*."

He blinked once, slowly, like he was absorbing this. I bent down and traced my tongue over his lips, then pulled back.

As I watched, his eyes kindled and his chest expanded. He coasted his palms up the arms of my t-shirt to my neck. Then he leaned deeper into the back of the sofa and pulled me against him.

*Yes. Just yes.*

I kissed him for all I was worth.

One of his hands came down to push up the back of my shirt, tracking the planes of my back, skin-on-skin. Impatient for more, I reached down and pulled it over my head, dropping it on the sofa, then I grabbed the hem of Silas's shirt and did the same maneuver.

"Slow down," he reminded me. "We have as long as we want."

And he was right. He was right. But I didn't want to wait another second.

I slid a tiny bit closer so we were chest to chest. The heat of his skin in the chill of the room hardened my nipples, and when Silas kissed me this time, he was obviously as impatient as I was. His hands moved in broad circles across my back, one caressing my shoulder and one moving much lower, making wider and wider circles near my waist, pushing my sweatpants down an inch more every time.

"Kneel up," he instructed, and I complied.

He pushed my pants down until the band was tight around my thighs and my half-hard cock made contact with his bare stomach. *Holy hell.*

He grinned as he gripped tight and stroked me.

"You like this? I know you do. And I know what else you like." He sank down into the cushions, watching me the whole time.

I was so dazed by him that it took me way too long to get what he was doing, but once I did I shook my head and grabbed him by the hair, yanking him back up. "Not this," I told him. "Not today."

He raised one eyebrow at me and… I mean, okay, yes, fair enough. I had never refused a blow job before. But I wanted more. I wanted to show him that I was ready for more.

I reached into the pocket of my sweatpants and took out a small bottle of lube and a condom. "More prizes," I said hoarsely.

His gaze narrowed, but *oh*, did they get hot. Hotter than I'd ever seen them. His hands slid around to squeeze my ass. "I do love prizes."

"Thank God," I breathed, and the man laughed.

"So impatient," he chided, but he lifted his hips to rub his fabric-covered cock against mine, and I moaned, knowing he was every bit as excited as I was.

I undulated against him again and again, his cock rubbing against the cleft of my ass, my cock flush against his smooth stomach, while we stared at each other, our breath mingling.

This part wasn't new — we'd done it before. But never since we'd acknowledged what we were to each other. Never without the fear that had been holding us back. And without those barriers, the connection I'd felt to Silas from the first second I'd seen him on the damn road — that unquenchable spark that had opened me to love again when I'd been determined to cut myself off, the bond that had let the most commitment-cautious person in all the land finally feel safe enough to *fall* — was like a living thing between us.

My joy was his joy. My pain was his pain.

And, uh… apparently, my impatience was his impatience.

I tried to unzip his pants as best I could in this awkward position, but after a minute, he pushed me off his lap in frustration.

"Pants. *Off*," he said, lifting his hips to strip down his own jeans and boxers.

"Who's impatient now?" I teased, pulling my sweats all the way off.

"Less talking, more moving."

I could totally do that.

I straddled him again and he grabbed for the lube, dribbling it over his fingers and down the cleft of my ass, rubbing it over my opening.

"Please, please, please," I begged.

"Shhhh. I've got you," he whispered. He pushed his finger inside of me and I hissed.

*Oh, shit.* I squeezed my eyes closed. It had been so long. Forever, really. It was uncomfortable, no matter how much I wanted it, and I worried for a split second that Silas wouldn't continue. But when I opened my eyes he was watching me with this fierce possession on his face that almost made him look angry, and I knew that we were on the same page.

"More," I demanded the second the sting faded, and Silas complied, giving me exactly what I needed. He pulled me down to kiss him, his tongue rubbing against mine as two fingers entered my body from below, and I cried out as I rocked myself back against him. "So fucking good."

"You have no idea," he said. "How much I want to be inside you." He grabbed my right hand and wrapped it around his cock, which was burning hot and hard.

"Then God, what are you waiting for?" I moaned. It came out garbled, but he seemed to get the spirit of it anyway, because he withdrew his fingers from my ass with a groan, grabbed the condom from the sofa, and rolled it on faster than I'd imagined possible.

"Help me?" he said softly. His hands grabbed my ass on both sides, holding me open.

I leaned forward and kissed him while I grabbed his cock and rubbed it against my opening. *Fuck*, I wanted this. *Now.* But when I opened my eyes and looked down at him, time seemed to slow for a second. Like magic.

Like the answer to a prayer.

I'd often wished, over the past couple of years, for the ability to control time — to draw out the good moments and fast forward through bad ones. I was forever impatient when things were going well, wanting them to hurry up and get even *better* or suspiciously waiting for the other shoe to drop. When the bad times inevitably hit, I couldn't stop dwelling on them.

But in this moment of suspended time, I didn't want to be anywhere other than where I was, and I wanted nothing more than this — staring into Silas's eyes as we came together.

With his hands braced on my hips, Silas pushed his way inside me, rocking up into me with tiny thrusts that burned and stretched even as I sank down on him. It hurt, a little, and I let myself feel every second of the discomfort, because pain was part of the process, and beautiful, too. But when he finally bottomed out... holy shit, it was glorious.

"You feel amazing," Silas groaned, throwing his head back against the couch. "Everett, *God*."

I gripped his shoulders and bent forward just a tiny bit, loving the way he shifted inside me as I did, and kissed him. And then I started to move.

I lifted myself up, clenching my ass, then slid back down, loving Silas's groans and the way his hips lifted to meet mine in perfect synchronicity, arching my back as one of Silas's hands came up to tangle in my hair and the other came to my cock.

It didn't take long at all — I'd wanted it too damn much, and it was too damn good. I came so hard I felt my heart stutter in my chest and I erupted all over Silas's stomach, panting and still rocking.

Silas tensed a second later, his face contorted, and he screamed my name.

Si wrapped his arms around me and buried his face in my neck, his chest heaving like a bellows. He tipped us to one side and held me tight against him, while we calmed.

A few minutes or hours or days later, after removing the condom but before either of us had the wherewithal to get up and get clean, he pushed his head back into the sofa cushion just enough so that our eyes could meet and he grinned at me. "I love you," he said way too cheerfully. *Suspiciously* cheerfully.

I frowned. "I love you too?"

"I know you do," he said happily. "You know, Halloween is in, like, four days."

I shifted, bringing my leg over the top of his, and narrowed my eyes. "Uh… yes. I'm aware. Mrs. Daley was hanging cobwebs out on her fence, and…" A thought occurred to me. "You don't wanna hang cobwebs do you, babe? They take freakin' *forever* to take down, and I'd really rather just stick with a wreath for our place. We can go all out for Christmas. For the non-denominational Pageant of Lights or whatever the fuck it's called."

"*Parade*. Light Parade." He brushed a kiss against my lips. "Do you remember the night we met?"

"Okay, I'm not senile, and it was about ten minutes ago in the grand scheme of things. Why do you look so smug?"

He clasped a hand to his chest. "Smug? No, baby. Never. *Smart* is the word you're looking for. *Perceptive*."

"What did you do?"

"So suspicious, Everett. Always so suspicious. I just happened to make a bet with a guy I found on the side of the road."

"A bet? With me?" I thought back to that night and shook my head. "No. Although… I vaguely remember you saying nothing in O'Leary was like a psychological thriller, and we both know how *that* turned out."

"If you'll recall, I bet," Si repeated, not paying attention to my interruption, "that you'd be calling O'Leary home by Halloween… and here you are."

"Oh my God. So you're saying you planned the whole damn thing," I accused. "Really?"

He trailed a finger across my cheek and stared at me like I was the best and most important thing in the universe.

"You don't plan for miracles, Everett Maior. You just

hold onto them when they come." He kissed me soft and gentle…

And my stomach grumbled unmistakably.

Silas threw his head back and laughed, not remotely upset that the monster in my stomach had spoiled our moment. "I will spend the rest of my life feeding you, won't I?" He grinned. "Let's have apple cake."

And so we did, curled around each other on the sofa, all dirty and disheveled, enjoying the messy, imperfect miracles that you find when you let yourself fall.

———

Want more Silas and Everett? Head here for a bonus epilogue exclusively for newsletter subscribers → https:// readerlinks.com/l/4228310

ICYMI, grab the Love in O'Leary prequel novella, *The Date*, here → https://readerlinks.com/l/1570166

And don't miss *The Gift*, the second book in the Love in O'Leary series, available here → https://readerlinks.com/ l/1570164

# About May Archer

May is an M/M author who lives in Boston. She spends her days planning vacations, mainlining diet soda, avoiding the gym, reading M/M romance, and when all other forms of procrastination fail, writing it.

Visit her website at mayarcher.com to sign up for her newsletter to hear about sales and upcoming releases, freebies and behind the scenes info and more! Or join her Facebook group, Club May!

facebook.com/may.archer.author

instagram.com/mayarcherauthor

amazon.com/May-Archer/e/B075JQVGLX

bookbub.com/authors/may-archer